This Large Print Book carries the
Seal of Approval of N.A.V.H.

PRETTY REVENGE

EMILY LIEBERT

THORNDIKE PRESS
A part of Gale, a Cengage Company

GALE
A Cengage Company

Farmington Hills, Mich • San Francisco • New York • Waterville, Maine
Meriden, Conn • Mason, Ohio • Chicago

Copyright © 2019 by Emily Liebert.
Thorndike Press, a part of Gale, a Cengage Company.

Thorndike Press® Large Print Thriller.
The text of this Large Print edition is unabridged.
Other aspects of the book may vary from the original edition.
Set in 16 pt. Plantin.

LIBRARY OF CONGRESS CIP DATA ON FILE.
CATALOGUING IN PUBLICATION FOR THIS BOOK
IS AVAILABLE FROM THE LIBRARY OF CONGRESS

ISBN-13: 978-1-4328-7094-2 (hardcover alk. paper)

Published in 2019 by arrangement with Gallery Books, an imprint of Simon & Schuster, Inc.

Printed in Mexico
1 2 3 4 5 6 7 23 22 21 20 19

*For my parents,
Tom and Kyle Einhorn,
who support me unconditionally.
I love you.*

PROLOGUE

Not many people can isolate the singular moment in their life when things veered off course. When suddenly their existence — which may not have been perfect, but was at least reliable — abruptly swerved into oncoming traffic. My moment could have been the day my parents died. Or when I realized I'd never had a true friend.

But those aren't the days I'm thinking of.

Believe me, I know what I did was wrong. Or, at a minimum, I know it was immoral. I mean, *I lied to the police.* Still, my intentions were honest. Really, they were.

In fact, I remember everything about that night — the way the streets were slick with milky fog. The way a steady breath of air whistled in my ears. The way the chill infested my body as I stopped in front of her house, with its sagging rain gutters and weedy lawn.

I knew the house well. I had a direct view

7

of it from my second-floor bedroom, where I'd lived for nearly all of my twelve years. I'd watched the splintered front door dangle from a pair of corroded hinges and sway in the slightest breeze. I'd mourned the three cats that were buried under crooked gravestones in the strip of a front yard. And I'd spent hours imagining what was concealed in their decrepit shed, nailed shut by an X of reticent wooden planks.

I'd pitied the girl who lived there, with her silky red hair and tenacious blue eyes, but I'd also admired her. She was everything I wasn't and everything I wished I could be.

The problem was that I was so foolishly desperate for a friend, so eager to soothe the sting of loneliness, that when she showed up on my doorstep, I let her in, no questions asked.

I just wanted someone to *see me* for a change. Is that so much to ask?

I guess so.

Because my actions that night changed our lives forever.

And not for the better.

1
KERRIE

It felt like I'd been in that same spot for sixteen consecutive days, with a bottle of vodka and a large red Solo cup on the side table next to me. I'd watched three seasons of *Toddlers & Tiaras,* at least fifteen old episodes of *The Real Housewives of Beverly Hills,* and I'd endured roughly twenty-six commercials peddling drugs that treated depression, enough to know that I didn't have it, even though I wished there was a pill that could fix me. I'd lost my job, my purpose, and I had absolutely no idea what to do next. Just another demoralizing setback in my thirty short years.

"How long have you been out here?" Matthew emerged from the bedroom in too-tight white boxer briefs, grinding his eyes with his fists like a toddler. To say that Matthew is my boyfriend would be an overstatement. But to say he's my roommate wouldn't be right either. You know, because of the sex.

"I don't know." I shrugged, turning my attention back to the TV and silently praying that he wouldn't sit too close to me. His morning breath is unforgivable. I've just never cared enough to tell him.

"Do you want something to eat?" He reached his stubby fingers beneath the waistband of his underwear to claw at his ass and pick at God knows what. "One of my famous omelets?" He suggested, in a transparent attempt to lift my spirits. I might have been tempted if I didn't know where his hand had just been.

"No, I'm fine."

"Okay." He left it at that, padding his way slowly into our cube-size kitchen with its lazy lighting and tearful faucets.

"Do you know what's amazing?" I called after him, without diverting my attention from last week's episode of *Keeping Up with the Kardashians.*

"What's that?" he projected over the booming television — I prefer it loud, so Matthew doesn't feel compelled to make small talk.

"Kim Kardashian has no actual talent."

"Uh-huh." He came back into the room and sat down next to me on our weary brown sofa.

10

"Do you understand what I'm saying?"

"I think so."

Clearly, he didn't.

"My point is: she has this whole empire now. Clothing lines. Makeup. Perfume. You name it. And she got it just by being pretty and rich. I mean, obviously not as rich as she is now, but it's not like she's an actress or a musician. I bet she can't even carry a tune. Right?"

"Sure. I guess so." He agreed as a matter of habit. That's the nice thing about Matthew, he doesn't demand brainpower from his companions. I don't have to discuss current events, politics, losing my job, missing my nana, or my dead parents. I can just be. I can rot my brain streaming reality shows for twelve hours at a clip without any judgment at all. If you think about it, it's a gift. No pressure whatsoever.

"Maybe if I had an ass like hers . . ." I trailed off and Matthew remained silent, as he so often does. I looked at him then. He was smiling cautiously with his mouth closed. That smile made me feel sorry for him.

"I'm gonna go make breakfast." He headed back into the kitchen.

When I first met Matthew, I wasn't looking for a relationship. I'd dated only one guy before him. Skeeter, an unemployed douche bag whose motley fragrance — a blend of cigarettes, cinnamon-flavored gum, and Suave hair gel — kindled a clammy sensation between my thighs. As time went on, I realized that I might not be the only girl in Skeeter's life, and therefore was not actually his girlfriend. So I did what anyone else would do. I nosed through his text messages while he was in the shower. And there was my answer spelled out in the form of a sext-chain with our former classmate Angelina Delorian. I was humiliated, but not altogether surprised. I thought about sneaking into Angelina's apartment and filling her shampoo bottle with Elmer's glue, but then I remembered what my nana always told me: "Senseless revenge will whip its neck and snap you on the bottom." And that was the last thing I needed.

After that, I conditioned myself to be content with whatever circumstances life dealt me. That's why, when I came upon Matthew in front of the deli counter at the unsavory mini-mart next door to my old office, where most of the meat was an insipid shade of gray, I allowed him to strike up a conversation with me.

He'd been rocking from toe-to-heel and humming a tune I couldn't quite make out as he studied the chalkboard of that day's specials. What struck me immediately about Matthew was how nice he was. To everyone. Even Vito, the petulant busboy who limped around wiping down tables and muttering expletives under his breath.

I just stood there watching Matthew and his niceness, until he turned to me and said, "I like the way you ordered. Methodically." Then — just as my gaze fixed on the mortadella and its constellation of yellowing fat — he smiled genuinely and asked, "Would you like to have lunch with me?"

"Uh, okay," I replied, even though there was nothing sexy about the request.

I needed a man who wanted to pursue me. A man who was reliably in my corner. A man who — just by loving me — validated me to the rest of the world. And I hoped that Matthew would be that man.

Unfortunately, he never exactly lived up to that ideal.

"Do you want to maybe do something today?" He reappeared with a plate full of soggy eggs and a thinning cord of American cheese glued to his chin.

"Like what?" I asked, somewhat defensively.

"I don't know. Like go outside?" he offered. "I know you're super bummed about

13

losing your job, but you can't just watch TV forever." He was right, of course. So I ignored him.

I wish I could say that my relationship is fueled by thrill and passion. I wish I was waiting on pins and needles for him to call. I wish I had a chafing itch to analyze his every thought. The problem is, Matthew has nothing to withhold. What you see is what you get. We exist in each other's worlds, which has been fine until now. Maybe losing my job forced me to examine what else is left in my life.

There's nothing wrong with my relationship. We never fight. We never even bicker.

For this reason, I'm sure that what happened next on that run-of-the-mill Sunday morning just as I'd switched the channel to *Access New York* came as an unwelcome intermission in Matthew's humdrum existence.

"Are you okay?" he asked. My skin must have blanched, because he actually noticed that something wasn't right. "Do you want to watch something else? A movie, maybe?" he offered, as he placed a timid hand on my forearm.

"No." I shook my head frantically as I raised the volume and positioned myself on the edge of the couch, angling my body

14

toward the screen. I'd gone completely numb the second I heard *her* voice. I never would have recognized her otherwise; nothing about her appearance made sense. Her vibrant red hair had been dimmed to a hushed shade of blond. Her once ivory complexion had adopted a golden hue. And while her eyes were still the same, wide set and blue — just like my mother's — there was an unmistakable reserve behind them.

"You look like you've seen a ghost." He wasn't far off. Still, he had no idea. To him, she was just another attractive face. To me, she was *everything.* Some switch inside me flicked on.

Host: Now that you've shared your tips for looking and feeling your best on your big day, Jordana, tell us a little more about Jordana Pierson Wedding Concierge.

TBWRML (or as I call her, That Bitch Who Ruined My Life): Think of us as *Lifestyles of the Rich and Famous* marries New York City's chicest brides and grooms. Our job is to source the best of the best of everything. If you can dream it, we can make it happen. No request is too outrageous. I assure you,

15

we've handled some major wish lists and have never disappointed.

Host: So, you're kind of like the fairy godmother of weddings!

TBWRML: Exactly.

Host: Rumor has it you landed the wedding of the year, maybe even the decade. Can you fill us in? Our viewers are *dying* to know every last detail!

TBWRML: The rumor is true. My clients Tatiana Doonan and William Blunt will have The Wedding of the *Century*. And no one could deserve it more. Unfortunately, that's all I can divulge for now. As you can imagine, everything else is top secret.

Host: Can't you give our viewers just a little hint?

TBWRML: Sorry, Amanda, you know my lips are sealed.

Host: *Right.* But is it fair to say that an event of this magnitude could make or break a career?

TBWRML: It certainly is.

Host: That must be very stressful.

TBWRML: I love what I do, so I prefer to think of it as a challenge. I have every confidence we'll rise to the occasion.

Host: And you do this all by yourself?

TBWRML: To this point, I have. Although the phone has been ringing off the hook, so I'm currently looking for an assistant.

Host: Ooh! Now there's an amazing job opportunity. Line up, ladies and gentlemen! Before we cut to a commercial break, tell us — who *is* the ideal candidate to work with Jordana Pierson on The Wedding of the Century?

TBWRML: Well, let's see. They'd have to be smart. And think fast on their feet. Of course, a strong work ethic is crucial too.

"I have a strong work ethic."

"What's that?" Matthew regarded me oddly. I didn't realize I'd spoken aloud, or

17

that he was still right next to me.

"And she owes me."

"Huh?" he asked, justifiably confused.

Because, why wouldn't he be? Matthew had no idea that Jordana — I guess that's what she's calling herself these days — took *everything* from me. My faith. My goodwill. I tried to help her, but she helped herself instead. At my expense. And at my nana's expense.

Just seeing her churned my insides. But it also inspired me. To finally do something for myself, rather than sit back idly waiting for the pitfalls of life to rain in my lap.

This was my chance to finally set myself on the right track. To straighten out all my wrong turns.

"I'm moving to New York," I said, my eyes still focused on her face, so familiar yet so foreign at the same time.

Matthew nodded, unaware that I actually meant it.

And unaware that he wasn't coming with me.

2
JORDANA

"Jordana!" Amanda McCormick, the host of *Access New York,* bolted toward me, her crispy blond hair cast into a helmet, framing her reedy nose and hollow cheekbones. "You were fabulous! A natural talent!" She winked.

I find winking to be the most genuine way to convey insincerity.

"Thank you," I said, nodding and smiling graciously at Amanda. I do a lot of that. It's part of the job of being me. I've spent days sharpening that affectation. Authenticity isn't easy to contrive. But I've had no choice. Not if I want to keep my secrets safe and sound.

"Most people aren't comfortable in front of the camera." She hesitated for a second, expecting an answer, even though it wasn't a question. It's taken me two decades to figure out that the less you say, the fewer lies you have to sustain. But I am here to promote my business.

"You're too kind, really."

"Believe me, I know. I do it almost every day." Another short pause. "It's not easy."

"I'm sure," I said with a smile I hoped was compassionate enough.

"All right, then." She took three deliberate steps backward, disappointed but undeterred by my reluctance to chitchat. "Well, we'd love to have you on the show again. Maybe you can bring some of those gorgeous white dresses with you, and I can model them! Here comes the bride," she cooed. "Wouldn't that be *so much* fun?"

So much. "That sounds fantastic, thank you." I looked down at my phone, which was exploding with text messages and emails.

"Oh, no need to thank *me,*" Amanda purred, and pressed her hand to her chest.

"I truly appreciate it," I acknowledged again, then added, "You're a pro." Even though I despise small talk, I do respect success and ambition.

And it's important to make people feel significant. In fact, I spend most of my time pretending to like people. I feign interest in their superficial charitable organizations, their paltry children, and their entitlement to plastic surgery. I send flowers post procedure, because it would be a crime against humanity for a nose job or an eye lift to go unsung. I offer containers of chicken soup, even though I know they'll never be consumed. It's called self-preservation.

Kind of ironic, then, that my chosen career path is an industry steeped in pleasing people, isn't it? Presumably happy people. That's the thing, though. Very few of them are actually happy. Like the brides who alter their gowns up to a dozen times, frantic in their pursuit to decipher why nothing "feels right." *It's not the dress, sweetheart. It's your fiancé. He'll still be screwing your maid of honor no matter how much lace you're shrouded in.* And the ones who lose thirty pounds, whittling themselves into prepubescence by their final fitting, refusing a glass of water, because they didn't read the calorie count on the bottle it came from. Denying their body is the swiftest way to deny their doom. In a calculated offense, I've been known to torture some of those bitches with an open box of sticky buns from Levain Bakery. *Oops, how did those get here?*

"That's what I tell myself." Amanda rolled her eyes and lowered her voice. "As a woman, I have to work twice as hard as the men around here. And I make half of what my male cohosts do. You know what I mean?"

"I hear you," I replied in an attempt to convey solidarity. And also because she's right.

"I love meeting strong chicks like you, who are kicking ass and taking names. Keep doing what you're doing. You're obviously very good at it. Don't be a stranger, okay?"

"I won't."

"Great." She waved at me before leaving.

I waved back as I thought about what Amanda said. I am kicking ass and taking names. And I do have an innate knack for my line of work. I suppose because I'm not preoccupied by the romance of it. I see my clients for who they really are and I know how to get them to trust me. They admire my refined taste. And my ability to turn glitter into gold. They think I'm one of them.

Still, my job is the one thing I have that allows me to maintain my sense of self. It's a hiding place. Right out in the open. Where everyone can see the me I want them to see. My personal safety net, in more ways than one. For now.

Because every girl needs an escape plan.

Trust me, I know.

3
JORDANA

When I arrived at my showroom — despite the cold weather — Tatiana Doonan and her mother, Caroline, were already idling outside in front of the Doonan family Range Rover, with its tinted windows and aftermarket Hella lights.

"Jordana," Caroline reprimanded, stroking the fur on her mink coat. She pronounces my name JorDONNA, I assume because it sounds less pedestrian. "You're late." She tapped a polished red talon on the face of her diamond bezel watch. It was thirty seconds past our scheduled appointment. I probably should have taken a cab, but sometimes I prefer the rebellion of riding the subway. My husband, John, has warned me against it at least a dozen times. To him, the subway system is the large intestine of New York City, where feces are stored before defecation. If only he knew there was a bum living at the Eighty-Sixth

Street station who freely excretes right there on the platform. Good for him.

"My sincerest apologies, Caroline. I know how important your time is." Interactions with people like Caroline used to provoke me, until I realized that I could treat this sort of toxic relation as a game. So now I say and do what I know clients like her want to hear. I sniff their asses. I wipe them clean. And then I sew a square of the toilet paper into the bride's gown and charge them for it.

Fine, not really, but it is tempting. There are so many inventive ways to convey a big fat fuck you without actually articulating it. Every now and then I feel a responsibility to put these ridiculous people in their place. But I have to be very careful how I choose to do it.

"Would you like a glass of champagne?" I offered before she had to ask. Rich people don't like to appear greedy. Neither do alcoholics.

"That would be lovely." They followed me inside. "For my trouble." Caroline's mouth curled at the corners, but the smile didn't reach her eyes. It never does.

"Of course. My apologies again." I filled two glasses, though I knew Tatiana wouldn't partake. She's the kind of drunk who only indulges after five o'clock, because that's when she deems it acceptable. In other words, she's still young. I give it three years until she's wolfing Ativan and Zoloft at ten in the morning, chasing them with Tito's, and pondering why her husband and their Austrian au pair share the same sexually transmitted disease. I'm not making this shit up. It happens.

"Here you go." I handed a flute to each of them.

"Thank you." Tatiana accepted it and then, as expected, placed it on the side table, while Caroline glugged hers down.

Arthur Doonan, Caroline's husband and the patriarch of their elite cult — two brothers and a homely sister — founded one of the most lucrative global investment firms in Manhattan. He sits on the boards of the Museum of Modern Art, the American Museum of Natural History, Lincoln Center, the Robin Hood Foundation, and Mount Sinai Medical Center. He doesn't appreciate art or music or give a crap about sick people, but they massage his résumé nicely. And Caroline wouldn't have it any other way. Because then she'd have no reason to host ladies' luncheons at the Four Seasons, procure racks of spangled dresses from Bergdorf Goodman, and start guzzling chardonnay at noon, which would be a real buzzkill for a socialite such as herself.

People like Arthur and Caroline are among the breed of men and women who plug their faces with poison and glide into the skin of slain animals when the weather dips below fifty degrees. They rub elbows with the mommies who pretend to be loyal servants to their children, while snorting coke in the bathroom stall at their preschool. They clink glasses with the men who collect exotic sports cars and heavy platinum watches to compensate for their snack-size penises and ebbing hairlines. Not to mention the fathers who steal home late at night because they're working so hard. So *hard* that just an hour earlier, their dicks were being suctioned in the supply closet by a nineteen-year-old intern. And finally, let's not forget the nannies who discharge their blood, sweat, and tears for these families while Mom's coming and going and Dad's just cumming. Hypocrisy is a cunning thief.

Regardless, Tatiana is one very important bitch. I mean bride. She's the ripe red apple who's still white knuckling her parents' branches for fear of deteriorating into the arms of her fiancé, who owns only two homes — Hamptons and Manhattan — to their seven. *The horror.* I haven't met the elusive William yet, but as you can imagine, I'm waiting with bated breath to air-kiss the man who's freely marrying into this cult.

"Your first dress will be ready next Wednesday," I announced, bracing myself for Caroline's incredulity.

"Are you kidding me?" Her eyes bulged like a Kewpie doll's, as I pierced my tongue with my teeth. I find that the sting of self-inflicted discomfort can go a long way toward achieving an objective. The flavor of blood is strangely empowering.

"Mom, take a fucking chill pill." Tatiana quieted Caroline's indignation with a flip of her wrist, which was stacked to her elbow with at least ten thousand dollars in Hermès bangles.

Tatiana is anything but traditionally beautiful. But she is Manhattan-girl attractive. This means that her wiry brown hair has been yanked into obedience and streaked with golden highlights. Her eyebrows have been waxed into the elegant arch of a gymnast's back. Her lips have been surgically engorged. Her skin has been lasered à la a third-degree-burn victim's before the molting process begins. And her body has been sculpted by none other than Tracy Anderson herself. Tatiana's physical maintenance is a full-time job. If she carries her

27

own children, I'll be astounded.

"*Language,*" Caroline admonished. The elder Doonan does not condone swearing. At least not in public. Such a pity, really. I hope she and Arthur are heavy into sado-masochism behind closed doors. Now *that* would endear her to me.

"What's the story?" Tatiana asked, politely enough, as she heroically diverted her attention from scrolling through Instagram to herself for a hot minute. She's not nearly as malevolent as Caroline is.

"There's nothing to worry about. The dress will be here ahead of schedule," I reassured. "Our original timetable had it arriving next Friday. But it will be here Wednesday. I promise you. Why don't we talk about the flowers?"

"Great."

"Fine," Caroline relented, folding her arms across her chest to demonstrate her displeasure. I'm excruciatingly familiar with her type. She needs to feel one step ahead of everyone and everything, while remaining wholly immobile.

"Excellent, let's sit down and I can show you some photographs."

"Actually, I tore some ideas out of bridal magazines." Tatiana began to riffle through her Louis Vuitton purse, which was just large enough to hold three tiny teacup dogs.

"No need," Caroline cut in before Tatiana could locate the loose pages. "It'll be red roses."

"Mom," Tatiana protested. "I thought we talked —"

"Red roses it is." She held up her hand like a school crossing guard. "Thousands of them."

"Red roses," I repeated, well aware that in Caroline's mind, this was her wedding, not Tatiana's. I come across that a lot. "Now let's talk about the music."

Two hours later, once Caroline had made the rest of Tatiana's decisions for her, and I'd sent them each off with a bottle of Dom Pérignon, I began to chip away at the swelling volume of work confronting me.

As a wedding concierge, it's my responsibility to plait every detail of my brides' and grooms' big days into a tight braid. *Please* don't mistake me for one of those robotic event planners. I don't bustle dresses. I don't powder noses. And I don't dab tears.

But I do handle everything else — the gowns for the bride and her minions, the tuxedos for the groom and his fellow date rapists, the centerpieces, the bouquets, the rings, the music, the food, and so much more. I'm the eyes and ears of the entire operation. Not to mention the final decision maker. Most of the couples I work with don't have time to sniff flowers or sample cake. Either that or they just don't want to. And, the good news is, they don't have to. That's where I come in. I think for them and like them. That second part is key.

In other words, even if their taste is tacky, I make it happen anyway. And I keep my mouth shut. Hell, I once hired Charo to perform at an after party in Atlantic City. Quintessential proof that money doesn't always connote class. Regardless, outlandish requests are my forte. I've procured invitations that were plated in solid gold and edged with pavé diamonds. *Not* cubic zirconia. Real fucking diamonds. I've acquired white truffles from France that cost thousands of dollars a pound. And I've had royal Bengal tigers flown in from India on a private jet and chauffeured in an armored Hummer to my studio.

The bottom line is that I choreograph dream weddings for Manhattan's most spoiled of spoiled brats.

And I need help, because ever since it was made public that I'd be handling the Doonan-Blunt wedding, I've been contacted by a surge of new brides and grooms *in desperate need* of the grandest, splashiest, over-the-top extravaganza that they can conceive of. Or that I can conceive of for them.

The problem is, I don't always play well with others. So while I know I can't do everything myself, I'm equally reluctant to rely on anyone else. Still, I'm forcing myself to hoe through applicants for the assistant job.

In hindsight, announcing it on television may not have been the wisest strategy. There are already sixty-six emails in my inbox from twentysomething ladder climbers. Clearly, it's not hard to come across a gofer in this city. But to find someone with a functioning brain and a realistic comprehension of what the word *discipline* actually means . . . that's another story.

As I scrolled through the cover letters, I realized quickly that the pool was perilously shallow. Thirteen of them had used an emoji in their cover letter. Loathsome. *Delete.*

And nearly all the others had described *ad nauseam* their ideal wedding dress, bouquet, and color scheme. As if it mattered.

It wasn't until the sixty-third email that things got interesting. It read:

Mrs. Pierson,

My name is Olivia Lewis. I just relocated to New York City and I'm in search of an assistant job. I have five years' experience with administrative tasks and general office management. I'm smart, organized, and willing to do whatever it takes to help you continue to grow your company. Please find attached a recent project I worked on for my former employer. I'm free to come in and interview this week. Should you feel I'm the right person for the job, I can start immediately. I look forward to hearing from you.

Sincerely,

Olivia Lewis

Willing to do whatever. *Oh, Olivia. You have no idea.* And not one mention of lilies or lace. I consulted my calendar and wrote back instantly.

Olivia,

Congratulations on moving to the greatest city in the world. I'm sure it will fulfill all your expectations. I'd love for you to come in Friday morning. Does eleven o'clock work? I look forward to your confirmation and to meeting you in person.

Sincerely,
Jordana

I pressed send without a second thought. She's the one. I'm certain of it. At least by comparison to her vacuous competition. Either way, my instincts have always served me better than my intellect.

Olivia Lewis will work for me. She just doesn't know it yet.

4
KERRIE

I gaped at my reflection. Who would have imagined I could be this *attractive*? Certainly not me. And certainly not anyone from my old life in Connecticut. Thankfully, Blake, my new hairstylist, knew better. He works at Equinox, a fancy-schmancy gym with a full-service spa inside, which I found by doing a quick search online. There are something like thirty clubs all over the city, so I figured, *how bad could it be?* None of the gyms I've belonged to had a spa. I was lucky if they had toilet paper in the bathroom.

"Wow!" I exclaimed, rotating my head from side to side in an attempt to capture every angle.

"You like?" Blake beamed at himself in the mirror and then yawned. "Sorry. I barely got a wink of sleep." He'd already shared with me that he'd had a horrific fight with his twenty-two-year-old-boyfriend, Marco

— who was infuriatingly immature — the previous night, and that he wasn't sure he could stay with Marco for much longer. *What with being twenty-five and so wise.*

"It looks amazing, thank you."

"Sit tight. We're not done yet." He stilled me with his hands and then flipped his swooping bangs off his face. "So much work to be done."

I glanced around the salon with its white-washed walls, light wood floors, framed black mirrors, and budding orchids on every console. I watched and listened to the women around me. I couldn't help but notice the way they smiled without expression. The way they touched without feeling. And the way they spoke without meaning. It's almost impossible to believe that the Jordan I knew is one of these people now.

When I'd first met Blake, amid the cucumber water, fresh fruit, and heated hand towels (love those!), I'd been skeptical when he declared himself a creative genius. As he peered over my shoulder at my frowsy reflection, bearing the pout of someone who'd just sucked on a lemon, I was incredulous.

"Maybe some auburn highlights," I offered, per my research in *Us Weekly.*

"No way." He shook his head defiantly

and then dismissed me with a flick of his wrist. "Blond. Golden blond. Like the sun kissed your head," he countered.

"I never thought I could pull off being a blonde. Just call me Marilyn Monroe!" I tried to lighten the mood. It didn't work. Marco, who was texting him every thirty seconds, had already done him in. "Whatever you think, though. I'm sure you know best." I wasn't sure, but I didn't care as long as he was capable of transforming me from Kerrie into Olivia.

"You need a body bronzer treatment when we're done," he informed me, before flagging down his colleague Danika — another twentysomething with sharp features and a churlish posture — whom he called a "floating assistant."

"Okay," I replied, as I let them work their magic. After coloring my hair, Blake sheared it into long layers and smoothed it with a flat iron. Then he sent me to the aesthetician for a wax and a HydraFacial. Next, to a stout Russian broad named Katya for a stone therapy massage. Because all that pampering can really take a toll. And finally, I had the body bronzer treatment. When I was ready to leave, Blake gave me the name of a makeup artist — a friend of his — who worked at Scott J. Aveda Salon (right around the corner!), who would widen my eyes and flush my cheeks within an hour.

I nearly hyperventilated when they handed me the bill for eight-hundred-plus dollars, but once I stepped outside onto the heaving streets of Manhattan, I forgot all about it. Because I blended in. For the first time, like Jordana, I was one of *them.* Or at least that's how I felt, which, as I understand it, is half the battle. My nana used to say, "The most beautiful thing you can wear is confidence," which translated into a load of nonsense when I was growing up. Although now I think she may have been on to something.

After my makeup application with Lily — who had three nose rings and a barbell-like device impaling her tongue — I headed straight for a small boutique around the corner from my apartment for my *Pretty Woman* moment. I know. So trite. But at least I was footing my own bill. I'd admired the mannequins in the window, adorned in clothes I'd only seen in my reality TV binges. I figured I'd just point to each one and buy a few complete ensembles, which is exactly what I did. To my delight, I was rewarded by one of the salesgirls with a glass of champagne and a chocolate truffle. It's remarkable how generous people are when there's enough money being spent.

Free food. Free liquor. Being Olivia isn't so bad.

Only, when I got home that afternoon, my sole companion was Kerrie, who is not used to being pampered or fussed over. I'm not going to lie, it's going to be a challenge to evolve through this transformation. But there's no way I could show up at Jordana's office looking like my former self and say, "Hi, I'm Kerrie O'Malley. Remember me?" That would just be stupid.

As I thought more about it, I stared out the window of my twelfth-floor apartment at the shard of life beneath me. Then I filled a large red Solo cup with tap water from the kitchen sink and surveyed the vacant space surrounding me. It was curiously simple to rent a suitable place on the fly in New York City. Just a few clicks and a phone call, and I'd committed to a one-bedroom located between Lexington and Third Avenue on Eighty-Fifth Street, which — from what little research I had time to conduct — appears to be a prime location.

I do have a very small nest egg thanks to the payoff from my nana's life insurance. Unfortunately, the money was never invested, but it was deposited into an account for me until I was ready to be fiscally independent, which I'm thankful for now so

I can put it to good use. I am well aware that it won't sustain me forever, though, especially in New York, so time is of the essence. It's do-or-die. Either I succeed — and Jordana will repay what she took from us, which will keep me financially afloat until I figure out what to do next — or I fail and skulk back to Connecticut with an empty bank account and my tail between my legs. I cannot let that happen.

That's why I'm here. And that's why I'm changing my identity. The fact is, sometimes deceit is an algorithm for truth. Or, plainly stated, a girl's gotta do what a girl's gotta do, no matter the height of the stakes.

Fortunately, Olivia Lewis was my mother's name, and it also happens to be the name recorded on my birth certificate. Olivia Kerrie Lewis. When I was born, my parents decided to call me Kerrie so I'd have my own identity. And O'Malley was my nana's last name, which I assumed after my parents' deaths, to avoid confusion at school. But Nana never went to the trouble of having my last name legally changed.

I think Olivia Lewis sounds majestic. It slips off the tongue like warm butter. I just need to figure out who Olivia Lewis is, because this life is so foreign to me. As I imagine her, she's delicate and refined. She walks with her head held high and her shoulders rolled back. She handwrites thank-you notes on dense ivory stock edged in gold leaf (I have no idea what gold leaf is. Does it grow on a tree?). And sips kir royales (or something posh like that) on the French Riviera, shaded by one of those wide-brim straw hats with grosgrain ribbon to buffer her delicate complexion. Olivia Lewis is someone who people notice; someone they want to indulge. She's like so many of the heroines I've read about in romance novels, or the characters — some fictional, some not — I've watched in Hallmark movies and reality shows. A species that's been both fascinating and remote to me. Both aspirational and inspirational. Thank God I spent years with my nose in books and my eyes glued to a television screen. My particular vault of knowledge is finally being put to good use!

The thing is, once I saw Jordana on TV, I knew I had no choice but to take action. I owe it to my nana. And I owe it to myself. I need to figure out who I really am, freed from the constraints Jordan placed on me.

And if Jordan Butler can transform herself into Jordana Pierson, then Kerrie O'Malley can certainly become Olivia Lewis.

Only one thing left to do before my new

identity is complete: I have to figure out what I'm up against. Jordan was tough. But Jordana might be tougher. I'm neither. But I think I'm smarter. And that's something.

Of course, once Jordana hires me — she will, I'm as sure of it as I've ever been about anything in my life — I'll need to gain her trust. Then, and only then, can I start to sabotage her life the way she did mine. I can finally expose who she really is, where she really comes from, and what she's really capable of to everyone she loves, everyone whose respect she craves, including her husband.

Jordana took everything from me, and now I'm going to take everything from her.

5
JORDANA

I stepped outside onto my terrace and let the bitter wind slap me in the face. The callous air was refreshing, even though the rest of my body was shivering. Sometimes it's still hard to believe that I've come this far. That the luxury of hovering over Park Avenue, stories above the motions of everyday existence, is mine, all mine.

So what if I had to perjure myself to get here? Everyone has a dirty little secret. At least one.

My husband, John, came home late last night with pink cheeks and a limp dick. Ask me what else is new. I'd purchased a brand-new black-lace number from Agent Provocateur that afternoon, and I'd waited up so I could seduce him, only to find out that he'd already been drained of desire by someone other than me. The practical side of my brain knows that it's our unspoken covenant, but that doesn't always soothe

the sting when I realize he's been with another woman. As a broad concept, I'm able to convince myself it's okay. It's when the evidence is right there in front of me that I question my convictions.

This morning I tried my hand at it again. Quite literally. I slithered my fingers up the inside of his thigh and my tongue along the margin of his ear. But he turned his back on me. The nerve.

"Can't you see that I'm busy?" He toyed with his iPhone.

"It'll only take a few minutes." I traced the tip of his dick, which was still apathetic. "Let me." Repulsive, but I have needs too. Really, what do these other women offer that I don't? I've given enough head to know that my skills are sharp. And I'm not exactly a reluctant fuck.

"Jordana. I'm in the middle of something." He inched farther away before throwing the covers to the side and rising to his feet. His dimpled ass mocked me. "I have critical work issues that need to be dealt with now." He swaggered toward the bathroom.

Once I heard the shower running, I engaged in a little hedonism of my own. Like I said, I have needs. And they're aching to be indulged.

After that, I joined him in the bathroom

43

and faced myself in the mirror. The self-gratification had left me feeling blanker than before. "I'm interviewing someone for the assistant position on Friday," I projected over the pulsing water. He didn't reply. "Did you hear me?"

"What's that?" he asked impassively, stepping onto the bath mat and toweling himself off. John used to be a prime specimen of a man. He worked hard at it too — carving and chiseling every muscle. Now, looking at him standing naked in front of me, I can no longer see the outline of his abs or the bulge of his biceps. He's gone soft and bloated. It doesn't matter. A fat, gray-haired rich man is still a rich man.

"I said I have an interview for an assistant on Friday."

"That's nice." He dropped his towel on the floor and moved into the bedroom. I followed. I refuse to be placated, even if he pays the bills. I fulfill my duties. That should entitle me to a little courtesy.

"It is nice. I could really use some extra help with things growing as they are. I can't do everything myself."

"I thought you said that the company wasn't making any money." He finished getting dressed, knotting his Gucci tie around his neck like a noose. Or is that my wishful thinking?

"It's not, yet, but that's because I need a second pair of hands," I lied. "Anyway, there was something about this girl's email. You know when you just have a feeling that someone's going to be right? That things are about to change for the better."

"Sure," he replied absently.

"Obviously, the Doonan project is a beast of a job. Not to mention my other weddings, which are challenges in and of themselves. I'm optimistic that this girl will be able to shoulder some of the overflow while I focus on the vital organs."

"Well, we definitely don't want to disappoint Arthur. Or Caroline." John has been rubbing elbows with the Doonans for two decades. Arthur used to play golf with John's late father, Mortimer Pierson, and John's mother, Betty, and Caroline still lunch at Fred's when there's an agenda to break bread over. Even though they don't actually eat bread.

Not to mention that John works for Arthur now, which he likes to remind me is the reason why I was hired in the first place. Watch him take credit for the whole thing.

Most everyone in New York City — from the pedestrians to the jet-setters — knows who Arthur and Caroline Doonan are. In fact, most of them want to be Arthur and Caroline, however misguided an objective that is. Even if John doesn't give a shit about my business, he'll hold my feet to the coals if I screw up this wedding. If so much as one hair on Tatiana's head is out of place, I'll be disgraced and discredited just like that. There is no social purgatory.

"Listen, I need my dry cleaning picked up today. And I need you to get Mary a birthday present." Mary, John's secretary, is sixty-three years old, as overweight as her age, and her skin is pleated like a shar-pei's. She's absolutely perfect in every way.

"I do have a busy day, but of course I'll make time. Anything for Mary." This, too, is exactly why I need an assistant.

"Excellent." He pecked me on the forehead. "I'll see you."

"Will you be home for dinner?"

"Unlikely." I tracked his footsteps down the hallway and into the foyer, where I'd left his briefcase. Ever the obedient wife.

"We can eat late. I don't mind. I'll have Chef make your favorite steak and potatoes."

"Don't count on it." He draped his coat over the crook of his arm. "In fact, don't wait up for me at all. I'm sure I have an evening meeting or two."

46

"You'll let me know?" My jaw stiffened as I adjusted his suit jacket and brushed an invisible speck of lint from the lapel.

"This is me letting you know, Jordana." One definitive nod and the conversation was sealed shut. "I'll see you tomorrow."

"See you tomorrow." I closed the door behind him and then spit out under my breath, *"You fucking prick."*

6
KERRIE

Five hours before my eight o'clock alarm, I woke up drenched in my own perspiration, but still quivering beneath my down comforter. I felt dizzy. Queasy. Confused. Fearful of my own self-doubt and betrayed by my feeble resolve.

Maybe I'd made a mistake moving to New York City. Maybe I put too much faith in karma. What if my big idea to seek revenge isn't enough? What if Jordana knows it's me in an instant? What if there's someone else more qualified for the job and I don't even get hired? There's a distinct possibility that I depleted my savings and overturned my life for nothing more than failure in the form of a makeover.

These are the thoughts that thrashed around in my head as I dipped in and out of the caressing arms of sleep — unable to linger there — until my filmy curtains could no longer restrain the light of day.

I missed Matthew. Enough to stretch my arms and legs across his side of the bed. I couldn't help but replay the day I left him. He'd slung his head and hunched his shoulders, while I bundled my things into two large metal suitcases that had belonged to my nana. Then he hugged me good-bye and said he hoped we'd stay in touch, even though we both knew that we wouldn't. Three years together and it was that easy to walk away.

I forced myself out of bed and into the bathroom, where the mirror spoke unkindly to me. My hair was no longer smooth and straight, but damp and coarse at the ends. My makeup, which had been so artfully applied, was now blotchy and smeared around my eyes, which were bloodshot and bloated. I shouldn't have eaten all that Chinese takeout last night. MSG is the thief of beauty, according to *Into The Gloss.* Why didn't I listen?

What if I can't do this? I believed I could be this other person and fix my life with one decision, but now that seems crazy. *Am I crazy?* That pretty girl at the salon isn't who I really am. But if I fail, I'll have to go back to Litchfield, humiliated, and beg Matthew to take me back into his home and his heart, because if I can't pull this off, then maybe that is the life that was meant for me. Maybe that is the best I deserve.

I splashed cold water on my face. Then I brushed my teeth and stepped into the running shower, allowing the scalding downpour to work its magic. I considered canceling the interview. People get pneumonia. Their pets pass away. *Their parents get killed in a car crash.* It happens. All of it. I know. Except canceling would raise a red flag, and Jordana might not be willing to reschedule if I change my mind. *Refocus, Kerr — Olivia.* Jordana cost me my nana's life savings and my most prized possession. More than that, though, she stripped me of my faith, my future, and — if I'm being perfectly honest — I hold her responsible for Nana's death. She filched my capacity to trust. I would have done anything for her. She knew that. I may have let her take it all if she'd just asked. I may have offered it to her if she'd stopped to think about anyone other than herself before being so careless. She didn't, though, because her selfishness and her greed dwarfed her respect for me. And I need to reclaim that respect. If I want a life worth living.

I stayed in the shower until I was as withered on the outside as I was on the inside. But somehow I summoned my resolve. I dressed myself in one of my new outfits — a black pencil skirt, a red silk blouse that buttoned up the back, a gold wrist cuff, and a pair of the highest patent leather pumps I've ever worn, in a color the saleswoman called "cashmere," which isn't really a color at all. I did my best to wrestle my hair into docility the way Blake had. And attempted to contour my face with the extensive collection of makeup I was told was the bare minimum to achieving the "no makeup look." The result was not nearly as polished as what the professionals had executed, but it would have to be good enough.

Fortunately, when I was sixteen years old, I broke my already crooked nose by riding my bike down a side alley behind Mc-Donald's and hitting a pothole in the road. (I was starving. And it was a shortcut.) Mercifully, health insurance covered the plastic surgery required to fix it, and now my nose is straight and bump-free. Second, while I was working for my old boss, she decided to try adult braces on the inside of her teeth. She offered to pay for mine as well, since I'd recently played a critical role in landing a huge account. The orthodontist even threw in a free whitening. It's pretty amazing how those things alone can alter your whole appearance. And now, with the addition of my new makeover, I truly look nothing like the twelve-year-old girl Jordana met nearly two decades ago.

Even though I still had an hour to kill, I gave myself another once-over and decided I was ready. I thought about eating something, and then reconsidered. It seemed too dangerous a prospect, given my nervous nausea. I also considered throwing back a shot of vodka to calm my nerves, though that seemed riskier. I needed to quiet my anxiety and keep a clear, keen mind in order to face Jordana.

Jordan I felt like I knew, even though I only spent one night with her. At the very least, I understood the roles we were cast in. I was the bored, lonely, plain girl down the street who looked up to her. And she was the captivating older girl, living in the decrepit house with the scary father, who had no idea who I was. Jordana, on the other hand, is a stranger to me.

I decided to walk. To inhale the crisp, cool air — polluted or not. Never mind my toe-crunching heels. Never mind that the waistband of my skirt had already dented my abdomen. No pain. No gain. Isn't that what they say? I believe that. And if I'm correct, so must Jordana. We're more alike than she might think. I'll prove that to her.

As I traversed the city streets, glancing periodically at a map I'd found on my cell phone, I tuned my focus to anything but her. The homeless people languishing beneath logo'd awnings. The swollen pigeons tapping at cubes of stale bread. The taxis buzzing through traffic like bumblebees on speed. And the people. All the people. Oblivious to one another in their pursuit of constant movement. Just the other day, I read that Manhattan is the most linguistically diverse city in the world. There are eight hundred languages spoken here, which means four in every ten households communicate in a dialect other than English. I found that intriguing, because I consider myself to be pretty smart, and I can't even name two hundred different languages.

Jordana's office is located on Sixty-Ninth Street between Madison and Fifth Avenue, which isn't too far from my apartment, so before long, I'd arrived at the unassuming three-story building with two seven-foot windows flanking a double door of the same height. The only other descriptive features were two modern sconces and two large potted trees surrounding the entrance. I inhaled fortitude and exhaled uncertainty. Then I rang the buzzer and waited. A full minute passed. Sixty whole seconds that extended to an eternity, as my heart pounded like a migraine. So much for fortitude.

Could she have forgotten about our meeting? A burning sensation rose in my chest. I pressed the button again, this time more tenaciously. And I waited. Maybe this was my out. God's way of telling me I made the wrong decision; I didn't deserve better. I rang the bell once again and then retreated, sick with defeat.

"Olivia?" Not a second later, her voice smacked me in the back. I nearly didn't respond. I'm not used to being called that yet.

"Yes?" I turned around. And there she was. Jordan. Jordana. I wouldn't have been able to pick her out in a police lineup if I hadn't heard her voice on TV. She was as breathtaking as ever, though, even without her red hair. My knees trembled as I watched her watch me.

"My apologies. I was just finishing up a call with one of our *lovely* brides." She waved me toward her. "Please join me." I followed her inside, where she directed me to a desk in the far corner of the loft-like studio, which bore a striking resemblance to Equinox's salon. I'm beginning to realize that empty white space is the mark of afflu-ence. Although you'd think with all that money there'd be more stuff. Like some kind of pricey knickknacks. Nana was a big fan of knickknacks. "Can I offer you some-thing to drink?"

"No thank you. I'm fine." She sat down, and I did the same. She hadn't looked at me yet. Not *really* looked. Even though I couldn't keep my eyes off her.

"I'm going to get to the point, since my schedule is tight." Her gaze met mine. At long last, the moment of truth. "I need someone who's intelligent, capable, orga-nized, and can think on her feet. No bullshit. We're here to design dreams, and anything short of that is an epic failure."

"Of course. I'm all of those things and more." My throat felt arid and raw. I swal-lowed a couple of times in an attempt to lubricate it with my own saliva. I should have asked for some water.

"Good." Her mouth warped into a sly smile. "And I see you have plenty of experi-ence as an assistant."

"Yes. Five years."

"What kind of company was it?"

"We made products for parents with little kids — there was a cup that held a drink and snack in one, a portable baby bottle warmer, and a changing pad that folded into a square about the size of my hand. Kind of like origami." I didn't mention that the company was based in Torrington, Connecticut, the largest city in Litchfield County, which isn't really saying much, considering how close it is to New York City and Boston. Or that, prior to that, I'd spent years filling prescriptions at the local pharmacy and waiting tables at Friendly's, which had mainly consisted of stripping human hair off tacky ketchup bottles.

"I see." She paused. "Did you like it there?"

"I did. I like working." What I wanted to tell her was that my mind thrives on the daily calisthenics of having a job. That everything from the menial tasks to the big picture of innovation inspire me, like I'm channeling the brainpower my father passed down to me into productivity. So much so that weekends nag at me. They seem vacant and clumsy in their attempt to compete with Monday mornings, which signal five days of feeling like I'm part of something and that people depend on me. I need that. It's all I've got.

"Then why did you leave?" Good question.

"My boss, Nancy, sold the company.

When she hired me, she said it was her baby and that she'd never let it go, but you know how it is." *Sometimes life boots you in the ass. Dead end after dead end.* "Though I don't fault her for her decision. I mean —"

She cut me off. "Do you do drugs?"

"No, not at all." I shook my head.

"Are you a heavy drinker?"

"Definitely not."

"Can you work late hours *and* some weekends?"

"Absolutely."

"What kind of salary do you expect?"

"Whatever you can afford." I knew it was an absurd answer, but I didn't care.

"Pay is in cash to start. No benefits." Interesting.

"That's fine."

Jordana stared at me for a moment, and I remained perfectly still, terrified that she might be trying to place me. But then she scribbled something on a sheet of paper in front of her and said, "Excellent. Let's give this a try. When can you start?"

"That's all?" Thank God she didn't ask for a reference. That could have been tricky. I'd taken a small precautionary measure by listing only an email address for Nancy, a fake one that routed to me, not her. If Jordana had inquired about her telephone number, I was planning to say that she was traveling internationally for six months — a celebratory gift to herself after the contracts were signed. I figured that would at least buy me some time. But this was almost *too* easy.

"That's all."

"You don't want to know anything more about me?" I'd gone to great lengths to contrive an invulnerable persona. I finally had a family. A heritage. Olivia grew up in Palm Beach with golden retrievers, a heated swimming pool, and a duck pond. Because, why not?

"I don't have the luxury of squandering time. How about Monday?"

"Sure."

"Wonderful." She stood up abruptly. "You can see yourself out?"

"Yes." I didn't know whether to shake her hand or just leave, so I did the latter.

"Oh, and Olivia," she called after me. "Appearance is everything in this industry. Red doesn't flatter your complexion. I'd suggest a deep blue or even a dark green. You understand."

"Okay." I waited a beat for her to say something else. But she didn't. She didn't have to.

And she had absolutely no idea who I

58

really was, which was exactly the way I wanted it and exactly the way I needed it to stay. For the time being.

As the door closed behind me, I tilted my chin toward the sun.

It's my time to shine.

7
JORDANA

I knew it! Olivia was everything I expected her to be. Eager and obedient. Even better, she accepted me at face value. Of course, she had no reason not to. But for some reason, it still surprises me that my facade is so believable.

The fact is, most people are too consumed with themselves to pay close enough attention to the world around them. Not me. I'm a carnivore for details. I want to know what's molded someone from a malleable ball of clay into the hardened form of a human being. I want to know their untold truths. There are so many within the circles I rove, and I'm good at extracting them.

These skills aren't easy to develop, though. They're the outcome of years of religiously calculating my father's moods. Years of monitoring the ebb and flow of his anger. So that now I know how to react and how not to, how to convince people that I'll keep their secrets safe, because one false move, and suddenly you're exposed. I can't risk that.

It's part of what makes me so good at my jobs: playing the devoted wife, and playing therapist to my most discerning clients. I once had a bride tell me, minutes before she walked down the aisle, that she was four months pregnant and no one knew, least of all her fiancé. Then there was a mother-of-the-groom who confided that her son was marrying for money and that he had a five-year exit plan. There was also a maid of honor who admitted that she had an ax to grind with the bride (her so-called best friend), so she planned to fuck the groom during cocktail hour. *This* is the world I live in. It's also why I need someone to help me. I simply can't be everything to everyone at all times.

I logged onto my computer and opened a Microsoft Word document, so I could start a list of responsibilities for Olivia, when the phone rang. Another reason why I need an assistant.

"Jordana Pierson Wedding Concierge."

"Jordana? It's Alexa Griffin."

"Hello, Alexa. How are you?" I sat back in my chair. Alexa is one of my neediest brides. The first time I met her, she asked if I was

61

on call 24-7. Just in case she was anxious about something at, say, two in the morning.

"I could be better," she sighed.

"Is there something I can help you with?"

"I hope so. It's my veil."

"Okay. What about it?"

"I think it's too long."

"I thought you wanted cathedral length. You said it was the most dramatic."

"I know, but . . ."

"But, what?"

"Have you ever heard of a birdcage style?"

"Of course, but that's the complete opposite of what you wanted. Birdcage veils only cover your eyes, sometimes jaw line. They're more like a lace bandeau. You do know that, right?"

"I do. It's just that my friend Lara said they're super in now. And that got me thinking. I don't want to look too conservative or, even worse, outdated."

"Alexa, elegance is timeless. I think you'll regret following a trend on your wedding day."

"So you don't like them?"

"No. I think they're tacky, if you want my honest opinion."

"Oh God, really?"

"Really."

"Okay, okay. I'm sure you're right. In fact, now that you mention it, Lara is a little tacky sometimes. She has these sunglasses that have rhinestones all over them. I mean, *rhinestones*. Is it 1985?"

"I think you're making the correct decision."

"Thank you."

"Any time."

"Okay, I'll talk to you later."

Once we'd hung up, I began to wonder why Alexa is as neurotic as she is. How does one become so fretful that they can't make a single decision without questioning it a million times? What's the difference between the way her mind looks on the inside and the way mine does? Does she have dirty little secrets too? As much I want to understand her, it takes discipline not to school her on what real-life problems actually are.

The thing is, if I want to succeed in this business, I have to empathize with her trivial concerns and the equally frivolous concerns of all my clients. I'm not complaining. My lifestyle isn't exactly a hardship. I have my husband, John, to thank for that. Of course, I'd sooner let him screw me to a wall than offer gratitude. Appreciation doesn't suit me. It smacks of obedience, which was my mother's style, not mine. Maybe that's why

I taste bile most of the time.

I dialed John's number and Mary answered. "Good morning, Mrs. Pierson."

"Hi, Mary."

"How are you?"

"Fine, thank you." I didn't ask how she was. I don't have to. "Is he in?"

"Let me just take a peek." She breathed heavily through the receiver. Mary is one hot dog away from a heart attack. "He certainly is. Let me transfer you."

I waited a few seconds before John came on the line. "What's up?" His tone was terse. John expects that if I call him during the day, there better be a damn good reason.

"She was fantastic!" I announced.

"Who's 'she'?"

"Olivia. My new assistant."

He exhaled. "Is that it?"

"This is a big deal for me. For my company," I explained, even though I knew he cared more about where he was going for lunch.

"It had better be, because I'm not going to stand by while you waste your time for much longer. You're not earning a dime. And regardless, we certainly don't need the money." John makes no secret of the fact the he resents my career. He also hates when I use the word *career* to describe what

64

he believes to be more of a hobby. Like Soul Cycle. He wants a wife who stays at home, devotes her time to taking care of him, and dabbles in occasional charity work. But that's not me. And by the way, I am earning a dime. Much more than that. He just doesn't know it.

"Well, I have high hopes," I replied, undeterred by his cynicism.

Sure, John and I pretend to like each other. Our arms girdle each other's waists in front of the camera at public events. We smile — wide and white — as the light bulbs glint, capturing the veneer we've perfected. But it's all bullshit.

No one's willing to admit that behind closed doors their husband's a philanderer. That they wince at the shrill squeals of their own children. And that they bleed every penny they earn, so that one day when their children grow up, their inheritance will be a legacy of debt. Within my gilded group, subsisting beyond one's means trumps fiscal responsibility any day.

"If that's all, then," he grumbled.

"That's all." We hung up without saying good-bye. John doesn't care about me. He doesn't even know me. Not the real me.

I'll tell you, it involves preparation and perseverance to bury your past. To study and replicate customs that aren't inborn. For example, when I was growing up, Santa Claus didn't visit our house at Christmas time. There was no lustrous spruce tree. No plump pink ham. I was told that naughty girls didn't deserve presents, mainly because my parents couldn't afford them.

Now the holiday season signals jaunts to Aspen by private charter, where lapdogs model mink coats and slurp Perrier from sterling silver saucers.

It may not be who I once was. But it's who I am now, even if it feels suffocating most of the time. Still, I need to hold my head high.

Because one day, it will all be worth it.

8
KERRIE

Once the buzz of triumph had subsided, a sudden surge of discouragement took its place. Jordana hadn't recognized me at all. It may sound hypocritical, but even though I wanted — no, *needed* — her to believe that I'm Olivia, there's a part of me that's disappointed. Just the sound of her voice, seeing her again, tugged the memories of that night from the depths of our pooled history, which is why I nearly blew my cover. I was so overwhelmed that I almost seized her by the shoulders and demanded, *Do you know what you did to me?! Do you see me?!*

But I didn't. I managed to contain my composure. And as a result, I have a foot officially in the door, which means I'm going to overlook the fact that I obviously meant much less to her than she did to me.

I have little recollection of my walk home from the interview. I was wholly oblivious

67

to the swift pulse of my surroundings. As the cars and trucks swiveled past me and the pedestrians swept by with their oversize purses and briefcases, I ambled forward, preoccupied by Jordana's every word, her every movement. I analyzed everything she'd said. Every expression she'd made. And I didn't stop, even once I was safely sequestered in my apartment, alone with my thoughts. I was so distracted, in fact, that it took me a minute to realize that the banging in my head was actually someone knocking on my door.

"Who is it?" I asked, peering through the peephole.

"It's me, Sara. Your neighbor." She smiled even though she couldn't see me.

I met Sara just the other day, in the mailroom of our building. She was attempting to pacify her son, who was screaming at the top of his lungs, so I didn't expect her to talk to me, but when she did, I introduced myself as Olivia. She seems sweet, if not desperate for the company of an adult. You always hear about New Yorkers being assholes, but Sara doesn't come off that way at all. Maybe because she stays at home and doesn't participate in many grown-up conversations. Unfortunately, her son makes Satan look like Mary's little lamb, which I found out the hard way when she asked if I could hold him for a minute, and he clawed the back of my neck with his jagged fingernails.

Regardless, in an effort to act more like Olivia would, I invited her to stop by for a drink.

"Oh, sorry. Hold on a second." I unlocked the double bolts, released the metal chain, and let her in. Apparently, you can never be too safe in a building without a doorman. "Hey. How are you?" She appeared less tousled than she had the other day. Probably because her mini demon wasn't in tow. "Welcome to apartment 12C."

"Thanks." She followed me inside.

"Drink?" I offered.

"Glass of wine?" She arched an eyebrow.

"That I can do." I nodded. "If you ask to borrow milk or eggs, though, you're out of luck. I'm on the takeout food plan until I get myself to a supermarket."

"I haven't seen the inside of a supermarket in a year. Do you know what it's like to wheel a child through the produce aisle?" In that moment, I realized just how different our lives were, and then did a quick scan of the apartment to make sure there wasn't any dirty underwear on the floor or photographs of Jordana on my computer screen.

"You can order all your groceries online. I can show you how to do it if you want. They'll even bring them upstairs if you tip well."

"Wow, that's awesome." I'm already getting used to this city lifestyle. Everything on demand. "I may take you up on that." I handed her a generous plastic cup of Pinot Grigio and motioned for her to sit in one of the two chairs I'd purchased at a furniture store around the corner. They were floor samples, covered in a neutral gray linen fabric, and the store was going out of business, so the price was right. Plus, the guy said he'd deliver them for an extra forty bucks.

I may have to buy one of those I ♡ NY T-shirts.

"These are comfortable." Her whole body slumped into the sunken cushion.

"Can I offer you some pretzels? That's all I've got."

"Nah, I'm good. Thanks." She blew her thick bangs off her forehead and sighed. Sara is much more attractive when she's not scowling. Her black hair, green eyes, and ivory complexion exude a modern Snow White vibe. "I can't tell you how nice it is to talk to someone without being interrupted by crying or projectile vomit."

"I'm sure." I tried to sound empathetic, but I don't understand the first thing about caring for a child full-time. "Where is . . ."

"Dante."

"Right." Did she tell me that before?

"My mother took him to his music class. Thank God. It's the most insufferable hour of my week. All they do is smash tambourines, shake little plastic eggs, and sing 'Row, Row, Row Your Boat' ten thousand times in a row, row, row."

I glanced at a photograph of my own mother on the side table I'd picked up at the same store as the chairs. She never had the chance to take me to music class.

Don't worry, though, growing up without parents isn't as tragic as it sounds. Despite the fact that I've been told my father was a self-effacing genius and my mother had a magnetic personality rivaled by Hollywood starlets. Apparently, she was someone people *wanted* to get to know. My nana always said, as striking as she was to look at, she was equally effervescent in a way you can't contrive. "All she had to do was smile and the whole universe would light up." Maybe if my mother had had the chance to raise me, I would have absorbed some of that effervescence. Maybe then I'd sparkle too.

Unfortunately, I never had the opportunity

71

to find out. My parents died just shy of my second birthday. I wish I could say that theirs was a cinematic demise. But it was nothing more than a clichéd car wreck. And an unwarranted one, at that. While my mother was engaging and vivacious, she was also a dreamer, someone who tuned out the vital details. So much so that she failed to mention to my father the need for brake fluid in her car, which turned out to be a fatal faux pas when a drunk driver entered stage left during a Saturday afternoon date while I was with the sitter.

Do I blame her for the crash? Yup. That's the simple truth. But time has dampened my resentment. At some point, I managed to iron my smothering hostility into a gauzy self-pity.

"I really need to start bringing a flask with me." Sara hooted, which drew me back to the present.

"It must be kind of cute, though. Dante is adorable," I said, even though he's not.

"You think?" She frowned. "I don't see it. I mean obviously people tell me that all the time, but I just assumed they were trying to be nice."

"Eh, you're probably right."

She snorted. "I appreciate the honesty. Really, I do."

"Well then, if it's any consolation, I think all babies are kind of ugly."

"Completely."

"I'm sure it feels good to have a break once in a while."

"Um, *yeah.*" She leaned forward conspiratorially. "Can I tell you something?"

"Sure." I nodded.

"I don't really like him."

"You don't really like whom?" I whispered, since she was.

"Dante." She laughed. "I don't like my own fucking kid! There, I said it."

"I'm sure that's not true."

"Maybe. But you know who I like even less? Who I really can't fucking stand?"

"Who?"

"My husband. That bastard was the one who wanted a kid in the first place. And why the hell not, right? He doesn't have to lift a finger. I do *everything.* I had a life before this. I worked at *The Wall Street Journal.* I wore high heels. Like really, really high ones. I had a department of twenty-three people who all reported to me. And not once. Not one fucking time in the ten years that I worked there did I sing 'Row, Row, Row Your Boat.' " She paused to refill her lungs with air and then continued. "*Now* Joel leaves at six in the morning and doesn't come home until after Dante is already asleep. And do you know why he leaves so early? Which I assure you he never did before we had a child."

"Why?"

"To work out!" she trilled. "The fat fuck actually hauls his ass out of bed to go to the gym, when I haven't so much as seen a treadmill or a dumbbell in a year. I used to have a killer body. I was a *machine.*"

"That sucks." *By all means, don't hold back on my account.*

"A little unsolicited advice?"

"Why not?"

"Parenting is overrated. I don't recommend it."

"Don't worry. I wasn't planning on it." Was I? I never gave it much thought when I was with Matthew.

"What about you? What's your story?" Her face softened.

"My story?" I cleared my throat. I wouldn't mind having a friend, even if we have little in common, but the only story I could tell her was a lie; the truth would make me sound like a psychopath.

"Like, do you have a boyfriend?" She glanced at my left hand. "Obviously you're not married. Lucky you."

"Nope. I kind of had one. For a while,

74

but . . . you know."

"Tell me. I'm *obsessed* with hearing about other people's baggage. I'm a frustrated therapist at heart. And believe me, I know that all men are total fucks. Even my father is a fuck. Dante is just a little fuck in training."

"Actually, my ex was a nice guy." She rolled her eyes. "I mean, he had his faults." The people pleaser in me added.

"Of course." She nodded expectantly, ready to dismantle poor Matthew limb by limb.

"It just didn't work out. He was almost *too* nice."

"Ugh, that's the worst! When you want to be like, 'Buddy, grow a set.' " Sara's phone rang inside her purse, but she ignored it. "So you're back on the market?"

"I guess." Another thing I haven't considered. I've been so focused on Jordana that dating hasn't been on my radar. Not even remotely. "Although I'm not really looking right now."

"Good for you. I'd give anything to be single again. Most of my girlfriends would never admit it, but I think they would too." She leaned back in the chair and crossed her legs. "You said you're not from around here, right?"

"Right. I just moved to Manhattan."

"*Perfect!* Promise me you'll let me take you out on the town. I need to leave my apartment with someone who doesn't have a pacifier, for a change, and you need someone to officially introduce you to this city."

Her cell rang again.

"Crap." Sara glanced at the incoming number and then answered. "What is it?" she snapped. "Oh, for Christ's sake, Mom. Just start running the bath" — she rolled her eyes again — "and I'll be there in five minutes." She grunted before standing up and slinging her bag over her shoulder. "My genius of a mother struggled to think of a solution when the baby shit himself. Aren't you jealous of my glamorous life?"

"So jealous." I trailed her toward the front door.

"Thanks for letting me vent. You probably think I'm crazy. I don't actually hate my child. Only my husband." She winked. "*Kidding.* It's just a lot. You'll see one day."

"I get it." I smiled, even though I didn't get it at all.

"Anyway, to be continued. We are *so* going out for drinks. And dancing! My treat."

"Sure. That sounds great."

"Okay. See you soon." She cocked her

head. "By the way, you look amazing. And that's a great blouse. Red is your color."

9

JORDANA

By the time I reached my office, Olivia was waiting for me outside, trying too hard to appear alert and purposeful. She's a trier, which I appreciate. I'm one too, in certain ways. Visually, there's work to be done, even though I do believe she's put forth some effort. Still, you can always tell when someone's moved to the city from out of town, even if only from an hour north in the suburbs. In her case it's Florida, which is a worst-case scenario. Today she's wearing black slacks that are begging for a decent tailoring job and a flowing blue silk top in the same style as the red one she wore to her interview. At any rate, all things considered, she's not bad-looking. Her features are simple — brown eyes, brown hair with blond highlights that I can tell were expensive, and a narrow, pointed nose that doesn't complicate anything. She's not fat. Or thin. Just average, like the rest of her. I'll have to set her up with my personal shopper at some point. But for now, there's far too much to accomplish.

"Let's go inside and get you up to speed." I unlocked the door, and she followed me in.

"Great." She bobbed her head.

I sat down and motioned for her to do the same. I'm going to have to teach her not to stare. At least not so obviously.

"Here's the deal. We have a number of weddings in the pipeline, but there are three that we're handling right now. Lucy Noble and Donald Cooper. Alexa Griffin and Grey Wilder. And Tatiana Doonan and William Blunt." I paused while she scribbled furiously in a notebook. "Lucy is a prosecutor for one of the top law firms in the country. I've only met her twice. Donald, aside from being a little dim, is actually lovely to deal with. You'll develop an affection for him in the way you would an abandoned puppy. Their wedding is in five months and practically everything is in place."

"Okay," Olivia acknowledged.

"Alexa and Grey are also a nice couple. He's a hedge fund guy and has left all the decision-making to Alexa, who needs a lot of coddling. Not because she's difficult, but because she's an innately nervous person. It will make you anxious at first, but you'll get used to it. The key is to reassure her over and over again that the choices she's made are — without a doubt — the best in every way. Their wedding is in seven months. So that's those two."

"Right." Her pen moved back and forth across the page.

"As for the Doonan-Blunt wedding, it is *by far* the most important of the three. *By far.* Everything hinges on this event being absolutely perfect. My reputation. The continued success of the company. And possibly my marriage. The Doonans are long-time friends of my husband, John's, family. And John works for Arthur."

"Got it."

"Do you know who Arthur and Caroline Doonan are?"

"Yes."

"Tell me what you know."

"Okay, sure." She cleared her throat. "Arthur owns a major investment firm called A. Doonan and is a board member for a handful of charitable organizations. Caroline is a socialite and also very philanthropic. From what I can tell, she helps raise money by throwing extravagant parties. They have four kids — Tatiana is the youngest — and six grandchildren."

"Sure, I understand."

"It's black tie, so the groom will be in a Giorgio Armani tuxedo, as will Arthur. And Caroline has customized a beaded, floor-length number that's over the top, as are her breasts, which I believe are brand-new. You'll see. Just don't gasp when you do. I already made that mistake. The flowers will be designed by Ron Wendt. Red roses, red roses, and more red roses. Again, not my taste." I exhaled. "I believe I've hit some of the main points, but there's a lot more. *A lot.* Fireworks at the after party, a whiskey tasting at the rehearsal dinner, a celebrity magician, and so on. I'll show you where the binders are so you can fill in the holes. Any questions before I throw you to the wolves?"

"How do you envision my role? As in, are there daily tasks I should follow through with? Is there a to-do list of some kind that I can relieve you of?" Eager beaver. I'm giddy!

"I haven't had the chance to complete a list, but the main thing is handling the flood of calls that are coming in since the announcement of the Doonan-Blunt wedding. Aside from that, just follow my lead. Once we get to know each other better, I'm sure we'll find a rhythm and develop a division of labor. Can you handle that?"

"I'm on it." She's confident. With any luck, not to a fault.

"This may seem overwhelming at first," I baited.

"Not at all."

"Well, then. If you're as capable as you are cool, we're going to get along famously. I want you to be able to trust me. And it's imperative for me to be able to trust you."

"I'm counting on that." Olivia smiled placidly. "In fact, there's nothing I'd like more."

I smiled back. "That makes two of us."

10
KERRIE

Once Jordana stepped out for lunch, I took the opportunity to thoroughly observe my new surroundings and fully digest where I was and what I was doing. Finally being here, working for her, feels dizzying and impetuous. It's the binge without the purge; there's so much to absorb.

The thing about the job interview is that it went by so quickly. There was no time to dwell on what was happening, while it was happening. But now that I have unlimited access to her, I can really dig in and hit the ground running.

She's noticed me watching her. I've caught her in the act. Only, I can't tell if she's watching me back. And if she is, is it because she's sizing me up or because I was watching her in the first place? *Or,* is it because she's beginning to recognize me? It's been eighteen years. I've slimmed down considerably. My features have sharpened, as has my mind. My nose is no longer crooked. My teeth no longer overlap. My hair is shorter and lighter, and my skin is finally unblemished. Though my face is still mine. If eyes are the windows to the soul, then she doesn't see me at all. She probably never did.

I sat down at my desk and picked up a list of our go-to vendors, which Jordana left for me. Ron Wendt Design was number one. I recognized his name as Tatiana and William's florist, so I pulled up his website.

There's a fraction of my brain that's rooting for Jordana to figure out who I am before I set her life off course the way she did mine. A small part of me wants her to remember what *I did for her* and what *she did to me* in return. But there's a much larger section of my brain that's energized by the anticipation of shocking her. And of maintaining the upper hand until I'm ready for her to know. Now that I'm Olivia, I have a deeper understanding of why Kerrie was who she was — a spectator. Maybe even a bystander. Albeit a bystander who wore comfortable shoes.

Olivia, on the other hand, rises high-and-mighty in one-hundred-and-fifty-dollar pumps, which are chafing my heels and savaging my toes. It doesn't help that

Jordana calibrates the temperature to seventy-six degrees, swelling my feet and moistening my armpits. I'm a hog in heat to her delicate swan.

I got up and walked around the office, gazing at the sketches of bridal gowns on the walls, running my fingers along the expensive furniture, and riffling through the filing cabinets. I sniffed the sweet scent of white lilies cascading from a tall crystal vase on the entryway console, as I wondered what my nana would think if she could see me now — fighting for her. She's been on my mind often lately. She is, of course, where this all began.

If only she'd been as prudent about where she squirreled her money as she was about spending it. Nana was a planner. She set aside a designated portion of her paycheck every week for what she called my college fund, which was reflected by a detailed budget she outlined at the beginning of each month. She didn't believe in banks. Nana always said, "Hold your money close to your heart," which — to her — meant storing it in the bottom drawer of her bedroom dresser.

Every Sunday she would open that drawer and take out just enough cash for grocery shopping, so she could prepare and freeze our dinners for the week. This meant the entire house, all thirteen-hundred-square-feet of it, would be permeated with vying aromas for a zesty twelve-hour span. She'd invite me to hop up onto a barstool next to her so we could work side by side, crafting a velvety chicken pot pie for Monday and a stout meat sauce for Tuesday's linguini, although neither contested her jarringly pungent tuna casserole for Friday.

While Nana insisted that it was important for me to know my way around the kitchen, what she cared most about was that I got good grades in school. As luck would have it, my studies were the one thing that came as naturally to me as the acne on my chin. Nana said I inherited both from my father, who — unlike my mother — did not have a flawless complexion or his head stuck in the clouds. Apparently, he used to read to me from the encyclopedia every night when I was a baby, and by the time I was eighteen months old he was encouraging me to watch *Jeopardy!* beside him on the couch. It's still one of my favorite shows.

In third grade I overheard my teacher, Mr. Abraham, tell my nana, "Kerrie has an inspiring gift, not only for the English language, but for math and science as well." (Thank you, Alex Trebek!) After that, she enrolled me in an advanced program and insisted that I plan to take every honors class available throughout high school, with the goal of attending Yale University when I graduated. Nana said it was one of the finest educational institutions in the country and close enough to Bridgeport for regular visits. Sometimes, on a sunny Sunday afternoon, we'd drive up there listening to show tunes, her favorite. Then we'd stop for lunch in New Haven before meandering around the campus. Nana would say things like, "You could live in *that* dormitory right there!" and "Look how smart everyone is! They all have their noses buried in books."

I returned to my desk, in case Jordana came back sooner than expected, and stared at the screen, with its vibrant photos of celebrations so spectacular it was hard to believe they were real. I read the bold print: EVENT DESIGN MANAGEMENT & PRODUCTION, LUXURY BRAND EXPERIENCES, PRIVATE PARTIES & SOCIAL GALAS, TECH AND FORTUNE 500 EVENTS, WEDDINGS.

It's a world I've never been exposed to — all the money and prestige. And a world that Jordan hadn't been exposed to, at least not when I knew her. When did that change? When did she transform into a woman so distant from the girl she used to be? Did someone tell her that being Jordan wasn't good enough?

I suppose that's one of the things I loved most about my nana — she never pressured me to be anyone but myself. She didn't force me to play soccer or tennis or any other sport. She didn't suggest that I try out for a role in the school play or dance recital. She didn't push me to invite my friends to sleep over. Because she knew I didn't have any friends. The truth was, as the girls my age began caring about things like popularity and started developing crushes on boys, I was content occupying myself with a book or a good TV show. While they were interested in gossiping about who was wearing what, where they were going, and whom they were going with, I was more interested in learning about the world outside of school and outside of my little town, from the confines of my bedroom.

Fortunately, my nana recognized what my strength was — academics — and she drew that to the forefront. She got me like nobody else did, at least for the twelve years she was mine.

I sat still for a moment and squeezed my eyes shut. I pictured Nana smiling down at me, as she so often did. And it made me hate Jordana that much more. I should have been less trusting. I should have seen her for who she really was. *A thief.*

I was the one to blame. I invited her into our home.

I opened my eyes again and started scrolling through pictures of a Red, White, and Blue party Ron Wendt had conceived. The tables were covered in bright blue fabric, with a long line of thin white vases spraying hundreds of red flowers, from one end to the other. At each place, there were white plates with gold scalloped edges and bowls brimming with strawberries and blueberries, in keeping with the theme. It's almost impossible to believe that this level of perfection exists. It's even more impossible to believe that it's my job to work with people whose July 4 barbecues cost more than the house I grew up in. But here I am. Employed by the woman who took everything from me.

I didn't have the chance to make things right for my nana while she was alive. But I can sure as hell honor her spirit now that she's gone. I've wasted enough of my life going through the motions without purpose. I let indifference and lethargy hobble me.

Nana may have believed that senseless revenge will "whip its neck and snap you on the bottom." Well then, it's a good thing this isn't senseless, because I'm more motivated than ever.

I took one more look around. And laughed bitterly. This time I'm the one who's been invited in. And I'll be the one who takes everything.

11

JORDANA

"Don't look around, the place is a mess. Stan is such a slob." Cathy ushered me inside her feebly lit apartment, located in a prewar building on the Upper West Side. It's a far cry from across town. Though the anonymity it provides is a relief.

"It's not that bad." I looked around. Their dark purple chenille sofa was mostly shredded, fully torn in spots. Stan's T-shirts and jackets were tossed over rickety wooden chairs that appeared burdened by the extra weight. And there was a selection of coffee-stained mugs littering just about every vacant surface. "I thought you had a housekeeper."

"Maria?" Cathy shook her head. "Her father got sick last year and she had to return to El Salvador to help take care of him. She said she was coming back, but you know how it goes."

"That's sad. I always liked her."

"Me too." I followed Cathy into the kitchen and watched her sweep her hand across the table. A flurry of crumbs trickled to the floor. "Have a seat. I got us all salads from the place around the corner." She opened the refrigerator door, which had a Chinese takeout menu, the number for a local plumber, and a list of emergency contacts fastened to it with magnets she'd collected from her travels. There was one in the shape of a key lime pie from Key West. And another that read, EVERYTHING IS BIGGER IN TEXAS! She set a plastic container packed with lettuce, vegetables, and grilled chicken at each of our places. "Can I interest you in some tea?"

"I'm good with water." I smiled and sat down.

"Stan, lunchtime!" Cathy hollered.

Cathy and Stan Paulson were the first people I met when I relocated to New York City eighteen years ago. They owned the very crappy building I moved into and they took pity on me, thank God. If not for their generosity in allowing my rent to be late and, on a few occasions, go unpaid altogether, I'm not sure I would have survived. Every week Cathy would show up at my shithole of a studio with a tray of lasagna or a few weeks' supply of toilet paper. She'd swear she overcooked or overbought, but I knew that wasn't the case.

Just three years before I'd arrived on their doorstep, Cathy and Stan had lost their daughter — who was exactly my age — to a treacherous, lifelong battle with leukemia. And apparently I reminded them of her, which worked out well for both of us. I needed them in the same way they needed me.

Cathy and Stan are the *only* people in my new life who know who I really am and the price that I'd pay if my true identity was revealed. They know that I've lied to my husband about everything, including the fact that Jordana Pierson Wedding Concierge has been making money since the first year it opened. If John knew that, then I wouldn't be able to save my funds for a rainy day. They also know that he's been threatening to shut down my company because he feels it distracts me from being as dutiful a wife as he deserves, which Cathy believes is one of the reasons John cheats. Whereas I think that's because he's an insecure asshole.

Either way, it's paramount that John remains in the dark about my past. And that the Doonan-Blunt wedding is executed to the level of perfection that Caroline Doonan expects. If it's not, John will put his foot down once and for all and I'll either have to confess, or my little cash cow will be all out of milk.

Cathy and Stan have guarded my secrets for nearly two decades. And for that I adore them.

"Well, I'm glad you could make it today. It's been a while," Cathy reprimanded in her gentle way.

"I know. I've been so busy with work." I opened the lid of my salad and scrunched my nose at the wilted slices of yellow pepper. "Unfortunately, I can't stay long, either. I have a major client coming in this afternoon and I hired a new assistant. It's her first day."

"The Doonans?" Cathy tucked a strand of her kinky brown hair behind her ear and sat down across from me with her cup of tea. She's one of those 1970s hippies who never graduated to the next century. Long bohemian skirt, chunky beaded necklace, no bra, and unshaven legs and armpits. She doesn't believe in deodorant, either. She says it's toxic, like rich people, even though she and Stan both have successful careers and, as a result, plenty of expendable income.

"Yes."

"Must be interesting."

"Eh. They're all alike."

"Yeah, but from an analytical perspective." In addition to being my old landlord, Cathy is also a family counselor. "Don't you ever wonder how people like that look at themselves in the mirror?"

"Of course."

"And yet you continue to immerse yourself in it." She lifted a forkful of salad to her mouth. "Though I guess there are some perks." She motioned to my Birkin bag. One of many.

"You know it's not as glamorous as it appears."

Don't get me wrong, I know how fortunate I am. But I slogged and hustled to get here. It took a unique brand of dedication to call the vast space I live in, with its white oak floors, milled baseboards, and trimless lighting, my home. I adore all four thousand rambling square feet of it — from the broad rectangular foyer bordered with inlayed wooden shelves to the meticulously landscaped wraparound terrace overlooking Park Avenue. I love the eat-in chef's kitchen with its glass-front professional refrigerator, imposing Calacatta marble island, and one-hundred-and-fifty-bottle-capacity wine cooler. And the four-poster bed sheathed in Charlotte Thomas bespoke sheets woven

97

with the finest Egyptian cotton. There's actually twenty-two-karat gold laced into the fabric!

Do I require this level of wealth? No. But I'm not complaining now that I have it.

"Maybe." Cathy arched an overgrown eyebrow. She thinks it's insane that women inflict pain on themselves to achieve aesthetic perfection. She also wears clothing from thrift shops, even though she can afford to shop at Bergdorf Goodman.

"Cathy."

"What?"

"You know I'm not really one of them."

"Sure, sure." She leaned back in her chair. "Stan!"

"What's all the shouting about? I'm right here." Stan appeared in white tennis shorts and a blue golf shirt. He beamed at me, and I beamed right back. He's the closest thing I've ever had to a real father. "Look at this beautiful girl." I stood up, and he pulled me into a warm embrace. "You're even more gorgeous than the last time I saw you, if that's possible."

"Such a charmer." I laughed and sat back down. Stan sat next to me and rested his hand on my knee.

Cathy rolled her eyes. "You think he says those things to me?" She and Stan have been together so long, they finish each other's sentences. And they're always bickering, but there's never any malice behind it.

"Did I not bring you flowers the other day?"

"Yes you did."

"See, I am a good husband."

"You're a gem," Cathy said, placating him. "Speaking of which, how's that husband of yours?" Cathy and Stan have never actually met John. For obvious reasons.

"He's fine."

"Still fucking anything with a vagina?"

"Jesus, Cathy." Stan moved his hand to my back. "Can we table the vagina talk until after lunch?"

"Those were her exact words, last time I saw her."

"They were," I acknowledged. I wasn't in the mood to talk about John's roaming penis.

Cathy's well aware that, while I have no intention of staying with John forever, his extracurricular activities curdle my insides. If only because I don't like to play second fiddle. She knows silver medals don't wear well on me. But it's worth it. He doesn't have to be attentive or faithful, as long as he veils his indiscretions and pads our bank account. I don't even need him to love me.

I tell myself it's easier that way. I try to view it as survival of the fittest. Charles Darwin, eat your heart out. I've worked too hard to get where I am to end up like my mother. To be trodden under the thumb of a man. That's why I have a career. A girl needs a backup plan in the form of her own savings. It affords me autonomy, regardless of what I have now. Because I know all too well how things can change in an instant, especially when there's an ironclad prenup in place.

I'd prefer not to focus on that, though. Besides, I have plenty to think about: three big weddings *and* a new assistant.

"I don't know how you do it." Cathy shook her head.

"Do what?"

"Pretend to be someone you're not. It must be exhausting."

"She doesn't have to pretend when she's with us." Stan said, pointing out the obvious. "She's perfect just the way she is."

"Thank you, Stan." I gave his arm a squeeze. "Wow, have you been working out again?"

"It's all the tennis." He smiled proudly. "I keep encouraging Cathy to get out there with me —"

"But I have two left feet," Cathy finished for him.

"So she says." He shrugged.

"And I'm not wearing —"

"One of those ridiculous skirts. I know." Stan rolled his eyes.

"So tell me about your new assistant. Is she fancy too?" Cathy changed the subject.

"Actually, no, she's not. Although I think she's trying to be, which is good." I picked up a piece of cucumber, noticed the browning around the edge, and dropped it back into the salad. Cathy stared at me in silent judgment.

"But you like her?"

"Today is only her first day. She seems great so far. I feel very optimistic for the first time in a while."

"I like to hear that." Cathy smiled.

"Me too." Stan spoke around a mouthful of lettuce.

"We don't need to see everything you're eating," Cathy scolded.

"She kind of fell into my lap." I checked my watch. Somehow, I only had twenty-five minutes to get across town and nineteen blocks south. "It may be too good to be true."

"In my experience, if it seems that way, it usually is," Cathy said. I thought about her words, and then stood up, leaving my salad and glass of tap water intact. "But we'll hope for the best. Your instincts have always been on point, which is one of the things I love most about you."

Cathy stood too and opened her arms wide to hug me. Then Stan did the same.

"I learned from the best." I reached for my purse and looped it around my wrist.

"I can't believe you have to leave already." Stan held me at arm's length. "Promise you won't be a stranger."

"I won't. I'm so sorry. When we made the plans, I had no idea that I'd have such a small window. But I didn't want to cancel on you."

"*Again,* you mean?" Cathy feigned insult.

"Yes, again. I'm the worst."

"Never the worst, but we were beginning to think you'd forgotten about us altogether," Stan added.

"Impossible."

"Lunch next week?" Cathy asked.

"You've got it."

"You bring the food." Cathy motioned to my untouched salad. "Then maybe you'll eat something. You're too skinny." We walked toward their front door, and Stan opened it to see me off.

"Tell that pompous husband of yours he better treat you well or he'll have to answer to me," he said.

I laughed. "I would, if only he knew you existed."

"We love you," Cathy called as I walked down the hallway toward the elevator.

"I love you guys too," I called back.

It's been too long since I said that to someone.

Or since someone said it to me.

12
KERRIE

"William, how delightful to finally meet you!" Jordana gushed, as she steered Tatiana and her fiancé into the studio.

One of the many things my old boss Nancy impressed on me is that clients can be a lot like children. You have to smile wide at them even if your car's been stolen and your credit card bills are overdue. You have to raise your voice an octave too high even though your instinct is to discharge a guttural sob. And you never — no matter the circumstance — lose your cool. The customer is always right. Even when they're wrong.

"I'd like to introduce both of you to the newest member of my team, Olivia. She just started today, but I've brought her up to speed on everything and she's as committed as I am to making your special day spectacular." Jordana looked to me for confirmation.

"It's very nice to meet you." I nodded and extended my arm dutifully. William took my hand. Tatiana smiled halfheartedly. "I'm so excited to work with you. Consider me your faithful servant."

"Faithful servant, huh?" William shook his head and laughed at the same time. "I don't think I've ever had one of those before."

"I guess it's your lucky day, then." I'm ashamed to admit that I blushed. Physically, William is exactly what you'd expect. He's handsome like a pure-bred German shepherd — tall and slender, with thick black hair that's greased and groomed. His eyes are dark but welcoming. His teeth are gleaming. And his navy suit appears to have cost at least my month's rent, probably double. What I didn't count on was his affable nature.

"You said the dress arrived early?" Tatiana toyed with a blinding diamond *T* necklace that dipped into her cleavage. "I hope it fits."

"Sweetie, relax." William stroked her back. "It'll be fine."

"I can't relax. This isn't any old dress. It's my *wedding gown.* It's probably the most important piece of clothing I'll ever wear. In my entire life. It can't be fine. It has to be *perfect.*"

"It will be. Don't worry," William said, attempting to alleviate her anxiety again.

"That's easy for you to say. You don't have my mother breathing down your neck."

"Can I offer anyone a glass of champagne?" Jordana interjected.

"I'd love one, thank you," William accepted.

"No thank you," Tatiana declined.

"I'll go get the dress and the champagne," I offered, and slipped into the back room. When I returned, William was seated alone on our white linen sofa, waiting patiently for the big reveal. Apparently, Tatiana isn't superstitious.

"They're in the dressing room." He motioned to his left, and I handed him his glass.

"Here it is!" I called out, as Jordana reached around the side of the black velvet curtain. I gave her the garment bag. I wasn't sure exactly what to do with myself, so I walked back over to the filing cabinet I'd been organizing before they arrived and kept quiet. *Do not speak unless spoken to.* Jordana was very clear about that, and I'm prepared to listen to every directive she sets forth. I need to keep this job. And I need her to trust me. Trust is essential in order to achieve sabotage.

"So what were you doing before this?" It took me a second to realize William was talking to me.

"What's that?" I teetered on my heels and nearly lost my balance.

"Jordana said this is your first day."

"Yes, right. It is." I fidgeted with one of the folders labeled LUCY NOBLE DRESS SKETCHES. "I just moved to New York City."

"From where?"

"Florida."

William is much cuter in person than he was in the photos I found online. I had to do some more research before meeting the Doonans firsthand. In fact, I did quite a bit of investigating into Jordana and her husband, John, too. I wanted to gather as much information about everyone as I could. After all, as Thomas Jefferson said, knowledge is power.

Obviously, I already knew a few things about Jordan Butler — where she grew up, what she did that night, and how she robbed us, but nothing more. An initial internet search revealed a house tour on ELLE Decor that featured Jordana's *amazing* apartment on Park Avenue, which is over three times as big as the home I grew up in. It said they gutted the interior when they first purchased it. Their architect and designer both called the style "enriched minimalism," whatever that means. You can tell from the photos that everything they own is classy, and the visual world they live in is unflawed, right down to the all-white, spotless living room. I'm guessing they don't eat on their couch. I'm also guessing their couch is *not* from Pottery Barn or Crate&Barrel.

The pictures showed Jordana smiling demurely on her wraparound terrace, with John's arm curled around her waist. The caption called him a *hot-shot financier* and said that he's a managing director at A. Doonan, LLC, Arthur Doonan's global investment firm, which Jordana had already told me. Still, it was proof in print that they're super wealthy, as if that wasn't apparent from the images alone. The writer waited until the final paragraph to mention Jordana's eponymous bridal concierge service.

Of course they were not shy about repeating that Jordana and John are expected guests at all of the city's "see and be seen" events, where I can only assume that socialites shovel caviar and slurp scotch to benefit the poverty-stricken. I've never tasted caviar, but it sounds repulsive. Fish eggs?! Really?

Caviar or not, the bottom line is that

Jordana has been living out every small-town girl's fantasy of opulence and success.

It's hard not to be enamored by the glamour, even though jealousy is tearing me apart inside.

Unfortunately, there were no similar profiles of Tatiana and William as a couple. There were a number of clips announcing their engagement. *A Royal Fairytale! Seeing Green for a White Wedding!* (the *S* was a dollar sign). And I did happen upon a short, professional bio of William, who works for a prominent hedge fund. There was also a lot of information on Tatiana's parents. Honestly, there were so many photos of all of them in gowns and tuxedos, fondling champagne glasses, that my vision started to blur.

"Where about in Florida?" I closed the drawer to the filing cabinet and walked back over to where William was sitting. I didn't want to come off as rude.

"Palm Beach." I kept my voice low, since Jordana was only paces away behind the curtain with Tatiana. I wasn't sure if she'd approve of me chatting with William.

"I love Palm Beach. My mom and dad used to have a place there."

"That's nice." I was practically whispering, which was a little awkward.

"Yeah, I used to go down there all the time

when I was a kid. We had to sell it when my mom passed away. My father was too distraught to go back. And it was too much for me and my brother to take care of."

"I'm so sorry about your mother."

"Thank you. I appreciate that. It's definitely not easy losing a parent."

"I know." I nodded.

"Your mom too?"

"My mom and dad." I was too preoccupied with saying the right thing to remember to lie.

"Wow, that's rough. Well, then I'm sorry for *your* losses."

"It was a long time ago."

"ARE YOU READY?" Tatiana projected from the dressing room, even though we were in close range.

"As I'll ever be." William hid an impish smile.

She threw back the curtain. "What do you think? I'm not sure I like it." I spotted Jordana, off to the side, digging her fingernails into her forearm.

"What do you mean? It's gorgeous. You look breathtaking." William stood up and took two steps toward her.

Tatiana took two steps back. "You'd say that no matter what."

"I would not." But I suspected he would.

"Please, William." She turned around to examine herself in the mirror. "Tell the truth. Do I look fat?"

"Sweetie, come on. You could never look fat."

"Seriously, William." Tatiana locked eyes with my reflection. "What do you think, Olivia?"

"Me?" I pressed my hand to my chest.

"Yes, you. You have an opinion, don't you?"

"I think you're the most beautiful bride I've ever seen." The words spilled from my mouth on instinct.

"Really?" Tatiana's eyes widened, as Jordana smiled smugly.

"Yes. You're absolutely stunning."

"Are you sure you're not just saying that?" She slanted her head to one side, as if the new perspective might enhance her view of herself.

"Definitely. I have no reason to lie." At least not about this.

"Come to think of it, it's not so bad after all." Tatiana beamed and then twirled around, chasing her image at every angle.

"I'm glad we're all in agreement." William grinned.

"I am too," Jordana announced, nodding at me before turning back to Tatiana, "Let's get you out of it, then."

As they closed the curtain behind them again, I overheard Tatiana say, "I like the new girl."

And Jordana replied, "So do I."

William and I shared a smile.

13

JORDANA

Once Olivia had left for the day, I sat down at my desk with a stack of bills in my hands. It was already six o'clock, and I knew that John wouldn't be home for hours. I picked up the phone to call Alexa Griffin, who'd left three messages throughout the course of the afternoon, despite the fact that Olivia had told her I couldn't get back to her until the end of the day.

These people truly don't understand that their troubles are First World. They're unable to fathom that the urgency they're experiencing is actually entitlement. Why? Because they've never been denied anything, including immediate and undivided attention. To them, a stray flower is a legitimate offense. The harrowing decision between serving lobster or filet mignon, Dom Pérignon or Cristal, is a genuine struggle. And it's my job to pretend that I feel the same way. To pretend that I, too, am outraged by invitations that dare to arrive in an envelope, by mail.

"Jordana? *Thank God,*" Alexa answered immediately. "I'm freaking out. I feel like things are out of control. There are so many loose ends to tie up."

"We're taking care of everything. You have nothing to worry about."

"I know, I know. It's just that . . ."

"Why don't you tell me what's on your mind?" *Use your words, little girl.*

"Well, I started thinking that pink shouldn't be my color scheme. I've been to three weddings in the last six months that were pink, pink, pink. Everything. I mean, they were beautiful, but can I really have another pink wedding? It seems so unoriginal. And of course Grey doesn't care. He's like, 'Do whatever makes you happy.' But that's easier said than done. I don't want people to think I've *copied* them."

"I can't imagine people will think that. No one owns the rights to the color pink. And anyway, imitation is the sincerest form of flattery."

"Sure, but I can't be an *imitator.*" Instantly I regretted my choice of words.

"What did you have in mind, then?" I began mentally ticking off everything we'd have to change if Alexa decided to switch her color. It would be a nightmare. I can't let that happen.

"Maybe purple? Isn't it royal or something?"

"Kate didn't do purple. And if the duchess didn't do it, it can't be that royal."

"You're right. Purple is out. What about just white? All white."

"As long as you're okay with blending in."

"Oh no, no. That won't do." Alexa was silent for a moment. And then, "I could go bold with red. Red is sophisticated."

"You could."

"But?"

"Well, I happen to know that there's a very big wedding before yours and that's their color."

"Tatiana Doonan?" I also happen to know that Alexa and Tatiana are frenemies. Two years ago, Alexa somehow managed to snag the Balenciaga gown Tatiana wanted to wear to the Guggenheim Museum's Young Collectors Party. The feud was splashed all over the pages of the *New York Post*.

"You know I can't say."

"So it is Tatiana. Forget red. It's trashy anyway."

"Alexa, I don't want to push you into anything, but pink is feminine. It's soft. Tender. Aren't you always telling me that

115

Grey says you can come off as overwhelming sometimes?" *Imagine that.*

"Totally. He just said that this morning. He called me bridezilla." *If the shoe fits.*

"Exactly." Quickly I typed *meaning of pink* into my internet browser. " 'Pink is the universal color of love,' " I read directly off the screen. "Don't you think that's so romantic?"

"I hadn't thought about that."

"Not to mention that peonies are most spectacular in pink. And remember, since they're not in season in the fall, we're going to import them, which will really impress your guests. *No one* has pink peonies in October."

"True."

"In my opinion, with your luminous complexion, pink is the only way to go. Grey will be absolutely mesmerized by your radiance. He won't be able to keep his eyes off you."

"You're right! You're so right. I don't know what I was thinking. It's pink. It's always been pink, and that's the way it will stay." Crisis averted.

"Excellent. Is there anything else?"

"Yes, yes. Let me see. I made a few notes." I heard the crackling of paper through the receiver. "How are we doing with Adam

Levine and Lady Gaga? My heart is set on one of them. Adam is so hot. But Lady Gaga is a strong woman like I am." *Sure.*

"We're working hard on making a booking. I've put in calls to their managers. It'll come down to scheduling."

"Money is no object. I'll even swap the date if I have to."

"I understand. Let's not get ahead of ourselves." Changing the date is not an option. Not if Alexa expects to live long enough to walk down the aisle. "What else?"

"Can we go over the menu one more time? And the vows. I can't decide if we should write them or not. Obviously, I want to. But Grey thinks it's hokey. Also, what if it rains? Can they do fireworks in the rain? I have to have fireworks. It's kind of the thing now." Of course it is. Brides and grooms worldwide — from Arkansas to Afghanistan — are shelling out tens of thousands of dollars to transform their wedding into the Macy's 4th of July Fireworks show.

"Let's address each concern one at a time." I measured the tone of my voice so as not to sound the least bit perturbed by her flagrant privilege. By the time I got her off the phone a half hour later, I was roadkill.

Fireworks. The only fireworks I'd seen

growing up were the ones in the living room when my father drank too much. I took a deep breath and considered what Alexa Griffin and Grey Wilder, Lucy Noble and Donald Cooper, and Tatiana Doonan and William Blunt — or any one of the other couples I've worked with — would think if they knew where I really came from.

I let my mind ramble toward that time and place. A time and place that was just faint enough to feel untouchable. A life that no one would believe had been mine.

As I considered just how significantly things have changed for me, I slid my finger underneath the sealed flap of the electric bill and nicked it on the edge. A thin, clean slice. I watched the blood seep slowly to the surface, before soothing it with the tip of my tongue. I have a high tolerance for pain. But I didn't always.

Believe it or not, I wasn't conceived to be the warrior I've become. As a young girl, I was diffident, nervous even. For the first three months of kindergarten, I clung to my mom's leg until the teachers had to peel me off like a stubborn scab. My teacher tried to soothe me with cherry ice pops and Nilla wafers, even though my mother's presence was the only thing I wanted. Still, I went to school because I wanted to make her proud.

I wanted to be just like her.

It wasn't until my tenth birthday that my perception of her shifted. That was when I truly *saw* her for the first time. My mom was intent on throwing me a party at our house, with what money I'm not sure. While many people associate Connecticut with yacht clubs and grand estates perched on the shores of the Long Island Sound, Bridgeport, the city I grew up in — which is the largest in the state — is a far cry from the enchanted seaside towns of Fairfield County. The violent crime rate is among the highest in the nation. Rape, murder, armed robbery, assault with a deadly weapon. All that good stuff. Let's just say I wouldn't let my child walk the streets alone. If I had a child.

But somehow my mother always seemed oblivious to our dire circumstances. Either that or she thought she was protecting me from them. She was so determined to give me the best tenth birthday a girl could ask for, maybe because no one ever did anything nice for her. I remember her saying, "You only turn double digits once." She encouraged me to invite all my friends. "We'll have pizza and yellow cake with vanilla icing and chocolate filling — your favorite," she said. "We'll play pin the tail on the donkey and impale a piñata with a baseball bat until it showers Raisinets and M&M's." What had escaped her is that I didn't have any friends. Even at a young age, I didn't really like people. Except my mom. And I didn't want any special attention, cake or otherwise.

Still, she was committed. So she asked a few of her friends to bring their kids. And she spent way more than she should have. The party was executed perfectly. Even if it wasn't what I wanted, I enjoyed myself, because I could tell how happy it made my mother. Everyone, even my father, was in good spirits.

Until all the guests were gone and we were safely behind closed doors. That's when I saw my father's face fierce with anger and his hands balled into meaty fists. "What the hell did you think you were doing?" he demanded, narrowing his eyes at my mother. "You said it was going to be a little party, not a blowout. How much did all this cost?" he slurred, as my mom slowly retreated.

He didn't bother to dismiss me this time. I suppose, in his sick mind, double digits was also the age when watching him bang my mother's head against a wall was no longer inappropriate. I remember wanting to scream and cry, but nothing came out. I remember wanting to jump on his back and pull him away from her. But instead I watched him pick up the remainder of my birthday cake, which my mother had lovingly baked from scratch, and pitch it across the kitchen at her.

Later that afternoon, when I found a far more docile version of him sitting in his chair in the living room, I approached cautiously and said, "I'm sorry, Daddy. It was my mistake. I asked Mom to do all of that." I pinched the underside of my arm until the tears began to flow. "It's not her fault," I sobbed, hoping that he'd forgive her. But he didn't say anything. He just kept drinking his whiskey and watching TV.

I'm guessing Arthur Doonan never shamed Caroline when she wanted to throw a birthday party for Tatiana. And I'm certain he'd never throw a cake at her or anyone else. I'm also pretty sure that Caroline wouldn't take it if he did. That may be the one and only way I wish my mom had been more like her.

Still, despite her shortcomings, she used to say that happiness is a choice. She would sit on the side of my bed at night, enfolded in her white cotton robe dotted with ragged yellow daisies, and, after she'd tucked the covers beneath my chin, lean in close and tell me that you can't depend on other people to fill you with joy. You need to discover it within yourself and learn to nurture it the way you would a stray animal or a newborn baby.

I believed her then. I'm not sure anymore.

The amazing thing is that no matter how constricting the agony that stifled her, she loved my father unconditionally. She wasn't crazy. She was a victim of abuse.

I may seem no different now than she was then. My condition may appear equally degrading, but I don't think it is. Because, while I do turn the other cheek, my emotional equilibrium isn't at the mercy of John's impulse. I'm not as invested in him as my mother was in my dad. And John, good man though he's not, is not a monster.

When my father's temperament was hot, he scalded everything he touched. Including my mother. He lashed out verbally and physically. He even thrashed about in his sleep. Those were the mornings I'd find my mother on the floor of my bedroom, curled into a ball, hugging her bare legs to stay warm. I wish she'd realized that the best course of action — the only course of action — was to run. As fast and as far as she could.

That's what I did. That's how I ended up

where I am today.

I do wonder what happened after I left eighteen years ago. I did love my mother. And I do miss her. Sometimes it's all I can think about. Other times, months will pass without the recollection of her split lips, swollen eyes, and sunken cheeks haunting me.

I don't know why she didn't come looking for me. I left her an insurance policy — a fiscal safety net. He probably threatened her. He would have said anything to keep her under his thumb. I waited for my mother for years. I wanted her to save me and herself. Because she *loved* me. Because she *wanted* to find me. But she never showed up. And I moved on.

I erased the thought from my mind and sifted through the stack of bills in my hands. I marveled at just how many people I employ. Florists, photographers, musicians, dress designers. My connections are my success. They bridge the gap between one lifetime and another.

The past is safely behind me. I just need it to stay that way.

14
JORDANA

It's been just a few weeks since Olivia started working for me, and already she's come a long way. Much further than I thought she would, I'll admit.

She's smart. There's no doubt about that. And quick on her feet. She's developed a digital filing system that streamlines all of our orders across every category and item-izes them by the wedding they correspond to. She's tidied up the space by reposition-ing some of the furniture. She made the point that where we work is a mirror of what's happening inside us, and that our brides will be delighted by the energy of the space. I don't know where she gets this stuff, but I couldn't agree more.

Beyond what she's done to update the office, Olivia fetches my coffee each morning and knows exactly how I like it after being told only once — black with a touch of skim milk. Then at lunchtime, if I'm staying in, she'll appear with a ginger salad and tuna sashimi from my favorite Japanese restaurant nine blocks away. This relationship is more successful than my marriage! I still can't believe how easy it was to find her.

"Do you know where I can find the invoice for Alexa's wedding gown?" I opened and closed a few documents on my laptop, but no luck. While Olivia's new digital filing system has modernized my antiquated paper trail, it's going to take a while for me to get used to it. I'm what some might call *technologically challenged.* It wasn't until recently that I traded in my leather-bound planner for an online calendar. I don't own an iPad. And I have absolutely no idea what this "cloud" everyone speaks of is. Fortunately, Olivia does.

"Let me help you." She walked behind me and leaned over my shoulder. "Wow, your desktop is a mess."

"What does that mean?"

"You have all these random folders, but nothing is organized." She clicked around a bit, dragging things here and there. "You have to condense the ones that go with each wedding, now that everything is on here. Maybe title each of them with the bride's last name for consistency. Do you want me to do it for you?"

125

"No, that's okay. I'm sure I can figure it out," I said confidently, even though I was certain I could not.

"Like what's this one? Travel?"

"I think that's a list of resorts people have recommended to me. I keep them for myself and for honeymoon suggestions."

"Okay."

"And this? Vendors?"

"That's probably outdated."

"Can I delete it?"

"No! What if I need it for something?"

"All right. How about this one? CD?" She hovered her mouse over a folder at the bottom of my screen.

"Some documents John wanted me to print for him a while back. It's all financial nonsense."

"Does he need it anymore?"

"Who knows? Better to leave it." The phone rang then. "Can you please answer that?"

"Sure."

"If it's Caroline, tell here I'm not here and take a message."

"Hello. Jordana Pierson Wedding Concierge." A pause. "Let me see if Jordana is in. She may have stepped out for a minute." *Perfect.*

"Caroline?" I mouthed.

"William," she whispered, holding her hand over the receiver. I reached out my arm, and she passed it to me.

"Hello, William. So nice to hear from you. How are you?" I appreciate that William calls himself. He could easily have his assistant do it, as most men would. I don't think John even knows how to use the phone system in his office. "Oh, I see. That's no problem. Let me check. Hold on."

I consulted my new online calendar. I'll admit it is pretty easy once you get the hang of it. "Unfortunately, I'm not free after five o'clock next Wednesday. No, I'm so sorry. I have a gala to attend. Can we do it later in the week? I can make myself available either Thursday or Friday." He went on. "Oh, you're busy then, okay. I wish I could do Wednesday. But I really can't get out of attending that event." John already told me, in no uncertain terms, that I better be by his side that night. "Olivia? Well, this isn't really her purview. I see . . . yes, but I'm not sure . . . it's just that . . . it's more . . . all right. If that's what you'd prefer. Six thirty. Cartier. I'll let her know. Thank you for understanding. You have a wonderful day too."

"Everything okay?" Olivia sat back down at her own desk.

"It looks like you're going to have to cancel your plans for next Wednesday."

"I don't have any plans." She smoothed her blouse and straightened her posture. She's always adjusting herself in my presence. Though I have to admit, I've noticed a marked improvement in her appearance.

"Well, that's convenient." It occurred to me then that she may not have a life outside of work, which is strange for someone her age. She's never mentioned a significant other, and she's pretty tight-lipped about anything personal. If she weren't so one-dimensional, I'd be suspicious. "You're going shopping with William for his wedding band."

"Me?" Her cheeks turned pink. She better not have a crush on the groom.

"Yes, you. I know this is a first. And quite honestly, I'm not thrilled about it. I'd rather be there myself, but William had to reschedule, and of course next Wednesday is the only evening I can't make it happen. Can you handle it?"

"Absolutely. How hard can it be to pick a ring? Men are usually very decisive."

"True. Still, I'll put in a call to Cartier ahead of time to guide their selections for you. I'm sure Caroline will want him to have the latest and greatest. I hope, for your sake, that she doesn't come with him."

"Me too." Olivia shifted in her chair. Looks and growing self-assurance aside, we're still going to have to improve her social awkwardness. "I can't imagine having a mother-in-law like that."

"Wait until you meet Arthur Doonan."

"Worse?"

"Possibly. He'll charm you at first. He's very charismatic."

"And then?"

"Just stay on his good side. If he has one."

"He and Caroline must make quite a pair."

"They do. Though if there's one thing I've learned in this line of work, it's that marriages are complicated. And they're not always as they seem. I mean, they're not always bred from love or a desire for true companionship. We see a lot of . . . arrangements around here." Olivia nodded, but I could tell she didn't really understand. "I know that may seem harsh, but it's true. I don't suppose you've ever been married?"

"Nope, can't say that I have."

"Are you seeing anyone?" I probed. Normally I wouldn't waste my time, but there's something interesting about Olivia. She's so innocent. Life hasn't pummeled her yet.

"No."

"Well, there are plenty of men in Manhattan. You'll meet someone."

"It's actually fine. I was seeing someone, but we broke up when I moved here."

"Oh, I'm sorry to hear that."

"It was my decision. I needed a change."

"Then I'm not that sorry." I smiled. Nobody understands the need for a fresh start better than I do.

"Do you think Tatiana and William are in love?"

"I'm not sure, and frankly, it's not my business to care. What I do know is that — whether they love each other or not — the wedding must and will go on. At this point, anything short of that would be a catastrophic embarrassment."

"Of course." Olivia nodded.

"Remember this. It's one of my cardinal rules. *Never, ever* become invested in the relationships of our brides and grooms. We're not marriage counselors. Our job is to execute the wedding itself. Understood?"

"Yup."

"Listen, if Tatiana and William figure out they don't like each other in a few months, they'll get divorced, or they'll pay for an annulment and go on their merry ways. It happens. But it's not our problem."

"That's sad. Don't you think?" Olivia

stared at me, presumably searching for sentiment on my face.

"Maybe." Our eyes met then. I still can't escape the feeling that there's something so familiar about her. Like she's an old friend. If I had any old friends. "I mean, yes. It is sad. But it's just the way it is." I paused to find the right explanation. "Happiness isn't always a choice."

15
KERRIE

By six thirty the following Wednesday, I was standing beneath the succession of bold red awnings outside the Cartier building at 767 Fifth Avenue.

It's April, and springtime has officially blossomed in New York City.

In Litchfield County, the season signaled songbirds humming, woodpeckers drumming, owls hooting, trees and flowers budding, and the earthy aroma of the ground and ozone thawing — a heady concoction of soil, grass, and pollen that no amount of chemical wizardry could emulate. But not in Manhattan. And definitely not in the heart of Midtown.

As I waited for William, I thought about what Jordana said last week. That happiness isn't a choice. I think she's wrong. Because I'm finally on the path to being happy. After two decades spent marinating in my own misfortune, I'm choosing to take my life back. I refuse to allow the crappy circumstances that have defined me thus far to hinder me from moving forward.

I'm not going to feel sorry for myself anymore. I have a new purpose in seeking revenge on Jordana. I have a new job that I'm enjoying so far, and I'm living in the most amazing city in the world. I may have started out faking it, but this is going to be who I am now. And yes, I know that bad shit happens to everyone. I'm well aware that there are plenty of people who've suffered far worse than I have. It's sort of like when you have the flu and all you want to do is complain about the fact that you have the flu, but then someone points out that you should be thankful that *all you have* is the flu. Because it's impermanent. And you could be dying from a brain tumor instead.

I never believed that until now. I never saw past my own hardship. But here I am, taking a good long look at what surrounds me. And I like it. A lot.

I'm actually relieved that I saw Jordana on television that day. If I hadn't, I wouldn't have summoned the courage to leave. I wouldn't have convinced myself that I could do better, and that I deserved to do better. What Jordana did all those years ago was horrific, but I can still make things right.

I'm more motivated than ever. And let me tell you, it feels damn good to come out of my shell and define myself by my own ambition, for a change. Like this is who I was meant to be all along.

I sucked in a breath of air, coated with the fragrance of car exhaust fumes, moist gravel, hot dogs, and honey-roasted peanuts, as I delighted in the realization that Jordana is finally going to learn what it feels like to have someone ruin your life. And she's going to have to atone for her sins.

How many afternoons did I sit perched on my windowsill with my nose practically pressed against the glass, watching the beautiful, mysterious older girl from down the block?

Sometimes she'd do cartwheels across her lawn or just dance around in her stone-washed jean shorts, spaghetti-strap tank tops, and black knockoff Adidas trainers when no one else was home. Of course, there was nothing special about those replica Adidas trainers, except that they were hers. And except that I'd never owned a pair myself. Real or otherwise, they were way too cool for me. But not for Jordan.

During the hottest summer days, I could reliably find her camped out on a flimsy beach chair outside her dilapidated house, with a bottle of baby oil, a sheet of aluminum foil, and her cracked Sony Discman, which she probably picked out of the trash. Sometimes I spent hours observing her from a distance. Sometimes I used my father's old binoculars, so I could get a closer look and come one step closer to figuring out what she had that I didn't.

It's funny how the minutiae we recall from childhood isn't trifling because it's a window to a singular place in time. A series of moments that, when looped and threaded together, become the fabric of our youth. Memories that make us who we are today.

I knew I'd never be like Jordan. I was who I was. Plain. Boring. Mostly awkward. And while I probably should have cared — maybe even been jealous or resentful of her external confidence, despite what she endured behind closed doors — I was strangely content just knowing I could absorb her grandeur from a distance.

It's almost impossible to believe that the Jordana I work for now was that girl. She's a silhouette of her former self — an outline that's no longer colored in. Although the truth is, I know very little about the woman she's become. She rarely talks about her home life or her husband.

She has been very respectful of me as her

employee, though. She asks for my opinion about everything from color schemes to cake flavors. She's tasked me with being the liaison between her and all our vendors. And, most recently, she allowed me to transfer our bills from paper to online. If I didn't hate her, I might genuinely like her.

I'm learning we're similar in many ways. For starters, we're both introverts, but we're also both extroverted enough to satisfy our objectives. We could be friends. Though come to think of it, I'm probably too low on the social totem pole to qualify. That's another thing: I've never heard her mention so much as an acquaintance. Doesn't she have anyone to confide in? It goes without saying that she's denying her past. New name. New look. New *perfect* life. I haven't asked any questions, which has been a unique challenge for me, because I want to know *everything* about her.

Where does she tell people she's from? Does she admit that her mother and father are still alive and residing in the same home on Cherry Creek Lane? Has she gone back since that night? Does her husband know that Jordan ever existed, or is her entire relationship based on deceit? I'm counting on the latter. After all, I am learning what it means to start over as someone else. It's hard to keep everything in a straight line when you're operating as two different people.

Jordan. Jordana. Kerrie. Olivia. The four of us are a crowd. But she's beginning to trust me. I can tell. Which is really the whole point. The first stage of my plan — to get her to rely on me before I sabotage both her professional and personal lives — is evolving just as I'd hoped. Now I need to figure out what comes next.

Twenty minutes passed, as I transferred my weight from one high heel to the other, in an attempt to mitigate the torture I've slowly become accustomed to in the near five weeks that I've been here. I can't leave. I can't call Jordana — she made that very clear. She's at her swanky event with John, not to be disturbed unless "the circumstances are dire." I skipped lunch in favor of work and am, therefore, on the brink of irritability.

Until I notice William lacing his way down the busy sidewalk, waving frantically, with reddened cheeks and an inviting grin. Even though this is my job, it's hard to deny William's appeal. So far he's defied every stereotype I expected of him. He seems laidback, kind, and humble.

William stopped in front of me, his hands

on his hips and his torso tilted forward. He sucked in a mouthful of air and then exhaled exaggeratedly. "I feel awful that I'm so late. I thought my five o'clock meeting would never end." He panted as he returned to standing. "Then I couldn't get a cab and, once I did, there was so much traffic I could have jogged here faster. Which I did for the last ten blocks."

"It's really okay. It's not like I had anything better to do." True story.

"Mind if I have a sip of that?" He motioned to the bottle of Evian I was holding.

"Yeah, sure. Of course." I handed it to him. Normally it would gross me out to share my water with a virtual stranger, but oddly, I didn't mind. And anyway, what else could I say? *I'm afraid you might have cooties.* "Are you ready to go inside?"

"Ready as I'll ever be!" He smiled and reached for the door just as a uniformed security guard opened it for us. "After you." William indicated for me to go ahead.

Once I entered the lobby, my hand flew to my mouth as I took in the elaborate architecture, the imposing vaulted ceilings, and the sleek glass cabinets showcasing what must have been millions of dollars in watches, bracelets, earrings, and necklaces, all dribbling diamonds. "Holy shit."

"You've never been to Cartier before?" He smirked, evidently entertained by my inexperience.

"No, never."

"Not even the one on Worth Avenue?" He raised an eyebrow.

"Remind me where that is again? I'm still learning the lay of the land here."

"*Worth* Avenue. In Palm Beach. Didn't you say you were from there?"

"Oh yeah. Of course I know *that* Worth Avenue. But I've never been to the Cartier there, no."

"Well, you're here now. Shall we?" He directed me toward a saleswoman who was greeting customers with a spritz of Cartier's signature scent.

"Hello, we're here to meet with Samantha," I said, unfolding the piece of paper I'd scribbled her name on. "It's in regard to William Blunt's wedding band. I was told she'd be expecting us."

"Yes, of course. Follow me." She led us toward the back of the store and into a private room with a desk and three chairs. "She'll be right with you."

"Thank you." William nodded and we took a seat next to each other on one side of the desk.

"This is exciting, huh?" I widened my eyes.

"I suppose." He didn't look excited.

"It'll be fun," I encouraged.

"Can I admit something?" His brow creased.

"To me?"

"Yes, to you!" He shook his head, visibly amused.

"Oh, okay. Sure, go ahead."

"I'm a little nervous."

"Nervous about picking a ring?"

"I don't know. Kind of. I mean, there's that." His shoulders slumped forward.

"And?"

"The wedding. Walking down the aisle. Tatiana looking like she hasn't eaten in three months, which she barely has. There's so much *pressure,*" he sighed. "Caroline was insistent on rushing the wedding the minute we got engaged, so the planning has been a lot. To say the least. And I've only been tangentially involved. Typically couples have much more time."

"I'm sure it's just jitters. That's very natural." Suddenly I'm an expert on marital bliss.

"You know I wanted to elope?" he continued, as if we were lifelong friends. "Tatiana and I always said we didn't need anything

140

more than each other. That the two of us declaring our commitment was all that mattered."

"So what happened?"

"All *this* happened. If you haven't noticed, this is Caroline and Arthur's wedding, not ours." He threw his hands in the air and then let them drop into his lap. "I mean, do you have any idea how much this is going to cost?"

"Actually, I do." I've seen the numbers. In fact, I've been trying very hard not to show how irate they make me or say aloud how *fucking* astronomical they are. But let me tell you, they're end-world-hunger big. Still, William isn't paying for a cent of it. The Doonans are footing the bill. What does he care?

"Well, then you know how ridiculous the whole thing is."

"It's not ridiculous if it's what you and Tatiana want." *It is completely ridiculous.*

"That's just it. I'm not sure that it is what I want. I love Tatiana. We've been together since our sophomore year of college. She used to make fun of all the stuff her mother did — the ladies' lunches, the charity boards, the obsession over looking a certain way and being perceived as someone you're not — and now I'm afraid she's being

141

sucked in. Tatiana used to be more relaxed, more carefree."

"Really?" I wasn't buying it.

"Oh yeah. She used to let her hair air-dry and she wore practically no makeup. She went to fraternity parties and drank beer from a keg. Now she won't leave our apartment without her 'face on,' and if her champagne isn't a specific vintage or her purse isn't the newest style, it's like the universe is going to combust. Don't get me wrong, I like nice things too, I just don't *need* all of this. And I certainly don't care what people think."

"Then why don't you say something?"

"Say something? Yeah, right. It's too late now. Arthur and Caroline would throttle me."

"It's never too late to be happy. Happiness is a choice." Despite what Jordana may think.

He laughed. "If only it was that simple. This is why I wanted you to come with me today. I figured your outlook would be refreshing, since you're still pretty new at all this." Fair enough. "Jordana is fine, but she's a little too intense for my taste."

"I hear you. And thank you." I looked away to conceal a full-on flush, as the door to the room swung inward.

142

"Mr. Blunt. I'm Samantha Dupont." A woman in a crisp, cream-colored suit with long, straight black hair, rosy skin, and narrow green eyes entered and extended a stiff arm. "Welcome to Cartier. We're absolutely thrilled to be part of your big day," she said with a very unthrilled, austere expression. "Let's get started, shall we?"

William turned to me before answering. And I offered a nod of reassurance. "All right, let's do this."

As I listened to Samantha recite the bullet points on each ring she presented to William, I made note of how expensive they all were. Samantha didn't dare mention prices, but I could see the tags tucked furtively beneath them. *Three thousand seven hundred and fifty dollars!* I swallowed my rage.

What I've come to realize is that there's very little mention of what things cost where our brides and grooms are concerned. The assumption is that they can afford it. Whatever it is. Of course something as simple as a wedding band is a given.

I wonder what it would feel like to never have to worry about money. To be able to waltz into a store like Cartier and say, "I'll take three of those huge-ass diamond necklaces." Just like that. Where I grew up, people didn't have options. They had to put

143

in long, arduous hours on the job just to feed their families.

When I first moved to New York City and started working for Jordana, I had no idea how much everything was going to cost. Even in Litchfield, which was a step up from Bridgeport, things were infinitely cheaper. I estimated that I could maintain my current lifestyle for about three months — strangely, the exact amount of time until Tatiana and William's big day. Unfortunately, I've been spending more than I ever accounted for without even knowing it. Last time I checked my bank statement, funds were dwindling too quickly, which is *not* good. I'll definitely have to readjust some things in order to sustain myself.

"These are the final styles for you to choose from." Samantha spoke briskly as she placed the first of three small red-and-gold leather boxes on the desk and searched our faces for anticipation. Then she lifted the lid in slow motion and exhibited one of the rings as if it were the Holy Child. "This is from our LOVE collection. It's among our most coveted designs. You'll notice the oval shape and screw motif. Absolutely timeless. It comes in rose gold or yellow gold and with or without diamonds. We think the diamonds add that something special. That *effervescence.*"

"Thank you." William examined it closely before handing it back to Samantha, as he had the others. "I'm not sure. I feel like I've seen this on half my friends. And I'm not quite the effervescent type. No offense."

"No offense taken. It is extremely popular," Samantha replied curtly. Quite obviously, offense had been taken. She deposited the second ring directly into William's open palm. "This is the Trinity de Cartier. An undeniable classic. As you can see, it's three intertwined bands — pink gold, yellow gold, and white gold. It was created by Louis Cartier in 1924. The pink represents love, the yellow is for fidelity, and the white denotes friendship. It's also meant to signify both mystery and harmony. It's *iconic.*" *Who knew one ring could say so much?*

"It's nice." He didn't try it on, which I could tell rankled Samantha. "But again, not really my taste. Do you have anything a bit plainer?"

"Plainer?" Samantha emphasized the word as if William had just asked her to drop down on all fours and bark like a dog. Naked. In the middle of the store. During the holiday rush. I almost laughed at the absurdity.

145

"Yes, maybe something gold. Not too thick."

"We have this last one. It's simple, eighteen-karat pink gold, engraved with Cartier lettering, and inset with a .03 carat diamond. Very *unassuming.*" I looked down to conceal a mocking expression. Samantha wouldn't know *unassuming* if it sat in her lap. "Is something funny?" She caught me and her eyes bulged like a tree frog's.

"No, not at all." I bit my lip and shook my head at the same time.

"What are you thinking?" William turned toward me.

"Nothing, really. It's fine."

"Seriously, tell me," William insisted. "I want your opinion. That's why you're here, isn't it? To help me."

"Okay." I paused, and Samantha leered at me as she tugged on her elf-like ear with her thumb and forefinger. A reflexive twitch. She's nervous about something. "I guess I was thinking that *unassuming* wouldn't necessarily be the word I'd choose. You know, because it does say the name of the store on the top of the ring and there's that diamond, which — don't get me wrong — is sparkly and all . . ." Samantha cleared her throat deliberately. "You know what? I'm sure I have no idea what I'm talking about.

146

Don't listen to me. I'm not even married!"

"Exactly." Samantha nodded.

"I agree with Olivia," William said, ignoring her obvious irritation. "Are there any others we can see?"

"Well" — Samantha starched her posture — "we do have a few more, however . . ."

"However, what?" William challenged politely.

"However, these are the ones we think are best suited for you."

"Right, only what I'm telling you is that these are obviously *not* the ones best suited for me. I don't want any embellishments. At all."

"Why don't you try them on?" she urged, desperation creeping into her voice. "Sometimes a piece of jewelry can look entirely different once you're wearing it."

"Listen, Samantha," William began, and I could see he was frustrated. If this had been Caroline, she'd have launched a full-fledged fit already. But William isn't like that. He's respectful, even when it isn't warranted. "I don't want to waste your time. And I'm sure you don't want to waste mine." He waited for her confirmation.

But Samantha wasn't willing to concede. "I promise if you'll just give these a chance." She inched the velvet mat toward him.

"We'd really like to see the other varieties," I interjected. "Please." After all, it is my job to be the bride and groom's advocate. And I can tell William is a good egg, even if he is a Richie Rich like the rest of them.

"Of course. It's our mission to make our customers happy. The thing is, again, *we* really feel that one of the ones you've already seen will work."

"Do you mind if I ask who *we* is?" I pressed. "I know Jordana was going to call in some suggestions, but I'm sure she'd want William to have whatever he's comfortable with."

"Yes, I spoke to Jordana. Her recommendations were on point, as they always are. And you're correct, she did say that they were only meant to guide William to a ring he loves."

"Then what's the issue?"

"Well," Samantha started, pausing to find the right words. "William's lovely mother-in-law-to-be was in earlier this week. She's a valued longtime customer." She hesitated again. "We spent quite some time going through each item, and she felt *very* strongly that one of the ones I've showed you would be best. I did present her with some that were a little *plainer*. But she eliminated those at first glance. She believes something ornamental would be more appropriate. Something that will make a proud statement." Samantha's lips spread into a thin red line. She'd outed Caroline and was petrified to say another word. I can't say I blame her.

"Ah, I see now. That makes sense." William grimaced. "Samantha, I do understand your predicament here. And I'm sorry that you've been put in the middle of this. That said, I don't want something that makes a statement. My statement is marrying Tatiana, not a piece of jewelry. So I'd say we have a couple of options here. One, you can find some other rings you think will suit *my* preferences. Or two, Olivia and I can thank you for your time and be on our way. Since I'm feeling generous today, I'm going to let you choose." He smiled genuinely, after punting the proverbial ball into her court.

"I, I'm . . ." Samantha stammered. "I don't know what to say." Caroline had tied her to a bedpost, and William was tightening the leash.

"Then I think we have our answer. Right, Olivia?"

"Yes, right." He stood up, and I did the same.

"Thank you for your time, Samantha." He

clasped her hand firmly.

"Yes, thank you," I parroted, wondering what the hell had just happened and whether Jordana was going to have my head.

"Mr. Blunt . . . I . . . I'm so sorry. Are you sure one of these won't work?"

"Yes. And it's quite okay — not your fault. We'll just be going now."

"Bye." I waved clumsily and followed William through the store and out onto the sidewalk.

"Can you believe that?" He raked his fingers through his hair.

"No," I lied, but then thought better of it. It's not William I'm deceiving. "Yes, actually, I can. I'm really sorry."

"This is *exactly* what I was talking about before. I can't even pick my own damn wedding band." He exhaled. "Well, I'm not going to let it ruin this spectacular night. I'm starving. You?"

"Ravenous."

"What do you say we grab some pizza? I'll take you to my favorite joint."

"Oh, no, that's okay. I'll be fine."

"Come on."

"What about Tatiana?"

"She's out with her girlfriends. They're probably knee-deep in dirty martinis by now. Anyway, do you really think she eats pizza?" He cocked his head.

"No?"

"But you will?"

"I will."

"Great!" William raised his arm to hail a taxi. "Let's go before you change your mind."

16
JORDANA

The words *listen* and *silent* share all the same letters. Olivia told me that the other day. Isn't that fascinating? Two virtues that confound most everyone, especially those who roam the hallways of privilege. There's always so much to say. So much to prove. If you can't stay a chin hair ahead of the competition, well then you might as well surrender to obscurity. You're nobody if you're not someone.

Thus, here I am at this absurdly lavish gala, by my husband's side — ever the obedient wife — nodding and smiling as a symphony of horns toot, toot, toot around the table. Why do I inhale this gold-plated bullshit? Because I have to. It's part of the job of being a socialite. If you want to maintain a position of power, it's crucial to make people think you give a fuck about them. It's the same way I approach running my business. *Does your rear end resemble*

Pippa Middleton's? Absolutely. But better.

I'll tell you, though, it's one thing to be naive enough to yearn for this life — to lie awake in bed at night and plot your ascent — as I did when I first fled to New York. And it's another thing to live and breathe it every day the way I do now. I used to think that once I'd nosed my way in, things would be easier. I was wrong. It requires strength and perseverance, not to mention a coat of armor — like treading water in an ocean full of sharks. One false move and you'll be eaten alive.

To John's left is Sefton Horowitz. He's short, stout, stubbly, and — dare I say — vulgar. Excruciatingly vulgar. Oh, the delicacies I'm privy to about good old Sef and what he can accomplish with his tongue alone. Sefton is Jewish and his wife, Priscilla, *was* a WASP, until his parents gave her an ultimatum. No holy conversion, no holy matrimony. So now she flips potato latkes, stirs matzo ball soup, and eats gefilte fish to verify her commitment to the tribe. And then on Sundays she attends services at a Protestant church in Harlem while Sefton thinks she's at the gym. I suppose she does bicep curls with her Bible.

Next to Priscilla are Aerin and Preston Hendricks. They have five kids — all boys

— who attend The Dalton School, a top-tier private school in Manhattan, where the elementary students fashion collages from scraps of fur and the freshman girls smoke pot before first period. Aerin and Preston are climbers. Surface scratchers. They're so desperate to gain entrance into "the inner circle" that they'll claw at the epidermis until they graze an organ. Poor Aerin will never look the part. She's ten pounds shy of being twenty pounds overweight, with a tawny complexion and soggy brown eyes. She's tried every diet from South Beach to Taiwan, but she loves to eat and hates to exercise, which renders her a plump little piggy. Unfortunately, it just so happens that, on the side, Preston is serving his tennis pro more than one ball. With a lot of Love-Love in between.

The third couple at the table with us, to my right, are The Lelands. Alexandra and Claude. They're a little older than the rest of the group, though you'd never know by their appearance. They have twin boys who are seniors at the esteemed Collegiate School. Connor will be at Yale come September. Rocco will be at Washington University in St. Louis, although they won't willingly divulge that. Rocco's rejection from Yale (also Brown, Columbia, Univer-

sity of Pennsylvania, and Dartmouth) orbited the social rumor mill in a shock wave,
given that both his father and grandfather
are Yale alums and still couldn't get him in.
Isn't that about as invigorating as a lemon
sorbet?

"We're renting a twelve-thousand-square-
foot villa on the Amalfi coast this summer,"
Alexandra said to me, as she flattened her
palm to her chest to show off a diamond
ring the size of my dinner roll. *Guilt gift.* "It's
absolutely breathtaking."

"I'm sure it is," I conceded. "I'm jealous!"
If I had to hazard a guess, I'd say she's having a second face-lift. What kinder way to
recover than by sunning your black-and-
blue marks on the Sorrentine Peninsula?

"I knew you would be." She clapped her
hands together.

"What about you? Are you and John doing anything special? Or just the usual —
Aspen and Hamptons?"

"I'm not sure yet. I have the Doonan wedding in June, so I'm trying to get through
that." John squeezed my thigh beneath the
table. He doesn't like when I talk about my
job with the other wives.

"Oh, that's right! I always forget you're a
working girl."

At this, John cleared his throat and turned

155

toward us. "Well, we'll see how much longer that lasts," he said more to Alexandra than to me. And then went back to his conversation with Sefton.

These people wouldn't know "working girl" if it dented the bumper of their Mercedes G-Wagen.

"Clark is completely fluent in Cantonese," I overheard Aerin say to Priscilla. "He's only nine years old!"

"Good for him," Priscilla replied. "Can you believe my Lulu can sing 'The Star-Spangled Banner' backward? Isn't that a riot?"

But it doesn't stop there. After preschool, elementary, high school, and college, it's law school or business school. Or a job. And then it's what kind of job. For example, everyone knows that the girls who become teachers are just biding their time until they marry rich. You think they give a shit about those snotty little kindergartners? Not a chance in hell. They're just relieved to make it through the day without puke — someone's other than their own — on their most sensible Jimmy Choos.

It's exhausting. This is exactly why I don't want children. At least not anymore. I'm not going to lie; there was a time when I did. After John and I were married, I got pregnant within a few years, without really trying. It was a boy. Honestly, I wasn't sure how to feel. On the one hand I was terrified. Having been raised by an abusive father and a mother who'd fallen victim to his sadistic behavior, I hardly had positive role models. On the other hand, I knew a child would afford me a whole new level of security as John's wife, and maybe even an opportunity to right my parents' egregious wrongs. John, for his part, was just happy about the prospect of having a son to carry on his family name. We both knew he wouldn't actually care for the child in any way besides financial support. And I was okay with that. Who knows? I might have been a good mother.

Unfortunately, twenty weeks into the pregnancy, we flew to Deer Valley to go skiing with a group of John's friends and their wives. I barely knew how to ski — it's a wealthy person's sport — but I did it anyway. It was essential in order to fit in. On my third run down the bunny slope, I was minding my own business and cursing the fact that my fingers were frozen beyond feeling, when a two-hundred-pound man pummeled into me from behind. I fell straight forward onto my stomach and rolled directly into a tree. I don't remember much after that.

I never had the chance to mourn the loss of our baby. John wanted to put it behind us in the same way he would an unsatisfactory meal at a fine restaurant. He said it was a disappointment, but there was no discussion beyond a frown and a shake of his head. I tried for months to regain what I'd lost. I even mentioned the idea of fertility treatments. That was a mistake. John told me that *people like us* aren't impotent. He blamed me, I'm sure of it.

That was when I decided that one day I'd start my own business. I needed something I could control. Something that couldn't be taken away from me. And, as it turns out, being a wife and a boss has become enough for me. Certainly, I could rely on my husband's wealth. I could spend my days at The Spa at Mandarin Oriental. Or chitchatting with my girlfriends over a boozy lunch of lettuce-wrapped air at Gramercy Tavern. If I had girlfriends. But that's not who I am. Or who I'll ever be. My mother gave up her identity to live in my father's shadow. She handed over her life to him and he squeezed her dry until all that was left was pulp. She didn't have an out. There was no contingency plan until I left one for her, and even then, she was too fragile to take it. I'm smarter than that. I'm stronger than that.

Speaking of, she called tonight. Just as I was leaving the office to come here. Eighteen years later, and she finally picked up the phone.

When I saw that it was her, my stomach lurched and bile rose in my throat. I didn't answer. How could I? Her message sounded urgent. She implored me to get back to her. But what's there to say?

She's not going to give up, the message said to me, and I can't risk that she'll try to get to me through John. Surely she's seen photographs of us online. The glowing couple. She knows where I live and where I work. I'm an open book on the internet, which is mandatory. If you act like you have something to hide, the vultures will pick you to pieces. And I can't have that. I know the only way to stop her is to talk to her. It's inevitable. After nearly two decades of silence, what could be so important now? I need to know, even though I don't want to.

"Excuse me for a minute," I whispered to John, as the lights dimmed and a movie screen came to life. They liquor you up first, then try to siphon your cash with photos of impoverished children. *While you glug your champagne, check out three-year-old Lena, who's listless and dehydrated. Won't you pay for a clean glass of water?*

"Don't be long," he admonished.

"I just need to run to the ladies' room."

I slipped out of the banquet hall and stumbled upon an empty conference room a few doors down. I pulled my phone from my purse and dialed. Slowly. Reluctantly.

"Jordan?" She picked up on the first ring. I resisted the urge to correct her. She doesn't know Jordana.

"Hello."

"I'm so glad to hear from you. I . . . I wasn't sure if you'd be in touch."

"This is a courtesy call. What do you want?" Why else would she reach out if not for money?

"Your father . . ." Her voice caught in her throat. "Your father is very sick."

"Okay." I wish I could say it mattered. But I hate that fucker.

"This might be the *end,* Jordan. Do you understand?"

"I do." My eyes stung. I closed them and pinched the bridge of my nose between my thumb and forefinger.

"I need you to come home. Right away."

"For what?" I sniffed indignantly.

"To see him. To hear him. Maybe to say good-bye."

"I said good-bye a long time ago. When

he pointed a gun at me. Remember that?"

"Things have changed."

"I doubt that."

"You'll see." She was crying. Softly, but loud enough so I could hear. I do miss her, but not enough. "Come home, Jordan. I need you to come home. *Please.*"

"I can't. It's too late." I shook my head like the child I suddenly felt like. "It's too late," I repeated. "I have a new life now. And I have to go."

"Jor—" I hung up before she could say anything else. And before I allowed myself to grieve. For her. For him. For the part of me I left behind.

Then I straightened my posture and marched back into the banquet hall as Jordana Pierson. Where I belong.

17
KERRIE

"You all right?" William checked in with me as we snaked our way down Fifth Avenue, dodging the other cars and pedestrians by a breath.

"Yeah, sure. Why?"

"Well, you're white knuckling the door handle."

"Oh, that. I'll be fine."

"We're nearly there, hang tight," he reassured.

"Where are we going?" I was already worried that having dinner with William — on non-wedding-related business — was going to piss off Jordana. I could practically hear her whispering in my ear: *My cardinal rule is never, ever become invested in the relationships of our brides and grooms. We're not marriage counselors. Our job is to execute the wedding itself.*

"You'll see." William pulled his wallet from his back pocket as we rolled to a stop outside a restaurant called Kesté Pizza & Vino on Bleecker Street in Greenwich Village, where I've never been before.

"Wait, let me pay." I rummaged through my purse. "I can expense it."

"Don't be silly. Besides, you're not really on the clock anymore."

"Thank you."

"Stay put, I'll come around." He tipped the driver liberally, opened his own door, and then walked around to my side to do the same. No one's ever done that for me. Honestly, I kind of thought it only happened in movies.

"You ready for a treat?" He helped me out of the cab.

"As you said . . . ready as I'll ever be."

"Oh wow." I spoke with my mouth full, as a thinning cord of cheese strung from my lips to the fat, gooey slice of pizza I was holding in one hand. Right off the bat, William informed me that the sign of a true New Yorker is the single-hand fold. I'm practicing. "This may be the best thing I've ever eaten. Seriously."

"What did I tell you?" He smiled, pleased with himself. "They've been voted number one pizza by *New York* magazine, best pizza in the state by *Food Network Magazine,* and

Food and Wine ranked them among the top twenty-five best pizza places in the United States." He read from the scattered frames on the wall behind me.

"They should hire you to be their publicist."

"No kidding. I come here probably once a week."

"I can tell. Everyone knows you by name." As soon as we walked in there was a flamboyant commotion, as a half-dozen Italian guys besieged William in a voracious embrace. All at once.

"It's kind of like my version of *Cheers.* I'm the Norm of Kesté, which — by the way — means 'this is it' in Neapolitan."

"I love facts like that!" I took another bite. It *was* addictive. "Have you ever heard of the 'Pizza Principle'?"

"Nope."

"There's a theory that since the 1960s, the price of a slice has been about the same as a subway ride."

"I'm stealing that."

"Go right ahead." I took another, smaller bite. "I can't believe they have so many different kinds."

"Yup, fifty. Certainly more than Cartier."

"Right? That was completely insane. I thought we were being *Punk'd,* for a minute there. I can't believe she wouldn't even show us the other rings. I mean, I can, but . . ." I didn't want to say too much. Even though it feels like William and I are becoming friendly, he's still our client. More important, so is Caroline.

"It's discouraging." He reached for his beer and took a long swig. "And I have to say, if this is the way things are going to be in the long term, then —" He stopped mid-sentence as a man in a shiny blue suit with a slanting smirk on his face approached.

"Mr. Blunt. Stepping out with another woman already?" He slapped William on the back, but kept his squinty green eyes on me. "Spencer Grafton." He extended his hand, palm up.

"Olivia Lewis." Awkwardly, I placed my hand on top of his and he kissed it with his hot, wet mouth, which was crowded by swollen pink gums. Bleh.

"Olivia works with Jordana Pierson."

"Ah yes, John's wife and wedding planner extraordinaire. Binky's already told me we have to hire her, and I haven't even put a ring on it yet." He laughed arrogantly, and I couldn't help but notice, even in the forgiving lighting, that his face was flush with freckles and his hair was buttered to his forehead with perspiration. Binky is one lucky lady. "So, this is a work dinner?" He leered at me like I was a ripe piece of fruit he wanted to sink his teeth into.

"I'm not sure what you're insinuating, but yes, it is," I answered quickly and confidently. "Sometimes meeting outside the office is more convenient for our clients and also more conducive to decision-making." I smiled austerely. "We believe in making things as easy as we can for our brides and grooms, since their time is so precious. I'm sure someone as successful as yourself can understand that."

"Absolutely." He turned toward William. "She's a firecracker." Then toward me again. "Binky will be in touch when the time comes. If ever she's fortunate enough to become Mrs. Grafton." He winked. "Let's hit the links soon, buddy. Maybe a home and home?"

"Sure, sounds great." William nodded as Spencer swaggered back to his table. "Sorry about that."

"No need to apologize. He seems like a real stand-up guy."

"If by stand-up you mean douche bag, then yes."

"But he's a friend of yours?"

"In a matter of speaking." William leaned forward. "Welcome to my world."

"I'm sure it's not so bad, despite the douche bags."

"There are plenty of them, trust me."

"I'll take your word for it." I took the last sip of my beer. It was the second for both of us, and I was beginning to feel a little tipsy. "So, I should probably know this, but what's a home and home?"

"His country club and mine."

"Right, of course."

"You handled yourself well with Spencer. He tends to rub people the wrong way." He smiled genuinely and signaled to the waiter, who was taking another couple's order but acknowledged him at the same time. "Anyway, what I was saying before Spencer interrupted is that Caroline's involvement in this whole thing is becoming too much. She has to realize that this isn't about her. It's one thing if she wants to offer her opinion on the flowers or Tatiana's gown, but a man should be able to pick his own wedding band."

"I'm sure Caroline just wants you to have something perfect." I didn't have the heart to tell him that she will never, ever realize that this isn't about her.

"Perfect for who?"

"For whom," I corrected. I couldn't help myself.

"What?"

"It's *whom*. Perfect for whom." My cheeks burned. "Sorry, apparently when I drink I become a staunch grammarian."

"Well, in that case, we're just getting started. The lady and I will each have another," he said as the waiter approached.

"Oh no, no," I protested, but it was too late.

"What's the worst that can happen?" William shrugged.

"Um, let's see. I could get drunk. Say something stupid. And lose my job." I chugged the rest of my glass of water and inhaled half a garlic knot to absorb the liquor sloshing in my stomach.

"You're funny, Olivia." Two more sweating bottles of Peroni were set in front of us. "Do you really think I'd let you lose your job?"

"I don't know."

"Hey! Have some faith, huh?"

"Okay." I ate the remainder of the garlic knot and washed it down with another slug of beer. My extremities were beginning to tingle.

"Why don't you start by telling me more about yourself. I know you grew up in Palm Beach and that you just moved here. I know that your parents passed away a long time ago. That you work for Jordana. That we have the same taste in wedding bands, or at least the same distaste. And I know that you love Kesté's pizza, perhaps as much as I do. But that's about it. Beyond that, who is Olivia Lewis?" He propped his elbows on the table and angled his face toward me, giving me his undivided attention. "Let's have it."

"There's not really much to tell." My brain went numb as I riffled through it. It's hard enough to maintain a double life when I'm completely sober. "I promise I'm not very interesting."

"Come on, I doubt that. Everybody's got a story, and if we're going to work together, you might as well spill all the gory details now."

"Uh . . . okay." I summoned what little liquid courage I had. "As you said, I grew up in Palm Beach. My parents died when I was two, and my grandmother took me in."

"Are you close with her?"

"She passed away a long time ago now."

"I'm sorry. Were you? Close with her."

"Yes, very."

"Do you miss her?"

"All the time. More and more lately."

"I can understand that." He waited before continuing. "I feel like when we make big life changes, we miss the people who helped define who we were to begin with. Does that make sense or is it the beer talking?"

"That totally makes sense."

"For example, with everything going on with the wedding, I've been missing my mother a lot lately."

"How did she die?" I blurted, and then shook my head immediately. "No, no sorry, that was rude. I think I've had too much to drink."

"It's cool, really. I don't mind talking about her. Basically, she went to the doctor thinking she had bronchitis, which turned out to be Stage 4 lung cancer, and two weeks later she was gone."

"Wow, that's rough." Our eyes met for a second before I looked away.

"Yeah, she wasn't even a smoker."

"I'm sure that made it even harder."

"Maybe a little. What about your parents?"

"Car crash." No reason to lie about that.

"So you never really knew them at all."

"Not really. My only memories of my mom and dad, if you can call them memories, are what people have told me. And what I've seen in photos."

"I'm sorry. That has to be tough, too."

"It is. But sometimes I wonder if it's also easier."

"In what way?"

"Well, since I never got to know them, there's nothing for me to miss." I hiccupped. "Oh my God, that's so embarrassing."

"Oh, please. You think I've never hiccupped before? It's endearing." *Endearing.* There's an adjective that's never been used to describe me. Ever. More specifically, never by someone like William Blunt, who must have a group of fancy friends to do this kind of thing with. People like Spencer Grafton. "And I totally get what you mean. While I cherished the thirteen years I had with my mother, it definitely wasn't the ideal time to lose someone I depended on so much. Occasionally, I think about what she'd look like now. And what she'd think about the man I've become."

"I think about that too. You know, whether my parents would be proud of me."

"I bet they would." He nodded sincerely. "Even though you don't like to talk about yourself."

"How do you know that?"

"I just do." William tilted his head to the side. "Okay, so tell me, what were you doing before you came to New York? I want to know everything."

"Everything? That's a tall order." *And,*

unfortunately, not possible.

"I've got time." He grinned.

"Okay, then. I was working for a company that created products for kids and babies — like practical snack bottles and changing pads. Things that make parents' lives more streamlined."

"That sounds interesting. Did you like it?"

"I did, but the owner sold the venture."

"Is that why you moved?"

"I needed to do something different." *I needed revenge.*

"That's really brave," he said, as his eyes met mine. "How's it been working for Jordana?"

"Fun. And challenging at the same time. I didn't know that much about wedding planning before this, but I'm learning as I go. Strangely, I think I might have a knack for it. I'm someone who likes when there are a lot of moving parts that you have to weave together to create something major."

He laughed. "I bet you are. Super impressive, even more so now that I know you can hold your own against a prick like Spencer."

"I guess pricks are my specialty." I laughed with him.

"It's funny, this conversation reminds me of the way I used to be able to talk to Tatiana. It's so easy with you."

"I remind you of Tatiana?" I was flattered, even though I know Tatiana and I have nothing in common. In fact, she's everything I'm not. Sophisticated, cultured, rich. Engaged to William.

"A little, yeah. It's a compliment, don't worry." He thought for a moment, while he kept his eyes focused on me. "I used to be able to sit down with her over pizza and a beer and just say what was on my mind. She used to listen, like you do. But if I'm being truly honest, it hasn't been that way for longer than I realized."

"What about your friends? You must be able to talk to them."

"Not so much. Tatiana and I have the same social circle. Our families know each other — as do all their friends. It's kind of incestuous."

"Sounds . . . convenient."

"Good word choice." He smiled. "I like that I can say whatever I want to you because you're not intertwined with any of our lives, yet you're still exposed to it through your job. You have a unique perspective, which is so valuable — in more ways than one. You know what I mean?"

"I'm happy to help in any way I can. That's what I'm here for."

"Right. My faithful servant." He held up his beer and hesitated for a moment. "To friendship."

I did the same. "To friendship."

"And to things being uncomplicated for a change."

"To things being uncomplicated."

If only he knew.

18
KERRIE

"Hey, lady!" Sara rasped over the pounding pulse of the music. "Sorry I'm late. You look hot!"

When Sara and I had originally made the plan to meet at a bar two blocks away from our apartment, she said she'd meet me there since she'd be coming from downtown. So I decided to arrive a few minutes early, to save us two seats and to order a white wine for me and a vodka martini for her — extra olives. It was still early and the place was pretty empty. The "scene" on the weekend doesn't really amp up until ten or eleven. Fine by me. I'm not one for congested spaces. Extra surprising that I like this city so much, considering there's no space in Manhattan that isn't congested.

"Really? You think?" It had taken me forty-five minutes to riffle through the mess of pencil skirts and silk blouses in my cube-like closet.

After trying on three or four of the skirts and then unfolding a stack of jeans that were all shapeless and far too . . . *Kerrie,* I finally settled on a pair of fitted black pants that I coordinated with a silvery tank top, minus the blazer I'd typically wear over it, and the highest of high heels — par for the course in New York. I flat-ironed my hair, curling it at the ends as Blake trained me to do, and then I applied a little more makeup than I normally would during the week. I have no idea how people put in this much effort all the time. It must take Tatiana and Caroline hours to get ready just to step outside their apartments.

"Hell yeah! You're one fine piece of ass." Sara always tries to buoy my confidence. It almost feels like a normal friendship. You know, despite the fact that she has no idea who I really am.

"Thanks." I smiled. The thing is, I've lost a significant amount of weight since I moved here; the relentless pace of this city will do that to you. Sara told me it would be much less expensive to have a few pieces taken in than to buy a whole new wardrobe. And she was right. "What's with the conservative attire?" I'd noticed her crisp blue pantsuit and white button-down shirt immediately, mainly because she never wears anything like that. She's usually in workout pants and a T-shirt.

"Job interview." She swung her purse over the back of her stool and sat down next to me.

"On a Saturday?" I took a sip of wine.

"It was the only time he could do it. And the only time I knew Dante would be with Joel. He took him to his parents' house in Westchester. They live on seven acres with a swimming pool, a tennis court, and one of those offensive jungle gym things. The whole shebang."

"That sounds nice."

"Does it?"

"Sure, why not?" I thought about where I grew up. No one had those jungle gym things, offensive or otherwise. We were lucky if someone stole a tire and jerry-rigged it to a tree. It's pretty amazing that it's only been seven weeks since I moved here. And already my old life in Connecticut feels out of reach. Maybe even like it never existed. *This* is who I am now. *This* is who I was meant to be all along.

"Let's see. Maybe because his parents make me itch all over."

"That's not good." I laughed. "I take it you don't like them?"

"No, they're fine. I guess. His mother is

passive-aggressive as all hell. She'll say things like, 'Oh wow, Dante got a haircut. Do you think he likes it that short?' And I'm like, *No, bitch! I don't think he knows he fucking has hair!* Or she'll say, 'It must be lovely not to feel pressured to take off the baby weight.' And his father's about a hundred and three. He tells the same stories about his childhood on a loop. Over and over and over. It may be the only thing worse than sitting through Dante's music class."

"A hundred and three?" I raised an eyebrow.

"Okay, he's eighty-two, but you get my point."

"So how did it go? The interview."

"Eh." She slid an olive off the miniature plastic sword in her martini and popped it in her mouth.

"Eh?"

"Well, I mean, I killed it. Obviously. I'm a fucking rock star. But I won't get the job."

"Why not?"

"Because I haven't gotten one single job I've interviewed for in the last six months."

"That doesn't make sense."

"Sure it does. The world of print journalism isn't what it once was. There are fewer editorial positions out there than ever before. And I'm not some hungry, responsibility-free twentysomething anymore. I'm a mom." She drained her glass and signaled to the bartender for a refill.

"So?"

"So that's how I'm seen. You take one measly year off to raise your child so he actually knows that the nanny didn't birth him, and you're done." She shrugged. "Listen, I'm not a moron. I knew it wouldn't be easy. I never operated under the misconception that people would be knocking down my door. There's always someone younger and more eager to step up. Someone who doesn't demand as high of a salary or have to hightail it out the door when her kid has strep throat. But I was fucking amazing at my job. I honestly didn't think it would be this hard to break back in."

"That sucks." I thought about how effortless it was for me to land the job with Jordana, and how I've been keeping my head down at work lately, as I incrementally secure my position as Jordana's faithful employee. I may even become her trusted friend, with a healthy dose of maneuvering. I have to admit I'm struggling with that piece of it. I know that my purpose is to make Jordana pay for what she did, but I haven't figured out exactly how I'm going

179

to achieve that. I can't just come out and tell her who I am and threaten to expose her. What if she doesn't care? What if she threatens me right back? Something tells me she could ruin me in this "town" with a half-dozen well-placed phone calls. It may sound strange, but I'm realizing that there's a certain degree of intimacy in Manhattan, despite its 8.5 million inhabitants.

My lack of strategy has rendered me restless and doubtful. That's one of the reasons I finally carved out time to join Sara for a drink. We've both been so busy. Her with Dante. Me with Jordana. And even though she pops in somewhat regularly for quick catch-up sessions, this feels different. Like having a real friend.

"Yeah, it does suck. Especially since I've exhausted almost every contact on my list."

"So do you regret taking the time off?"

"Yes. No. I don't know. Hindsight is twenty-twenty; all that bullshit. And I can actually tolerate Dante most of the time, but — at this point — I feel like I could tolerate him better if I wasn't with him *all day long*. It's grueling. More so than being in an office. In the beginning, I felt guilty every time I hired a babysitter so I could run some errands alone. I used to agonize over whether or not I could leave him for the long hours that a full-time job requires. *What if I blink and he's thirty-five? What if I miss his school play because I'm on deadline?* Those were the kinds of questions I asked myself."

"I see how it's a tough decision."

"Believe me, I know I'm not alone in this. Most mothers struggle with the same stuff. *How do I balance everything? Am I a terrible parent if I don't stay home? Am I going to become insipid if I do?* All the 'lean in' crap." She traced air quotes with her fingers. "I just never thought that would be me. I've always had things figured out. So I assumed this wouldn't be any different."

"But now you do think you want to go back to work?"

"I know I do. I need to use my mind. Unfortunately, *Mickey Mouse Clubhouse* isn't enough stimulation for me, even though the theme song is pretty damn catchy."

"And Joel supports you?"

"Yeah, he does. Mainly because he knows what a pain in the ass it can be to take care of Dante. He's not the easiest kid, if you haven't noticed." The bartender returned with Sara's second martini, and Sara pressed her palms together in prayer, bowed in his direction, and said, "You're a god."

181

Then she winked at him and took a big slug of it before continuing. "I'm sure Joel wouldn't mind having a second income, either. He does well. But so did I. It would allow us to finally buy an apartment. Shit is expensive in this city we call home. It ain't Kansas, Dorothy."

"No kidding." My chest constricted at the reminder of my own waning financial situation.

She went on. "Then again, in the same way that I do, he wants one of us to be around for Dante and everything else that comes with having a child. He has mixed feelings about Dante being raised by a nanny. And since he's not quitting his job anytime soon, that leaves me."

"Right." The great thing about Sara is that she can ramble endlessly without interruption, which is convenient, especially when alcohol is involved.

"Anyway, they're sleeping at Joel's parents' for the night, so I'm a free woman for a change. Any hotties?" She scanned the room.

"What's your type?" I peered over my left shoulder and then my right.

"Not for me!" She slapped me on the arm a little harder than necessary. I had noticed a couple of cute-ish guys checking me out, which is new for me. "I'm talkin' about *you*. I assume you're not getting laid yet?"

"At the moment, no." I suppose I should care, but I don't.

"Such a shame." She shook her head. "Now is the time, my friend. Once you're an old married hag like me you'll wish you'd done a little more wading in the man pool. Trust me."

"I don't know. It's not really my focus right now." An image of William flashed in my mind.

"What is your focus?"

"My job." *Revenge.*

"The wedding planning?" She considered this. "So you're liking making dreams come true?"

"I am. The opportunity to work for Jordana has been . . ." I paused to find the right word. "Enlightening."

"Wait a minute. I didn't catch this the first time you told me, but you mean Jordana Pierson, right?"

"Yeah, why?"

"I know that name." She thought for a few seconds. "She's like a socialite, right? Married to John Pierson, managing director at Arthur Doonan's firm."

"Yes." The fact that she knew that much off the top of her head riled me. What the hell is so special about these people?

"I used to write about John and Arthur all the time. I told you I was a business editor at *The Wall Street Journal*. I mean, it's not like I know them personally, but Arthur Doonan is a total fucking crook. My colleagues and I pursued him for a long time, but there was never a paper trail or even a source willing to go on the record, which meant no evidence for a story. Man, I wanted to expose him. And then of course there's John Pierson. He may not be a crook like Arthur, but he's still an asshole. Word on the street is that he's a skirt chaser and a sexual harasser. Apparently, he sleeps with all the new interns and support staff to welcome them aboard, if you get my drift. Well, at least the pretty ones with perky tits. I told my bosses a million times, but do you think they gave a shit? Nope. They're all horny men too. They told me to stick to covering the serious facts."

"So John cheats on Jordana?" I clarified, even though that was obviously what she was saying. Regardless, I wanted to hear her spell it out.

"I'd say so. In fact, I'm pretty sure he'll nail anything with a hole. I bet she knows. The wives always do." She finished her second martini. "I never witnessed it with my own two eyes. But let's just say I wouldn't want to be married to a guy like that. Sometimes all the glitz and glamour — that big, fancy life — just isn't worth the price you pay."

"I guess." If what Sara was saying is true, then maybe Jordana doesn't exactly have it all. She probably staggered into a world of misery all on her own. On some level I already suspected that, but until now, I wasn't sure why. Did she know John was like that when they first met? When he proposed? When she walked down the aisle? Is that why she decided to devote her career to other people's eternal bliss? And why she thinks happiness isn't a choice? That's sad. Not that I feel too sorry for her.

"Such a blast from the past, I'll tell you," Sara mused. "Feels like forever ago." She gestured to the bartender again. The girl can hold her liquor. "There's this hotel down by Wall Street. What the hell is it called? It starts with an *A* . . . fuck, do I have mommy brain. Hold on, I'll come up with it."

"What about it?" I choked back my desperation.

"All the finance guys take women there. Interns. New hires. Assistants. Anyone who wants to ascend the ranks without actually

185

working for it. Supposedly the general manager is a real guys' guy and promises absolute discretion. So much for that, right?"

"Do you think he goes there? John, I mean."

She shrugged. "Hell if I know. Why? Are you thinking of blowing the whistle on him?"

"No!" *Maybe.*

"Easy there, tiger. I was just kidding. You don't want to get involved in that, especially with your boss. I'm sure a chick like her chooses to turn the other cheek."

"Yeah, yeah. Of course."

"Andaz!" Sara shouted, splashing her third drink on her blouse.

"What?"

"That's the name of the hotel. Andaz. I knew it would come to me. Real modern kind of place. Wall Street and Water."

"Interesting." I chugged my second glass of wine. Wall Street and Water.

"Anyway, enough about those jerk-offs." She motioned to the small patch of dance floor, which was wide open, save for two drunk women in midriff-baring tube tops, stumbling around and lip-syncing to the music. "You wanna get out there?"

"I don't think so. I'm pretty tired." I

186

couldn't get home fast enough to do more research on John and his possible connection to the Andaz.

"You're bailing on me already?" Sara rolled her eyes. "The night is young! Stay for one more drink and then I'll let you walk me back." She smirked. "As long as you don't try to take advantage of me."

"No worries there. I may not be getting laid, but I'm secure in my heterosexuality."

"Noted." She laughed rowdily and clinked my glass. "And cheers to that!"

By the time I'd escorted Sara to her apartment — there'd been a lot of faltering involved — it was just past ten o'clock. I ordered Chinese food and sat down at my computer with a container of sweet and sour chicken, to find out just how sweet or sour Jordana's life is. After typing every possible configuration of the words, "Andaz Hotel" and "John Pierson," disappointingly, I came up empty-handed.

So instead, I decided to log into Jordana's email. I watched her type in her password the other day when I was standing behind her at her desk. It's not the first time I've taken a peek, but I've yet to discover anything important or even curious. Just a bunch of back and forth with clients and vendors.

But before I did, I paused for a moment. I'm not sure if it was guilt or sympathy that caused my hesitation. I could have just gone to sleep and called it a night. Regardless, I forged forward.

I scanned through Jordana's emails one at a time. There were a handful from Caroline griping about this or that. There was one from William dated a few days before, explaining that, while we did not have the great fortune of selecting a ring he liked at Cartier, he was very impressed with me and looked forward to my continued company in his pursuit. *Company* seemed like a nice word to choose.

Finally, just as I was about to turn in, a new message appeared from Caroline Doonan.

Jordana,
It's urgent that I speak with you tomorrow. I know it's Sunday, but it can't wait. Call me first thing.

— Caroline

Urgent. When it comes to Caroline, that could mean just about anything from an ingrown toenail to World War Three. But I pressed delete anyway.

And it felt damn good.

19
KERRIE

As I sat at my desk, alive with anticipation, I thought about my fortune cookie from Saturday night: *He who hesitates is last.* I mean, if that's not a call to action, then what is?

The phone rang and I recognized the number of Caroline's seamstress, Nina, on the caller ID.

"Good morning, Jordana Pierson Wedding Concierge." The first thing Jordana told me about Nina is that she's extremely talented. The second thing she told me is that she's completely scatterbrained and very disorganized. I haven't had the pleasure of meeting her yet, which works to my advantage.

"Hi, Jordana. It's Nina" — I didn't correct her — "I'm checking in to confirm . . ." I heard a loud thud and an "Ow, shit!" A few seconds passed. "Sorry. I dropped the phone. My office is such a mess. So what I was saying is that I want to confirm that

189

Caroline Doonan's shrug is supposed to be black velvet, right?"

"Hold on." I didn't want to say too much, for fear of outing myself. Silently I pulled up the order on my computer. Black duchess satin. "Velvet is correct."

"It just seems like a heavy fabric for June."

"Yeah."

"But I know Caroline. She wants what she wants."

"Always."

"Okay then, thank you. Have a good one."

"You too." I hung up and smiled to myself. Now, that wasn't so hard. Caroline will be apoplectic. Nina will blame Jordana. Jordana will blame Nina. No one will even think to blame me. And I don't feel badly about it at all, especially because shrugs are completely absurd to begin with. They're like half a jacket. Honestly, I'd never even heard of one until I started working with these ridiculous people.

I walked around Jordana's desk to log into her email again. I figured I'd remove a few random appointments from her calendar — a bikini wax, a haircut, and a trip to the dentist. Nothing business related. And nothing too obvious. Just enough to encourage her to mistrust herself and — if I'm vigilant

— to rely on me even more than she already does.

The thing is, though, Jordana and I have developed a nice rhythm in the seven weeks since I started working for her. I'd hardly say we're best friends, but she definitely likes me. And Olivia likes her. I'm not softening or anything like that. It's just that it's gratifying to finally be acknowledged by her. To be appreciated once and for all.

Would you believe that the other day she practically swooned over my new shoes? Then she told me how impressed she's been by my dedication. And added that not only have I been an enormous help to her, but that our clients have noticed too.

In order to keep up appearances, I returned to Equinox's salon last week for a refresher. The full workup, even though it's not even remotely in my budget anymore. I had highlights and a trim with Blake. An eyebrow tweezing with a willowy blond named Renee, who smelled of lavender and vanilla extract. And a facial with Olga, a bulky Swedish woman with persuasive hips and legs that resembled Redwood trunks — on average the tallest trees in the world. Some can grow higher than the spire of Notre Dame Cathedral.

I even treated myself to another massage

with Katya. Because, why not? What's an extra two hundred dollars when you've already spent far more than you should?

While I was at the salon, I also spoke to Blake about working with some of our brides. It's important to maintain fresh and varied vendors for our clients. Jordana gave me another pat on the back for that.

I keep telling myself that this is my life now and I think I'm finally getting the hang of it, save for the overspending. Not to mention that people are noticing. A guy at the bodega around the corner said I looked like Jennifer Aniston. He may have been drunk, but so what? I'd be thrilled if I resembled her third cousin twice removed.

I was such a plain Jane when I was growing up, the girl that faded into the woodwork. Yet here I am today — single and successful in the city. The city that never sleeps. It's hard not to savor every minute of it. But I can't allow my self-interest to distract me. I need to focus all my attention on retribution.

I know it seems like such a prickly word. Still, I have to see this through. And appearances are part of that. I can't very well show up at places like Cartier with William looking unkempt.

The phone rang again, and I noticed it

was him, just at the same moment he'd popped into my mind. How serendipitous! I picked up quickly. "Jordana Pierson Wedding Concierge. How can I help you?" I answer that way, even when I know who it is. Jordana expects formality across the board.

After my wedding band shopping with William, she told me that he asked if I could be his point person for all things groom-related and that she agreed. I could tell it made her a little nervous, but with everything going on around here, she said she has to be able to count on me without hovering over my shoulder. *Exactly.*

"Is this my faithful servant?" I pictured William smirking. He has just one dimple on his left cheek, right beneath his eye. I wonder if Tatiana loves it. I do.

I laughed. "Present and accounted for. You're never going to let me live that down, huh?"

"Unlikely."

"Well then, what can I do for you today?"

"I saw the whiskey tasting in my calendar for this Friday. Just confirming that you're coming with me."

"I think I'm the one who's supposed to confirm with you."

"Slacker."

"Not a chance. I'll be there."

"Excellent. I could use a few drinks and a listening ear."

"I think I can manage that."

"Great. I really appreciate it."

"Of course." I nodded, even though I knew he couldn't see me. "Until Friday, then."

"Looking forward to it."

"I'm looking forward to it too." I hung up, feeling a little lighter. Maybe I was flirting just a bit. But only because I'm not stupid enough to think someone like William would ever look twice at me in that way. Regardless, it's nice to have a playful repartee with someone of the opposite sex. God knows I never had that with Matthew.

By the time Jordana arrived, I was in the thick of arranging a jewelry presentation for Lucy Noble and I'd long forgotten about my conversation with William. My armpits were damp and my eyelashes were sweating. On day one, Jordana told me never to adjust the thermostat under any circumstances. I already knew she was cold-blooded, but the heat can be oppressive. It's hard to think, much less strategize.

"Good morning." She blew past my desk, visibly distracted.

"Jordana." I hailed her down like a taxicab.

"Can it wait?" She'd already sat down at her computer and was stabbing at the keyboard like a concert pianist approaching her crescendo.

"I don't think so." I didn't move.

"What is it?" Finally, she looked up.

"Sorry, it's just that Caroline Doonan has called six times."

"About what?" She appeared strained and impatient, which irritated me. I can barely stomach her when she's being nice to me.

"She said there was some kind of big mistake with the flowers and that she emailed you over the weekend but didn't hear back."

"I have no idea what she's talking about. It's been red roses all along and that's the way it still is." Jordana dismissed me without actually doing so. "I'll call her back later."

"The last time I spoke to her she said she'd be here at noon." I consulted my watch. "Which is in two minutes."

"It must be my lucky day." Jordana balled her hands into fists.

"Is everything okay? I mean, are you okay? You seem . . ."

"I'm fine." She spread her fingers on the desk, flattened her palms, and pushed herself to her feet. "Thank you for asking."

"Of course. You can always talk to me if

—" Before I had the opportunity to probe any further, the front door flung open and Caroline stalked toward us with a serpentine glare and a bite that was sure to be al dente.

"So you *are* still alive, then." It wasn't a question. But she expected a response.

"Hello, Caroline. It's lovely to see you again." Jordana smiled. She mimics authenticity so skillfully it's almost authentic.

"I emailed you on Saturday night and I've been calling all day." She glowered at me, as if I hadn't relayed the messages.

"My sincerest apologies, but I never received your email. And I was in meetings outside the office until now."

"Unacceptable." She twisted one of the buttons on her Chanel suit. "There's been an enormous error. I'm absolutely livid. If this is the way you do business, then —"

"Caroline," Jordana cut her off. "Why don't we step into the back so we can speak privately."

"Very well," Caroline conceded. Grudgingly.

Once they'd closed the door behind them, I lingered right outside it, pretending to reorganize the filing cabinet I'd sorted at least three times already.

"We have a serious issue," I overheard Caroline declare, as if the Bubonic Plague was sweeping the Upper East Side. "I ran into Gail Foster at the American Cancer Society gala on Saturday evening. And she said that she ran into Ron Wendt in the Hamptons. Apparently, he told her that we're doing all *white* roses for the wedding. *White.*"

"I assure you that's not the case." Jordana maintained her composure.

"Well, you're wrong." It's amazing how many mistakes are made when planning a wedding, even ones I'm not responsible for. I sat back down at my desk and dialed Ron Wendt's office number.

"I'll take care of it," I heard Jordana say.

"Ron Wendt Design. This is Clarissa."

"Hi, Clarissa." I spoke softly so I could still hear Caroline and Jordana going at it. "This is Olivia Lewis at Jordana Pierson Wedding Concierge."

"Oh, hi Olivia!"

"Listen, Jordana needs a favor. Quickly. Can you help me out?"

"Of course. Anything for Jordana."

"Can you please fax over confirmation that the flowers for the Doonan wedding are red? All red roses."

"You've got it. I'll do that right now."

"Thank you. You're the best." I hung up and continued to eavesdrop.

"Jordana, I would appreciate if our vendors do not discuss the details of *my* wedding with anyone." I noted the use of *my*. Poor William. "Especially a loudmouth like Gail Foster."

"It's very hard for me to believe that Ron would be so indiscreet. He knows better than that."

"Are you calling me a liar?" Caroline's voice rose an octave.

"Absolutely not. I'm sure this is some kind of misunderstanding that will be solved today."

"It better be."

"I'll personally reconfirm that all the roses will be red. Each and every petal."

"Good. Because as you well know, I will not tolerate any more oversights. If every *last* thing isn't perfect, it will be the *last* wedding you ever plan." Frankly, I wasn't sure who to root for.

"I understand," Jordana appeased her. She had no choice. Caroline's upper hand was winged and waiting to swat her like a fruit fly if she didn't comply.

Just as I was about to skulk away — it seemed like the conversation was closed — the phone rang yet again. I lunged to answer it. No need to draw attention to the fact that I wasn't at my desk.

"Hello, Jordana Pierson Wedding Concierge."

"Hello, is Jordan there? I mean, Jordana." The woman corrected herself immediately and instantly my interest was piqued.

"Let me see if she's in. May I ask who's calling?"

"This is Gillian Butler." She coughed and then sniffed. "I'm her mother."

"I see. Can you please hold?" I pressed mute and placed the receiver down. "Gillian Butler," I said her name aloud. This woman who positively had no idea who I was, but yet we had one major thing in common — *Jordan* left both of us. I picked up again. "It turns out Jordana is in an important meeting at the moment. Can I take a message and have her get back to you as soon as she's available?"

"I don't believe you."

"What's that?"

"I don't believe you that she's not there. She can't avoid me forever." I closed my eyes and considered my options, of which there were none. I couldn't interrupt Jordana and Caroline. That would be inappropriate. Still, there was a large part of me that empathized with Gillian. I had to help her.

"I'm so sorry. I promise you I'll let her

know that you want to hear from her. Right now, I'm afraid that's the best I can do." At least it was the truth.

"I understand." She withdrew. "Would you mind passing along something to Jordana for me?"

"Of course not." I reached for a pen and a pad of paper. "I'm ready."

"Tell her that if she doesn't call me back today, I'll be at her apartment first thing tomorrow morning. And if she thinks I don't know where she lives, she's wrong."

"Is that all?"

"Yes." She practically whispered it, and I struggled to hear her over the sound of an incoming fax. "I'm sorry."

"You don't need to apologize." *You are the victim. We are the victims.* "She'll be in touch. You have my word."

As soon as we hung up, Jordana and Caroline resurfaced.

"Olivia, please get Ron Wendt's office on the phone. We need to confirm that all the flowers for the Doonan-Blunt wedding are red roses."

"Already done." I picked up the fax that had just come in and handed it to her. I watched her mouth curl into a satisfied grin.

"There you have it. Red roses in black and white." She showed it to Caroline, whose face warped into a scowl.

"Very well, then. You're off the hook for now," she sneered. "I'll be in touch."

Caroline stalked off without so much as an acknowledgment of my existence. And Jordana slumped back into her chair, appearing uncharacteristically defeated. I didn't care.

"While you were —" I began.

She shook her head. "I can't right now."

"I'm pretty sure you're going to want to see this."

She didn't say anything, so I just passed her the note I'd transcribed from her mother and turned back toward my desk.

"Olivia."

"Yes?" I swiveled to face her again.

"I may have to go out of town for a day. For work. I'm not sure when yet, since my next two weeks are an impossibility."

"Okay."

"I realize it's not ideal what with the Doonan-Blunt wedding sneaking up on us, but I don't think I have any other choice."

"Absolutely."

"I'll need you to oversee everything, including the other weddings. We can't let those fall by the wayside."

"Got it."

"Another thing."

"What's that?"

"Please don't say anything to anyone about my mother. She's —" Jordana paused for a second. "Troubled. She can't be trusted."

"My lips are sealed." I feigned understanding, despite my reflex to defend Gillian and to remind Jordana that she's lucky to even have a mom.

"You know what, I'm going to work from home for the rest of the afternoon. I need some peace and quiet." She closed her laptop, stood up, and slung her purse over her shoulder.

"Sure, I'll be here." She walked toward the door, stopped just short of it, and turned around.

"I almost forgot, the building manager is coming by to pick up this month's rent check. I've been so distracted that I forgot to mail it. He's a little annoyed and completely irrational, but that's another story. He said he'll be here around three. The envelope is in the second drawer on the right side of my desk. All you have to do is hand it to him."

"That sounds easy enough."

"Thank you." She smiled wearily. "By the way, excellent work with Caroline today. I assume you overheard her rant and called

Ron Wendt's office without being asked."

"Yes."

She nodded. "Well done. That's exactly what I needed you to do. It's really remarkable how easily you've adapted to this job, and how good you've become at it. Thank you for being an excellent assistant. And a friend." Our eyes met, and she lingered there for a moment.

But she didn't say anything else. So I just nodded back and replied, "You're welcome."

20
JORDANA

"Your old man is finally on his way out, huh?" Cathy leaned against the armrest of her sofa and coiled her legs beneath her. I sat across from her in a patchwork chair that still reeked of cat litter, even though their twenty-three-year-old Maine Coon, Dolly, passed away a few months ago. I abhor cats, mostly because my father doted on the ones we had when I was growing up. I never understood how he could display such tenderness for an animal, while being so cruel to his own family. He said it was because they didn't talk back to him the way we did. They showed him respect. There may have been something to that. Still, I developed a strange fondness for Cathy's cat, Dolly. She was one serious alpha bitch. "Frightening thing is, he's not much older than I am."

"Don't say that." I came straight to Cathy's apartment from my office. I needed to talk to someone about my mother's efforts to lure me home. Obviously, that person could not be John. And while I briefly considered confiding in Olivia — maybe just that my father was ill and that we've been estranged for a long time, nothing more — I knew it wouldn't have been a prudent decision. The simple fact that she knows my mother is alive hits too close to home.

"What? Aging is a bitch. We're all going to die at some point."

"You should write greeting cards, you know that. By the way, you have something green wedged between your front teeth." I couldn't look at it dangling there for another second. Death talk or not.

"Kale. I had a great salad for lunch." She picked it out with her nail. "So how are you feeling about everything?"

"Not good."

"That's not a feeling." Usually, when Cathy puts on her family counselor hat, I find it burdensome. But not today. Today, it's exactly what I need.

"I don't know. I feel pissed off. Angry. Resentful. How's that?"

"Better." She stood up and walked toward the kitchen. "Something to drink?"

"No thank you."

"I won't bother asking if you want something to eat." She returned with a glass of water for herself and fell back into the threadbare couch. "Are you sad?"

"No."

"That was a quick reply."

"You know I hate him."

"I do, my love." And I hate it even more when people call me that. I wonder why I've never told Cathy that it was my father's term of endearment for me, which was disorienting because — as far as I could tell — he didn't love much beyond his whiskey, his rifles, and his dinner on the table at precisely six o'clock or there'd be hell to pay. He used to say, "Jordan, *my love,* why don't you find something to busy your pretty little self with in the backyard while your mother and I have a talk?" Then he'd shove me along with a firmly pressed hand to the bottom. As a child, those words paralyzed me, but not for long enough to stay and watch. The thing is, if you witness something with your own two eyes, then you have to admit it's real. And acknowledging that my father split my mother's jaw with his fist more than once was more reality than I was primed to confront.

But I'm not going to think about that. Not today. Not anymore. I've come too far and tolerated too many of Cathy's therapy sessions to allow myself to slide beneath the sanity threshold. *Again.*

"Then what else is there to say?" Cathy's heard every detail of my story. When I first met her she wanted to call the Bridgeport Police and have my father arrested. I begged her not to. As much as I wanted to save my mother, I'd just extracted myself from the situation and I couldn't bear to think about commingling my new life with my old one. She respected my wishes, against her better judgment.

"Well, you can hate him and be sad at the same time." She took a sip of water. "That's completely normal."

"I don't care whether it's normal or not. I may not have all my feelings in order, but I'm certain that sadness isn't one of them."

"Okay." She shrugged. "Whatever you say."

"Do you think I should go home?"

"Funny you still call it that."

"You know what I'm saying."

"And you know my answer."

"Yes?"

"Yes."

"But why?" I was really hoping she'd say no. Or at the very least, that it was up to me.

207

"Because you never said good-bye, and now is your chance."

"Why do I have to say good-bye? Who's going to make me?"

"You asked what I think."

"I was happy when I left. You must remember that." I let my mind travel back in time, to when I first moved to New York City.

I was running. I wasn't sure what I was running toward, but I knew that whatever it was, it would be bigger and better. I had a substantial amount of cash, but no credit card — in other words, no trail. Fortunately, I found a scrapheap of an apartment. That's when I met Cathy and Stan, who said cash would be fine. I also met Gilda, a struggling hair-and-makeup artist living next door, who gifted me my first spray can of Mace. Gilda's brother was a line cook at one of the hottest new restaurants in Midtown, where all the bankers went to loosen their ties over thick cuts of steak and heaping portions of mashed potatoes. He introduced me to his boss, Leon.

Leon offered me a job on the spot as a hostess. I'll never forget how he foamed at the mouth like a rabid dog and said, "Oh, the boys will love you." Then he invited me to discuss the details of the job in his pinprick of an office, but I said I was fine right where I was. I've never been *that* naive.

During the week, the crowd consisted of rich, horny, overworked men who probably had small dicks and large trust funds. On the weekends, their wives would accompany them, flaunting their couture clothing and flashy diamond rings — the gaudier the better. I wanted so badly to be one of them. To be glamorous and refined. I wanted people to look at me and think, *She is someone.* Someone who's not fleeing from her impoverished past and struggling to make ends meet. I wanted to exchange my welcoming smile for a life that was effortless and comfortable. A life full of caviar wishes and champagne dreams.

Sure, I could have been persuaded into a liaison with the less faithful of those men, who would have lavished me with promises and praise and the expectation of a blow job in the back seat of their chauffeured Rolls Royce. But I wasn't looking for a cheap thrill or a wad of cash on the nightstand.

I wasn't a side dish. I was the main fucking course.

And I knew it.

"Are you sure you're not confusing happiness with relief?" Cathy asked. "If you want to know what I remember, it's a seventeen-year-old girl who was scared shitless, but ambitious as hell."

"So I'm going home."

"I'd offer to come with you."

"But I need to do this on my own."

"You do."

"I'm not going to see him."

"Then why go?"

"Because my mother won't leave me alone. And if I don't appease her, she threatened to come to New York."

"That sounds like a great reason." Cathy rolled her eyes.

"I realize you're being sarcastic, but it's the truth. She's making me. I can't very well let her come here and meet John. He thinks she's dead. And that I grew up in Westport, where the rich people live. Not Bridgeport, where the people who work for the people in Westport live."

"Maybe it's time to stop living a lie, then. Ever thought of that?"

"Don't be ridiculous. If John knew I wasn't everything he signed up for, he'd divorce me without a second thought." I imagined bringing him to my old neighborhood, where the houses did not have fresh paint jobs, pared lawns, and flower beds. Not even close. Our lawn was always weedy, with brown patches that had been dehydrated by the sun.

I wonder what it would have been like to be raised by normal parents who cared for me, both physically and emotionally. A normal family — where everyone goes to the movies together on Sunday afternoon. A family in which the mother's eyes weren't black and blue and her lips weren't split. I envision a father who was anyone but my own.

If things had been different then, would things be different now, too? Would I be in a loving relationship with two-point-three kids, a Goldendoodle, and a sports luxury vehicle with an I'M A PROUD SOCCER MOM! bumper sticker? I shook off the idea.

"I've always thought John sounded like a winner."

"It's not just him. If all the people we socialize with and all my clients found out about my past, they would disappear faster than vintage Gucci at an estate sale."

"God forbid." She looked at me disbelievingly.

"I'll get out eventually." I stared into my lap.

"I hope so. I don't know what you see in that husband of yours anyway."

But *I* remember what I saw the night I

211

met John: *money.*

A man I was casually dating at the time, Allen, had brought me as his date to the annual Juvenile Diabetes gala. I was looking especially radiant in a strapless red Valentino gown I'd swiped from the bargain bin at Bloomingdale's. When I found it, there was a gaping slash down one side and the saleswoman said it would never fall the way it was supposed to, thus the rock-bottom price. I didn't care. The opportunity to own a dress of that caliber was worth the investment to have it repaired. So I bought it and took it to a tailor around the corner from my apartment — a Japanese woman the size of my pinky finger who worked her magic. Then I asked Gilda to work hers. The results were everything I'd hoped for. My makeup was fresh but sophisticated, and my newly blond hair was coiled into loose ringlets that fell effortlessly around my face and down to my collarbone. Call it luck, but I knew exactly what I was doing.

I'd met Allen at the restaurant where I was working. He'd asked me out a number of times and I'd declined because he wasn't my type. Allen was an investment banker. Real buttoned-up on the surface. He wore wire-rimmed glasses low on his arched nose. And had hair misting from his nostrils, even though he was bald on top. Allen was a nattering fool when you tried to have a conversation with him that wasn't about stock prices and number crunching. But when he asked me to accompany him to a charity event, I knew I couldn't say no. It was my first entrée into a world I'd never been a part of.

Then in walked John. With Sylvia. She described herself as a powerhouse prosecutor, but I couldn't look past her sunken eyes and protruding forehead. I didn't care about her. All I cared about was that the opportunity had been handed to me. God must have said to himself, *Well, this girl's had a dreadful excuse for a life so far; time to throw her a bone.* I could practically hear him whispering it in my ear. So I pinched that bone between my teeth.

I sidled right up to John — who was handsome and clearly successful, and who had a full head of hair. I ignored my own companion and his, because our connection was instant. I told myself not to fall for him, but to focus on the big picture instead. To devote myself to keeping him happy in order to secure my silver spoon. I fluttered my eyelashes and grazed his thigh with my hand when no one was paying attention. I laughed too hard at his jokes and replied to every question he asked with the answer I knew he wanted — perfect little lies. By the time dessert arrived, John said he was ready to leave. I slept next to him in his bed that night, but I didn't have sex with him. I made him pursue me. I knew I'd lose him if I made it too easy.

John later told me that he'd been drawn to me because I didn't throw myself at him. And also because I was stunning to look at, confident, clever, and street-smart, unlike so many of the tediously banal women he'd dated prior to me. But I know that what really hooked him was my constant attention to his every whim. Men are like children. They need to be coddled and cared for above everyone else.

Four months later, we were married at seven o'clock in the evening at the Metropolitan Club on Sixtieth Street and Fifth Avenue. I was resplendent in a strapless Vera Wang ball gown. The bodice was embellished with thousands of Swarovski crystals and the skirt was bolstered with tulle and overlaid with lace. My hair was pulled back in a loose chignon and fastened with a two-tier, cathedral-length veil, which I wore shrouding my face. It's very important for the bride to appear virginal.

John, for his part, was dashing in a double-breasted Prada tuxedo he'd purchased specially for our big day. I carried long-stemmed, bloodred calla lilies, and guests dined on foie gras followed by lobster and filet mignon. We were the picture of wedded bliss before three hundred of John's friends and family. An audience of strangers to me.

Planning our wedding was my first foray into an industry I'd eventually take by storm. It afforded me a glimpse of how the insecurity and daydreams of rich people impel them to pour endless amounts of money into one fleeting event. While I didn't know back then that owning a concierge service was in my future, I did know that there was a prospect there. And I knew I'd be very good at it, if and when the time came.

"Forget John. This isn't about him," I said, returning from my reverie.

"Isn't it?"

"*Cathy.* I'm not in the mood for a lecture."

"Then you've come to the wrong place, honey."

"I am *not* seeing my father."

"So you said."

"I don't care what you think."

"Of course you do." Cathy stood up and so did I. "I adore you. You know that. And I'm sympathetic to your predicament. But I also believe that you know what you have to do." She opened her arms and I folded myself into them. "Sorry to cut this short. I have a paying client who will be here in five minutes."

"No, of course. Thank you for the impromptu therapy session."

"Anytime." She released me from her embrace. "Now, go on. You can do this. You're one of the strongest women I know."

"I'm not so sure about that." I shook my head.

"Well I am," she said with a nod. "Call me if you need me."

"I may take you up on that."

"Good." She walked me to the door. "And tell your mother that her daughter has someone looking out for her. Two people." Then she opened the door and smiled. "A mother needs to know that."

21
KERRIE

If there's one thing I've learned about whiskey tastings — because, as you might imagine, this is my first — it's that it's impossible *not* to end up marginally drunk. Of course, it wasn't my *intention* to get drunk. My *intention* was to remain focused and clearheaded. In part because I'm here in a professional capacity. Fortunately, William is three sheets further to the wind than I am, and he seems to find the whole thing entirely amusing, which is a relief because — for the last four days — I've been investing all my energy in stepping up my sabotage game and I'm ready to relax for a change.

Let's just say that the envelope with the rent check that the building manager picked up did not actually have the rent check in it. Somehow that made its way into the trash can on the corner of Eighty-Seventh Street. Go figure.

I also started tweaking details of the other weddings we're planning. For example, both Adam Levine and Lady Gaga, whom Alexa Griffin had her heart set on performing two songs apiece — *no expense spared* — passed on the opportunity. Their managers emailed Jordana, but somehow the messages got deleted. When Alexa checked in this afternoon, I said, "We're still working on it! Fingers crossed!" Once Jordana realizes, there will never be enough time to get another artist of equal caliber. Or likely even close. She'll be calling dive bars in the village in search of a halfway decent cover band. *Madame Levine anyone?*

Then there's Lucy Noble and Donald Cooper. Donald's mom, Mindy, phoned on Wednesday to tell me she's planning a surprise for their reception. I said, "Fabulous!" Who doesn't love surprises? Lucy. Especially when it comes to her mother-in-law-to-be, who's a sloppy drunk known for her inappropriate public displays. I'm only privy to this information because I read an email to Jordana from Lucy's fiancé, Donald, saying exactly that. *Oops.*

I know how all of this seems. And I'll admit there's a large part of me that feels icky that innocent people are being entangled in my mission, but I can't let myself be derailed. Hearing the urgency in Gillian Butler's voice amplified my thirst for revenge.

"Are you having fun yet?" William leaned toward me conspiratorially. We've been at a spot called The Flatiron Room for the last hour or so, drinking a lot and eating very little. It's located in the heart of New York City's Flatiron District — another area I've never been to before. It's so exciting discovering new neighborhoods!

The space is rich and masculine, with coffered ceilings, wood moldings, leather banquettes, and oversize chandeliers. Countless bottles of whiskey are showcased in see-through, back-lit cabinets surrounding us, and there's a grand stage with thick red velvet curtains, even though we're the only ones here. It's like everything around us is glowing beneath the softest candlelight. If I had to choose one word and one word only to describe the atmosphere, it would be *sexy*.

"I am having fun. I've never done anything like this." I took a sip of a thirty-year-old scotch blend and set my glass down on the table next to the others, as the liquid filled and warmed my chest. There are a few things I've gathered thus far. For one, whiskey can be spelled two different ways

— with or without an *e*. Who knew? And there are about a zillion different kinds of whiskey (or whisky) — Irish, American, Canadian, Japanese, and White, to name a few. There are whiskeys from the Highlands, the Lowlands, the islands, pretty much from everywhere across the globe. Also, and this was a revelation for me, scotch and bourbon are types of whiskey, too. Again, who knew?

"You've been missing out, then." William smiled and his eyes glinted.

"Clearly." I smiled back. Once our server had finished presenting our choices, he'd left us to our own devices — to sit for as long as we liked, and continue to taste. "This isn't where you're having the rehearsal dinner, though?" I slipped my heels off underneath the table and wiggled my toes.

William laughed. "No. The dinner is at Caroline's friends' apartments on Central Park South. It's spectacular, and the view is among the best in the city. Eric Ripert is cooking everything on site, and I heard Billy Joel is going to rattle off a couple of songs on their Steinway."

"Who's Eric Ripert?"

"You know, he owns Le Bernardin." He pronounced it with a terrible French accent, which was adorable.

"Can't say that I do, but I'll take your word for it."

"You have heard of Billy Joel, right?" He smirked.

"Very funny. My nana loved the song 'Only the Good Die Young.' " Ironic, I know.

"She had good taste. Anyway, we're just here to get an idea of which varieties we like for the private tasting that night. Can you imagine Caroline and Arthur hosting a party here?"

"I guess not. It's a really cool place, though."

"Exactly. And would you consider Caroline and Arthur cool?"

"I've never met Arthur, but definitely not Caroline." I picked up a different glass and sampled something called a Black Bull forty-year Duncan Taylor. It went down smooth. "But isn't your father throwing the rehearsal dinner?"

"He is, but he's just along for the ride like I am. Caroline's the ring leader, if you haven't noticed." William tilted his head back and finished off a rye called Dad's Hat, which seemed appropriate given the conversation.

"Right," I said, nodding soberly even though I was far from it. "I've definitely noticed."

"Arthur, on the other hand. He just signs the checks. I don't think he gives a crap about the actual wedding."

"Really?"

"Really."

"He must care about Tatiana's happiness. She's his daughter."

"One would think. But all Arthur really cares about is money and power and getting what he wants no matter the cost or the collateral damage. That's about it."

"Oh." I thought about what Jordana said about him, and also what Sara said at the bar about him being a crook. "He doesn't sound like the nicest guy."

"Nice?" William laughed. "That's definitely not how I'd describe him."

"Sorry."

"Eh, he is who he is. But enough about Arthur."

"Yeah, of course." I took that as a cue to drop the subject. "So I think we're set with most of your stuff for the wedding. My checklist is pretty much complete."

"That's awesome. Thank you so much for all of your help, Olivia. It's been really great knowing that you're on top of everything and that you have my best interest at heart."

"That's my job!" I declared, a little too enthusiastically.

"Yeah, but you've gone above and beyond. You've been a friend, too, and I truly appreciate it."

"Thank you," I practically whispered to overcompensate. And again reminded myself of Jordana's cardinal rule: *Never, ever become invested in the relationships of our brides and grooms.* "Is there anything else you want to go over? Like the time line for that day. Or which cigars you want for the men? Obviously, we still need to find you a ring." I searched my brain for any other outstanding *business* items, but everything was so fuzzy.

"You know what? Let's not talk about the wedding anymore. I know it sounds odd, since we're here for that reason, but lately it feels like it's been consuming my life and I need a break, if that's okay." He propped his elbows on either side of his plate and rested his chin in his palms, like a little kid would. "What about you?"

"What about me?"

"Are you planning to get married?" It seemed like a strange question, coming from someone who wanted to move away from the subject.

"I'll probably need a boyfriend first." The heat from my chest rose to my cheeks, which had to be bright red.

"You don't have a boyfriend?" He sounded surprised, which — in turn — surprised me.

"I did, but we broke up." I wanted William to know I'm not a complete loser.

"Oh, I'm really sorry."

"It's fine. It was my decision."

"Why?"

"Why?" I paused to find some clarity. On the one hand, I want to be honest with William. If we really are friends, like he says, I feel like I should be as truthful as I can be without revealing something that might give me away — as contrary as that sounds. "I guess I realized that I wasn't passionate about him in the way that I should be, you know, if I wanted to be with him forever."

"Forever is a long time." William looked past me with glazed eyes. I could tell he was thinking about something beyond me and Matthew. "Why else?"

"He didn't inspire me. We sort of found ourselves in a rut. And at some point I knew that if I didn't make a change, I might never figure out who I really want to be."

"That's so profound." He bobbed his head up and down in slow motion.

"I'm not sure about that." I snorted. Damn whiskey. "I think it just sounds that way because we've had a lot of alcohol."

"I don't know. It makes a lot of sense to

me." He shrugged but didn't say anything else, so I took the opportunity to draw the conversation back to business and away from Matthew.

"If we could just talk about the rehearsal dinner for a minute?"

"Okay," William relented, though he looked disinterested.

"Do you know which of the whiskeys you want me to order?" I asked. "I want to make note of them now. I'm a little concerned that they'll all blend together if we wait until tomorrow."

"You're probably right." He straightened up and attempted to look sober. "All right, so I'd say my favorites were the Irish, the Japanese, and the White. Also, there were a couple I liked from the Lowlands and the islands. Can you ask for a list of those?"

"Absolutely." I keyed his selections into my phone.

"Oh, and Dad's Hat. That one was delicious."

"I agree."

"So, your ex-boyfriend. He's back in Palm Beach?" Just when I thought he'd forgotten about Matthew . . .

"Yup." Or Connecticut. *Tomato, tom-ah-to.*

"Do you still speak to him?"

"Not since I left."

"How long were you together?"

"Three years."

"Wow." William was somewhat alert again. "And just like that you were able to walk away?"

"It was a long time coming. Sometimes you need a nudge; an impetus to propel you forward and dislodge you from a situation that's comfortable but not stimulating."

"You are so right." He studied my face. "You're really smart, Olivia. Where did you say you went to school?"

"I don't think I did. Nowhere prestigious." I looked down. "I'd hoped to go to Yale, but it didn't happen."

"Why not?"

"My plan got derailed." I couldn't very well tell him it was because my life — financial and emotional — went haywire when Nana died. That someone — *Jordana* — stole everything from us.

"Well, Yale or not, you seem to be doing well."

"I guess so."

"Come on! Give yourself a little credit. You ended a long-term relationship, moved away from home, landed a great job, and have the fabulous fortune of planning The

Wedding of the Century." We laughed together.

"Oh, you're calling it that now too?"

"Only in jest. But don't tell Caroline, she would *not* approve."

"Your secret is safe with me."

"Thank you." He sat still for a moment and then stood up abruptly, steadying himself on the back of his chair. "Shall we?" He bent his elbow so I could loop my arm through his.

"We shall." William stumbled a bit as we made our way out onto the street. I helped him into a cab, despite his insistence that it was ungentlemanly for him to leave first.

And then I stood there inhaling the balmy spring breeze and allowing the unrelenting vibration of the city to eddy around me.

I've arrived, I thought. *My plan is unfolding.*

Still, it's not enough. I need to move things forward faster. Tinkering with details of the weddings alone isn't going to achieve my goal. I'm just not sure what my next steps should be. And the clock is ticking.

I walked a few blocks, allowing my mind to ramble, as it often does. I thought about Jordana. About her poor mother. About how she must have felt when Jordana abandoned her. I thought about the fact that Jordana doesn't give a shit about anyone but herself

227

and her fancy life. I thought about Sara — a true friend and a genuine person. A wife and a mother just trying to figure things out for herself, without screwing anyone else in the process. I thought again about what she'd said about Arthur Doonan and the new insight I'd gleaned from William. And why it is that people like Jordana and Arthur seem invincible, while people like me and Sara have to struggle to get what we want.

That's when the idea came to me. In a flash of genius. Or it could have been the blurring effect of all the booze. Either way, if what I was thinking made sense, it could be the very thing that would solve all my problems. It would be a risk. But a risk worth taking.

I fished my cell phone out of my purse and texted Sara.

Meet me at my apartment in fifteen minutes.

Then I took one last breath of life, made my way toward the subway station, and headed home.

22
KERRIE

By the time I'd reached my front door, Sara was already there, sitting cross-legged in her pajamas on the intricately patterned industrial carpet that blankets my dimly lit hallway. *Ick.* Doesn't she realize that people have chewing gum stuck to the bottom of their shoes? Or that they may have stepped in yellow snow?

"It took you long enough," she grumbled.

"Sorry." I turned my keys in the locks and let us in. "Drink?" I could hardly wait to tell her my idea.

"No thanks."

"Really?" I set my purse down on the kitchen table and poured myself a tall glass of cold water from the sink. My body was still feverish from all the whiskey.

"Really. I'm not in the mood."

"Is everything okay? You seem cranky." I'd never seen Sara this irritable before. Come to think of it, I'd never seen her irritable at all. Sarcastic, often. Frenzied, most of the time. Entertaining, always. But never deadpan. It's not her shtick.

"The good news is that no one is sick or dying. I just had a crap day."

"Dante?" He's usually the culprit.

"Surprisingly, no. Just more job shit. Three more rejections. One of which I was really counting on. It's defeating."

"I'm sorry to hear that." She nestled her body into the corner of the couch. I took a seat on the very edge of the chair across from her. "Although I think I may be able to help you."

"Help me with what?" She hugged a throw pillow to her chest like it was a flotation device. Or a shield.

"Your job search." I took a few gulps of water and felt the cool liquid spread throughout my body before placing the glass on the coffee table.

"I appreciate that, but unless you have connections at a major newspaper . . ."

"Not exactly, just hear me out." I gestured for her to remain silent. "I know this is going to sound crazy. So don't discount it until I'm finished. Okay?"

"I guess." She let go of the pillow and started picking at her chipped manicure.

"Promise me."

230

"Oh my God, just say it!" She looked up and widened her eyes at me.

"I want to help you take down Arthur Doonan," I announced without flinching.

"What are you talking about?" She laughed but sat up a little straighter.

"This isn't funny. I can help you take him down. For real." I stood up to make my point.

"You sound like Arnold Schwarzenegger. It's hard *not* to find it comical."

"You said Arthur is a crook, right?" I continued, pacing back and forth.

"Yeah," she said with a nod.

"And you said you're absolutely sure, right?" I stopped in front of her.

"Yes. I already told you that. When I was at *The Wall Street Journal,* it was considered fact, even though no one could actually prove it."

"Well, then it's not really a fact, if you want to be literal."

"It's a fact." She rejected my attempt at accuracy.

"Then don't you think he should pay for his purported crimes?" I sat back down and leaned toward Sara. I looked her directly in the eyes with an expression that said, *I mean business.* Or at least I hoped it did.

"Of course I do, but it's not that simple,

Olivia. He's a giant in the financial world. A big-ass fucking giant."

"So I've been told."

"Have you? Because it's no joke. *He's* no joke. It's been said that Arthur has predicted every major turn in the stock market in the last twenty-five years. I know he owns a significant percentage of Manhattan commercial real estate. And he funds all sorts of shit, like really important *think tanks*. Mark Cuban might as well be his goddamn housekeeper!"

"I hear you," I acknowledged, even though I refused to let her intimations daunt me.

"He's untouchable," she added, in case I hadn't gotten it.

"So are you saying you wouldn't want to take him down if the opportunity presented itself?" I pressed on, undeterred.

"No, but —"

"And do you think that maybe, if you did take him down, you'd have editors knocking down your door to hire you?"

"I suppose. I mean, yeah, definitely. But people have been trying to *take him down,* as you say, for years. What makes you think I could even begin to do it on my own? I don't work in that space anymore."

"You wouldn't have to do it alone."

"What do you mean?"

"You'd have me." I grinned. "And *I* have personal access."

"Olivia, I'm so impressed that you'd even think of something like this." She smiled. A smile that was so genuine, it reaffirmed my instinct to help her. "But I could never put you in a position like that. You do realize you could lose your own job in the process."

"I do." Which is why, if Sara decides to get on board, I'll have to explain to her how Arthur's demise serves my purpose as well as hers. *That* is the genius of it.

"And that's *crazy*. You said it yourself."

"So what?"

"You have no idea who you'd be dealing with, Olivia. Screwing with Arthur Doonan isn't a game."

"I'm well aware that the stakes are high."

"To say the least. It seems pretty impossible, actually."

I felt spurned on her behalf. This wasn't the scrappy Sara I knew.

"We're friends, right?" I asked, even though our relationship is founded on lies.

"Of course."

"Do you trust me?"

"Sure."

"Then just think about it, okay?"

"Olivia." She stood up, and I did the same. "I'm so flattered that you want to help me.

It means a lot. I just don't see how this could work. And I kind of need to get back down to Dante. He's been really fussy all day, and Joel is trying to get some work done."

She started to walk toward the door, and I followed her. "Please just think about it."

"Okay," she conceded, and then turned around to hug me. An uncharacteristic display of affection. "I'm really glad you're in my life, Olivia."

"I feel the same way."

"I'll talk to you tomorrow. Sleep tight." She patted me on the arm.

"Sounds good." I smiled, sensing in that moment that I might be able to bring her around.

And also knowing that, if that was the case, I'd have to tell her everything.

23

JORDANA

"I won't be home until late tonight," I announced. I sensed John's shadow hovering behind me as I folded a light sweater into my bag. Connecticut can be chilly at night, even at the end of May.

Yes, I'm going. With just under three weeks left until the wedding that will either secure my position as the preeminent wedding concierge in New York City or eternally tarnish the reputation I've worked tirelessly to curate, I'm returning to where it all began.

Believe me when I say that anything else would be less excruciating. *Anything.* I'd rather be photographed in last season's Chanel at the Met Ball. Or be seated in the third row at New York Fashion Week. I'd even maroon myself on a desert island with Caroline Doonan and her lap dog.

"Oh?" John's attention was piqued.

"I'm going to Boston for the day," I

answered, even though he didn't ask. "There's a fabric store on Newbury Street that's supposed to be spectacular. One of my brides asked if I could meet her there in person to help design her gown." I stopped myself from saying any more. Providing too many details is what liars do. I know better.

"That's a lot of driving," he said.

"I'm fine with it."

"That's not the point," he bristled. "I'm sure I don't have to explain to you that time is money. So the question is: Is it necessary? Is it the best use of your whole day? Not: Are you fine with it?" John doesn't mind being apart. But he does mind when I'm the one to leave. I know this because, in the past six months alone, he's been working much later hours and taking more "business" trips than he has in the last five years. He says he's been meeting with Arthur Doonan, but I suspect otherwise. Either way, he doesn't complain then.

"I think it's necessary."

"There are no suitable fabric stores in Manhattan?"

"Of course there are, but this one is supposed to be the best. That's what my clients command. You know that."

"Well then, I suppose I can pick up my dry cleaning. And make myself dinner." His tone was light, though trodden with meaning.

"Don't be ridiculous." John is well aware that we have a housekeeper and a chef who are salaried to do these sorts of things, but he never communicates with them directly. He tells me what he wants done and then, miraculously, it happens. Or, more accurately, I anticipate his needs and desires and guarantee they're taken care of — by anyone but me. I don't even think he knows our housekeeper's name. And that we pay her cash under the table. He could get in trouble for that. Because of his line of work, John is meticulous about keeping his hands clean. It may be the one thing I admire about him. "Dora will pick up your suits and shirts and hang them in the closet, as she always does. And Chef will make you whatever you'd like for dinner." I avoided eye contact, which is another sure sign of a liar.

"Forget about it. I'll just go out." I didn't bother to ask with whom.

"Let me know if you change your mind."

"I hope the fabric store is worth it."

"I'm sure it will be."

I have no idea why my mother is so insistent that I come home now after eighteen years of radio silence. I have no idea

237

why she wants me to see my father before he dies. Or why she thinks I'd want to. Frankly, it's an insult. I cut out when I was seventeen. When he slapped me across the face and aimed a gun at my chest.

The thing is, she didn't give enough of a shit to try and find me until the man who tortured us decided he needed an eleventh-hour farewell. Have I thought about what my father's death means to me? Sure. Nothing. Just because we're genetically related does not make him family.

But, per usual, I bet my mother will forgive his felonies.

I'm not sure what John would say about me if I were dying. He barely knows me. And the me he does know isn't the real me anyway. Still, it would probably be a glowing epitaph. He'd use words like *charitable* and *altruistic.* After all, we do sprinkle our wealth around, and he wants everyone to know it. John actually sneers at people who donate anonymously. Because, why would someone bother being benevolent without recognition? What a waste of goodwill that would be.

"How about a little something to hold me over until tomorrow?" John whispered in my ear, calling me back from my reverie. He gripped my arms firmly and turned me toward him before pressing his lips determinedly to mine. Then he negotiated his tongue between my teeth and his hand up my skirt. There's always an urgency in his approach, especially when he feels marginalized. And once he's aroused, he must be sated.

"Is this what you had in mind?" I dropped to my knees, and his eyes widened with lust. He nodded, unbuckling his belt and allowing me to do the rest. Then he moaned like a horny adolescent.

Every smart woman knows a blow job is much more efficient than sex. And less messy.

"Oh God yeah . . . oh yeah . . . faster . . . harder. That's right, baby." He thrust his hips like a mechanical bull until releasing one last rapturous roar. "That was fucking amazing." He smiled lasciviously and swaggered into the bathroom to clean himself off.

"Don't you forget it," I called after him, reaching into my purse for a breath mint.

He didn't reply.

So I slipped out quietly. Without saying good-bye.

Sure, the time will come when I'm fed up with this life. When suffocation will nudge me toward liberation. I'm not there yet. But

I know I will be.

And when that time does come, I'll finally be able to break free. I'll finally be able to find peace.

That's all I've ever really wanted.

24
KERRIE

As first, Sara wasn't terribly enthusiastic about messing around in Arthur Doonan's business. That I anticipated. Then, this morning, when I spoke to her on the telephone, she restated that it really didn't seem like something that would end well for either of us.

Kerrie would have accepted that. She would have said something like, *Sure, I understand*. Or, *It probably wasn't a good idea in the first place*. That's what people pleasers do.

But now that I'm Olivia, my focus has become me. And I'm not prepared to back down that easily, especially when I know I'm on to something.

Since Jordana is out of the office, I asked Sara to meet me here, so I can help her understand how our objectives coincide. If we can prove that Arthur is guilty, which is the wild card — and it's a doozy — then both Jordana and John's names will be disgraced for being affiliated with a criminal, at which point I'll reveal everything about Jordana's past to her husband and all her "friends." John will also be out of a job. Sara, on the other hand, will be fielding lucrative offers left and right. Win-win.

Of course, if we're going to be in this together, there's something she needs to know. I'm aware that revealing myself to anyone is a gamble. It may even be a big mistake. But the only way we'll be able to operate as a team is if she understands my motives in the same way I understand hers. And anyway, now that I finally have a true friend, I'm going to try not to spoil it.

A *friend.* Oddly, the one thing I have that Jordana doesn't. Who knows? Maybe I would have been Jordana's friend if our pasts hadn't collided. If I'd applied for this job without knowing who she was or what she'd done. Day in and day out, it's a unique challenge to remember that she's my target, not my comrade. When your mission is to convince someone you hate to adore and respect you, there are times when fiction and reality become muddled. So I have to remind myself who she is. What she did. And how I need to make her pay.

"Hey lady!" Sara busted through the front

door in skinny jeans, a camo-printed T-shirt, and slides with the Gucci symbol stamped all over them. Her chin-length black hair was blown straight to cup her face, and for a change she appeared to be wearing a decent amount of makeup.

"Wow, you look awesome." I stood up and walked toward her.

"Thanks. I needed a pick-me-up after all that self-pity." She spread her arms. "No more pit-stained tops. No more rubber flip-flops from Duane Reade, though those fuckers are comfortable. I may be a stay-at-home mom, but I don't have to look like a bag lady. You get me?"

"I get you."

"This place is nice." She looked around. "A little sterile for my taste, but nice. You still like it here?"

"I do."

"Ha! Pun intended."

"Very funny." I rolled my eyes.

"So what's up? What's the big secret? I can't stay long. Dante is with a babysitter and she has to leave in an hour."

"Let's talk over here." I motioned to the white linen sofa and sat down. In order to lure Sara here, I'd told her that there was something major I had to tell her. Beyond my plan to take down Arthur Doonan.

"I'm definitely intrigued." She sat down too, but her eyes were still darting all over the place.

"I'm not exactly sure how to say this, so I'm just going to come out with it."

"Okay." Sara was finally paying attention.

"I'm not who you think I am. My name is Kerrie O'Malley, not Olivia Lewis."

"Excuse me?"

"Logistically speaking, Olivia Lewis was my mother's name and it was also the name on my birth certificate. Olivia Kerrie Lewis. But I've always gone by Kerrie, and O'Malley was my nana's last name, which I took after my parents died."

"That's it?"

"Not exactly. There's more. A lot." I explained everything to her, as she nodded and said things like *Holy shit!* and *No way!* And when I was done, there was a prolonged silence — which has never happened in the history of my relationship with Sara. "Say something. You're making me nervous."

"Give me a minute." She took a breath. "I feel like I should be pissed that you lied to me."

"I'm sorry."

"Apology accepted."

"That's all?"

"I don't know. What am I gonna do? Never talk to you again?" She shrugged. "Listen, Olivia. Kerrie. We've all got our stuff. You think my shit doesn't stink? I get it. I'd be furious as hell if I were you. I'd want revenge too." She thought for a second. "And she really hasn't recognized you?"

"Not that I know of. I look pretty different than I did when I was twelve. And it has been eighteen years. And she only met me one time."

"Wow." She shook her head. "It's just like that movie *Single White Female*. You know, the one where Jennifer Jason Leigh transforms herself into Bridget Fonda and then tries to steal her identity."

"Yes, I know that movie. But the difference is, I'm not looking to *be* Jordana. Believe me."

"Fine, maybe it's more like *The Hand That Rocks the Cradle*, where that crazy doctor molests Annabella Sciorra and then kills himself. And then his wife becomes Annabella's nanny so she can seek vengeance."

"A little closer, but I'm not a psychopath." *Am I?*

"This is wild."

"So you're really not mad at me?"

"Nah. I'm not a grudge holder. If I was,

Joel and I would have been divorced before we were married."

"And now do you see how we share the same goal?"

"What goal is that?"

"If we take down Arthur Doonan, Jordana and her husband will be collateral damage. You'll have your choice of jobs, and I'll have achieved retribution. I can't do it without you. I've made a little progress on my own, but it's nothing compared to the impact this could have if we work together."

"I'm not going to lie; it's tempting. It's just that saying it is one thing. And doing it is another."

"Okay then, answer me this: Before Dante was born, where did you used to be at seven o'clock in the morning?"

"That's easy. In the office, at my desk."

"And where are you now at seven o'clock in the morning?" I've heard her say this so many times. Now she needs to listen to her own words. I mean, *really* listen to them.

"In my apartment, drenched in projectile vomit, with congealed rice cereal in my hair."

"Right. And there are days that . . ."

"I don't talk to anyone except the cashier at CVS, where I go to buy children's gas medicine, not mascara."

"And why don't you buy mascara?"

"Because I don't wear mascara anymore!" I could tell I was riling her.

"Exactly! And why is that?"

"Because I DON'T HAVE A JOB!" She jumped to her feet. "You're right. You're so fucking right. I've spent the last six months practically begging people to hire me. People who, by the way, used to rank below me. And I have no one left to call. Clearly, my approach has failed."

"So then maybe it wouldn't hurt to try a new approach? What's the worst thing that could happen?"

"Well, lots of awful things could happen." She fell back onto the couch. "It could blow up in our faces. Like a massive explosion."

"Okay, *but* —" I sensed one coming.

"*But,* let's just say I agreed to this insanity." She paused before continuing. "And that you do have access to Arthur. It's not as if he's going to turn over his private files to you just like that. Didn't you say you haven't even met him?"

"True, but didn't you say you were a rockstar journalist?"

"Hell yeah. And I still have a few solid connections."

"Perfect. I'm thinking that while you start looking into Arthur, I can try to glean information from William, and maybe even Tatiana."

"That makes sense." Her eyes were dogged. "You'd have to probe gently, though. Make it seem off-the-cuff, like you're just casually interested. I'd leave Jordana and Caroline out of it for the time being. They'll be too suspicious. And given what you just confessed, you don't want Jordana to think there's anything unsavory going on."

"I can do that."

"I'm not going to lie, ruining Arthur Doonan would be a huge professional coup for me. I'd finally prove to all those assholes who've been rejecting me that I've still got what it takes to be a contender."

"Okay, Marlon Brando." I laughed, giddy with the impression that I was winning her over.

"Every single major newspaper in this country would offer me a job that I actually want," she added.

"Yup," I agreed.

"And all of this would stay between us," Sara confirmed.

"All of this would stay between us," I repeated.

"Pinky swear." She extended her hand toward me.

"Really?" I haven't done a pinky swear since I was ten.

"Really." We linked fingers. "I'll see you tonight at your place, as soon as Joel gets home. God, can you imagine if this actually worked?"

"I wouldn't have suggested it if I didn't."

Once Sara had gone, I returned to my desk and tried not to think about our new partnership in crime. There are still other weddings that need managing, and Jordana informed me that she's planning to take on more once William and Tatiana have sealed the deal.

My first order of business was to confirm that the bridesmaids' dresses for Lucy Noble and the groomsmen's tuxedos for Donald Cooper will arrive on time. Then I had to verify that their aerial photographer will be able to fly over her parents' estate in Amagansett at the precise time of their ceremony, which was no easy task, given all the FAA regulations in place. And finally, I had to secure a two-million-dollar diamond-and-ruby necklace that Fred Leighton is lending Lucy to go with her grandmother's ruby earrings. *Two million dollars!* Since Donald's father owns three professional sports teams and Lucy's sister is married to one of the Kennedys, their photos will be broadcast across various TV stations and featured in any number of national magazines and newspapers, so it's an obvious publicity opportunity for Fred. Fortunately, I was informed that the necklace is waiting for Lucy in the vault and will be polished to perfection before being delivered to her parents' home the morning of the wedding. Naturally, there will be a security guard present until the last guest has departed, at which time the necklace will be returned.

After I'd locked down those tasks and a few others for Lucy and Donald, I turned my attention to Alexa Griffin and Grey Wilder. Alexa has been calling every day. Her anxiety seems to intensify with each minute that the wedding grows closer. So I thought, instead of waiting for her to be in touch, what if I reached out to her? If nothing else, Jordana will appreciate my proactivity. I picked up the phone and dialed her cell number.

"Jordana? What's wrong?" She answered before it rang.

"Hi, Alexa. It's Olivia. And nothing is wrong. Nothing at all," I reassured.

"Oh, okay. That's a relief. I was worried when I saw your number." She didn't sound relieved.

"I just wanted to give you a ring to check in. You know, make sure you're feeling good about everything."

"Is there something not to feel good about?" She was breathing heavily.

"Not a single thing, everything is on track." Except Adam Levine and Lady Gaga. Though I imagine life will go on without them. *Somehow.* "Are you okay?"

"Yeah, fine. I'm on the treadmill. Six miles down, two to go."

"That's impressive. Good for you."

"Well, I can't very well look like a heifer in my gown. I've been eating like food is going out of style lately. It's like I can't stop myself. Last night I ate *pasta.* I mean, it was gluten-free, obviously." *Obviously.*

"You look amazing." Alexa can't be more than a size four.

"In clothing, maybe. But you haven't seen me naked. I have cellulite on my outer thighs. It's a nightmare. I'm going to the dermatologist next week to see what she can do about it."

"Believe me, I wish I looked like you," I said, even though it wasn't strictly true. Alexa does have a nice figure, but her facial features are a little severe for my taste.

"That's so nice, Olivia. And thank you for checking in. Jordana never does that."

"She's crazy busy. That's what I'm here for. Although I assure you, Jordana is doing whatever it takes to make sure your wedding is flawless," I added. It's one thing to do something proactive. But it would be a very different thing if, in doing so, I shed a negative light on Jordana.

"That's nice to hear," she panted.

"Okay, well, I'll let you get back to your workout. I'm here if you need anything." I chose not to mention that Jordana was out of town.

"Thanks, Olivia. I'll talk to you soon."

"Sure thing." We hung up and I smiled to myself. Alexa isn't so bad after all. She's just a normal girl, like the rest of us. Fine, a normal girl with a shitload of money. But still, she's got problems and insecurities, even if they are nitpicky. Either way, they're *her* problems and *her* insecurities. And it's my job to alleviate them. Which I actually have a knack for.

As it turns out, revenge or not, I'm great at what I do. And I really love it.

Imagine that.

25
JORDANA

Just as I was about to turn onto my old street, Cherry Creek Lane, my body began to rebel. My skin prickled. My hands shivered. My vision clouded. And my chest constricted, strangling my determination to accelerate. I pulled the car over to the side of the road to collect myself. I pressed my forehead against the steering wheel and focused on catching my breath, but each gasp was so elusive I could only hold on to it for a second.

I questioned whether I was as strong as Cathy said I was. And whether I could face my past after all. I felt shriveled and hollow like a raisin in the sun. Fear, plain and simple, that's what it was. And it had sidled up beside me vigilantly, careful not to alert me before it was too late.

I sucked in a mouthful of air and sat up straight. I rolled my neck to ease the pressure that had burrowed at the tip my spine.

That's when I saw it. Right there on the corner of Cherry Creek Lane and Honey Hollow Road, where it had always been. Her house. The girl who saved me.

Kerrie O'Malley. That was her name. She was only twelve years old at the time. A baby mouse. Soft and fuzzy. Squeaky and innocent. Meek. Except that she was smart. And intelligence should never be underestimated. For me, though, she was a liberator. She had no idea what she was getting herself into when she opened her door to me that night. Neither did I. But I had no other choice.

I am ashamed. I am unworthy of forgiveness. Just like my father.

I do wonder what happened to Kerrie. What damage I did.

Once I'd quieted my anxiety, I shifted the car back into drive and curved around the side of Kerrie's house until I reached number nine, which looked bizarrely the same, though much less slovenly, at least from the outside. The house had been repainted a gleaming white to match the others on the street, and the lawn was no longer patchy and overgrown with weeds. The gravestones of our former cats had been removed, as had the rickety old shed. And there was now a small bird bath with a fountain in its place.

As I walked up the stone path, which also looked to be brand-new, I could smell the aroma of something stewing in the oven. Probably something I haven't eaten in nearly twenty years — like a meaty lasagna or a shepherd's pie. Unfortunately, my appetite, at least for food, has been tempered by my commitment to preserve a certain appearance. Again, it's part of the job that's being me, Mrs. Jordana Pierson.

I hesitated before the front door, which was lacquered in a rich green gloss and much sturdier than the one I grew up with. I thought about letting myself in, when it occurred to me — I don't live here anymore. I'm a guest. Or, perhaps, an intruder. I didn't have the chance to think much further. As I reached for the shiny brass knocker — another new addition — the door swayed open, and there she was. Standing in front of me with moist eyes and a convivial grin that told me I was welcome. Even after all this time.

"Jordan." She whispered my name as if it was our secret. In a way it was. Then she took two steps backward, and I took two steps toward her.

"Mom." What else was there to say? I looked past her. For him.

"Your father is in the hospital." She shook her head. "He's not coming back. It's a matter of days, they said."

"I see." My muscles slackened slightly.

"Come in, come in." She took my bag and set it down on a bench in the entryway. I followed her into the kitchen, where, as expected, there was a full banquet of delicacies. The sort of things that I grew up eating. When I didn't know better. There was the expected hearty lasagna. Dinner rolls. Salads. And desserts — freshly baked pies and cookies. A tray of cannoli. It was enough to feed a small army of hungry soldiers. "Help yourself." She motioned to the assembly of aluminum vats, which seemed to multiply around me.

"You shouldn't have. This is way too much."

"I didn't. People have been bringing things by all week." She bowed her head. "You know, to pay their respects."

"He's not gone yet."

My mother winced. "Can I get you something?"

It was an awkward tango, to say the least. I sat down at the table, and she orbited me like a hawk, calculating my every movement.

"No."

"Not even a little something?" She reached into the cabinet for two plates and piled them high with lettuce.

"Salad, but only if you're eating." It's instinct to deny myself, though I'm so out of my element that I wonder if calories even count here. I wonder if anything counts here.

"Okay." She continued making both plates. "You're so tiny." She appraised me, careful not to linger too long. My own mother is afraid of me. I can't blame her. When you've spent the majority of your adult life being startled by the sound of your own heartbeat, what other choice do you have?

"The house looks better." While she brewed a pot of tea, I stood up and walked around the first floor, which isn't much larger than my bedroom in New York. Each room had been updated with more modern furniture. In the living room there was an oversize gray, ultra-suede sectional accented with jewel-toned throw pillows — orange, purple, and turquoise. There was also a glass coffee table where the splintered wooden one of my childhood had been. And a thick sisal rug covered the newly stained floor. Returning to the kitchen, I noticed that the cabinets had been refaced, all of the handles updated too. There was a tiled backsplash to complement the stovetop, and the appliances were ones I'd never seen before.

"Thank you. It's been a labor of love." My mother dressed the table with linens and silverware, and we sat down across from each other with our plates of salad and mugs of tea.

"I can tell." I observed her face. Really inspected it for the first time since I'd arrived. She appeared youthful, girlish even. Lighter and smoother. She'd dyed her gray hairs to match her natural chestnut color. Her eyes were wider. Her skin was luminous. "You look great." I knew the woman across from me, if only faintly from my earliest years. Before he aged her.

"Things have changed." She smiled weakly. A genuine smile, not the one she used to put on for my benefit.

"Oh?" What things? What could have changed? I suppose everything. Why is it that when we leave someplace that we've called home, we assume that nothing will be different when we return? That it will have been preserved in time, waiting for us to come back and defrost it.

"You'll see tomorrow." Was that a smirk I saw pass her lips? I've never seen my mother smirk. You have to be irreverent to smirk.

"I'm not staying until tomorrow. I'm here because you threatened me, remember?" The mood darkened once again. Enough of the niceties.

"But you have to go visit your father in the hospital."

"No I don't. And I won't."

"Jordan." She reached her hand out.

"Don't touch me." I recoiled. "And that's not my name anymore. I'm Jordana now." I pronounced it the way Caroline does. Jor-DONNA. "I'd prefer if you call me that."

"You seem so angry." She placed her hand back in her lap.

"You say that like you're surprised. Wouldn't you be angry if you were me?"

She was silent.

"I'm asking you, Mom. Can you blame me for being furious?"

"No." She hesitated. "It's just that . . ."

"It's just that what?" Did she expect me to forgive and forget that easily? Like she always had?

"It's been so long. I thought that maybe . . ."

"You thought that maybe what? That I'd have forgotten what he did to me? What he did to you? And the fact that you let it happen. Or maybe you thought I'd let it slip my mind that you never once came to look

259

for me, that you never once reached out to me until now? For fuck's sake, Mom, it's been eighteen years. EIGHTEEN YEARS!" I hurled the accusation at her. "Why now? Tell me. Do you really give a shit if I say good-bye to Dad on his deathbed? Do you really think he deserves that courtesy from me?"

She was silent again.

"Answer me! You owe me that." I slammed my hand on the table, alarming her.

"Because he asked me to find you." She looked away.

"*He* asked you to find me? That's really rich." I shook my head. "So in other words, you didn't give a crap about finding me. Not until it was important to him. Congratulations! Mother of the year."

"*Jordan.*"

"Jordana! It's *Jordana*!"

"I don't think I deserve to be spoken to this way."

"Don't you? Oh really? Well, I don't think I deserved to be abused as a child. I don't think I deserved parents who let me run away and never came looking for me. I expected that from him. But you? Obviously you figured out where I was at some point. And you still chose him over me!"

"Is that what you think?" Her voice was

barely audible. I'd bruised her. I didn't care.

"It's the truth!" My tone was fierce. "I was a child, for God's sake! You were supposed to protect me. He was a monster."

"Don't talk about your father that way, Jordan."

"Jordana!" I shrieked. "And I'll talk about him any way I'd like. I'm an adult. I get to do that. I'm not scared of him anymore."

"I'm sorry." She was sobbing now. "I'm so sorry."

"Sometimes sorry isn't enough," I admonished, even though I knew, deep down, that the last thing she needed was another person to rebuke her. She's had quite enough of that. And in the end, I was the one who ran. The one who left her behind without so much as a proper good-bye. What must that have felt like for her? To lose her daughter. To be alone. With him.

"You're right. I was just as bad as he was."

"That's not true. You know that. You were his victim, just like I was. But you made a lot of mistakes. Maybe too many mistakes." What if I let my resentment fade away and I don't recognize myself anymore? What if all I can feel is pity?

"I shouldn't have threatened you," she volunteered.

"No, you shouldn't have."

"For what it's worth, I wouldn't have gone to your apartment." She swabbed the corners of her eyes with a cloth napkin.

"Honestly, that reassurance isn't worth much. You got me here against my will."

"I know you have a new life now. Very glamorous." If only she knew.

"Please don't be a martyr. I worked hard to get where I am."

"No, I'm happy for you. I always wanted that for you. Something better. Something bigger. You were destined for that." She was still crying, but softly. "I couldn't give you that here. As much as I hate to say it, you did the right thing by leaving. I just wish —"

"Please don't." I held up my hand. I didn't want to have to feel remorse.

"Sorry." She sniffed one last time, cleared her throat, and then lifted her head. If nothing else, my mother's learned how to recover. "When I said things changed after you left. I want you to know they changed for the better."

"That's fantastic to hear. So basically, once you got rid of me, life was suddenly one big fucking party?"

"No, not at all. That's not what I meant." She looked me in the eyes. "I was heartbroken when you left. That's not something a parent just gets over, Jordana. You weren't the only one in pain."

"And again, Mom. I was a child. You were an adult. Don't serve me that bullshit."

"I don't want to fight with you."

"Fine, then just tell me what you want. I'm here now. What do you want from me? Money? I can write you a check and be on my way."

"No!" I'd insulted her. "I don't want a dime from you."

"Then what?"

"Please just stay the night."

"Are you joking?"

"No, I'm not. I'm asking you. I know you don't owe me anything."

"That's for sure."

"But I am still your mother. So, *please,*" she implored. "Even if you never do another thing for me again. And even if you don't want to see your father. It's been so long. And your room is ready for you."

"I don't think so. I didn't pack any clothing."

"You can borrow something of mine."

"You know your stuff will be way too big on me. And anyway, I'm extremely busy at work." I had plenty of excuses.

"*Please,* Jordana. If you do this for me, I'll never ask you for another favor. You'll never hear from me again." She was desperate.

"Let me call my husband and my office. I'll see what I can do." I held a stern face. "But I am *not* going to see Dad. And that is *not* negotiable. I hope you can respect that."

"I promise it'll be worth it if you change your mind."

"He's already dead to me."

She cringed. "I understand," she said, even if she didn't. "And thank you."

26
KERRIE

I consulted the calendar to make sure I was right. There *are* less than three weeks left until the Doonan-Blunt wedding.

Ilana, the bridal assistant at the Oscar de la Renta atelier, has left four messages on our answering machine attempting to confirm that Tatiana's *two* gowns are to be delivered to our office. In the last one, she said it was her final day on the job and that her colleague Melissa will be our point person moving forward. The thing is, Tatiana has three gowns, which presented me with an easy opportunity to carefully delete each message. By the time Jordana figures it out, Ilana will be long gone. And my hands will remain completely clean.

Now that I've disclosed my real identity to Sara and we share the common purpose of destroying Jordana *and* Arthur, it's pretty much all I've been able to think about. I reached into my purse for my wallet and pulled out a passport-size black-and-white photo of my nana. I keep it tucked into the compartment behind my cash, so I can look at it every so often, specifically in these moments when I'm doubting myself. I sat there for a few minutes just staring at her placid smile, the way her eyes glinted. It may have been the flash of the camera, but I prefer to believe it was her inner spirit shining through, as it always did.

I thought about how, when I was younger, I yearned for something to segregate me from the people who said things like, "My mom is my best friend." Or, "I'm such a Daddy's girl." The people to whom these things were givens. And these givens were irrefutable, because their memories were functioning archives of their shared pasts spiraling through the present and into the future like a spool of cotton candy. Sweet, airy, light. Easy. I've never been any of those things.

Sure, every now and then a flicker of a memory will ignite — a flimsy white blouse or a shock of brittle black hair — but I've come to realize that these flashes are merely recollections of old photographs or stories I was told by Nana. Even though, technically, I was an orphan, and we barely had the means to make ends meet, I always had a roof over my head.

Still, it wasn't like Daddy Warbucks was mowing the lawn.

It was Nana — and Nana only — who stepped in to reprise the roles of mother and father until her final curtain call. When they found her, with her arms folded across her chest, as the world disintegrated around her.

I was twelve years old. Lost and alone.

And it was all Jordan's fault.

I propped the photo on my computer keyboard and sat back in my chair, allowing the memories of that fateful night — when the sky was dim and the streets were clammy — to flood my brain. As I walked by her house, I had a direct view into the well-lit living room. They rarely kept their curtains drawn, odd considering all that they had to hide. Maybe her mother thought that if someone saw what was going on they'd report it to the authorities.

Everything happened in a heartbeat. Her mother and father were fighting. Gillian — I know her name now — looked like a modern-day June Cleaver in her yellow dress with pale blue flowers and a white apron tied around her waist. Jordan's dad was wearing a thick green army jacket and grasping a rifle in his left hand. The kind of rifle you use for hunting. It looked like he'd just arrived home. He was red in the face, his finger erect, nearly pressed against Gillian's forehead. I couldn't hear what he was saying or make out the movements of his mouth, but — whatever it was — she was cowering.

That was when Jordan entered the room. She tried to insert herself in between them. To pacify her father, as best I could tell. But without warning, he pulled his free hand back and whipped his palm across her face in one fluid motion. She cradled her cheek and bowed her head. I couldn't see if she was crying, but I wanted to cry for her.

What happened next was perhaps the most jarring. Jordan stood straight up to find her father's gun pointed at both of them. I braced myself for the shot. Held my body stiff, like I could already sense the reverberations in my skull. I couldn't move. I couldn't speak. I just closed my eyes and waited. But nothing came. No shot. I opened my eyes again and, when I did, I saw Jordan lift up a chair and lunge at her father with every morsel of strength she had. She thrust all one hundred-something pounds of herself at him, until he tumbled to the ground and out of my sight. That was when she saw me. Standing frozen outside the window.

Our gazes fixed on each other's, and I nodded. *It's going to be okay,* I communicated, without actually saying it. *You'll be safe with me.* I smiled and waved her toward me. And to my surprise, she came. She trusted me. Much in the same way she does now.

Jordan rushed out her front door and trailed me back to my house and — as I'd prayed she would — waited halfway down the block until my nana left for her night shift. That was when she knocked, and I invited her in.

"Are you hungry?" I asked. "Do you want a sweatshirt?" She was shocked and shivering. I didn't mention what I'd seen. She didn't either.

"Yes. Thank you." I couldn't take my eyes off her, this cool older girl who was in such dire straits, but I did, for just long enough to make her a grilled cheese sandwich and heat up a bowl of tomato soup. I stared at her while she ate, like she was some kind of otherworldly being. I couldn't figure out what made her so impeccable. She had that something. Either you have it or you don't. I don't. I never have.

"Are you okay?" I watched as she nibbled on the crust and spooned the soup into her perfect pink mouth. I noticed the constellation of freckles that trailed across her cheekbones and over the bridge of her nose. "I will be."

"Do you have someplace to stay tonight?"

"Not really." She shrugged. I'm ashamed to admit I was hoping she would say that. I wanted so badly to be an important character in her story. Someone she'd never forget.

"You can stay here."

"Really?" She coiled a section of her long red hair around her index finger and gnawed on her bottom lip.

"Sure."

"What about your parents?"

"I don't have parents. It's just me and Nana. And she won't be home until tomorrow morning. You can sleep in her bed as long as you make it up before you leave."

"That's really nice of you. You don't even know me."

"We're neighbors." I smiled. I couldn't tell her that I did know her. Or at least it felt like I did. "It's not like you're a complete stranger."

"That's true." She smiled back. If she was wondering why I was so eager to please her, she never said as much. "That's pretty." She pointed to my necklace.

"Thanks. It's my mother's engagement

ring." My nana gave it to me on my tenth birthday, strung on a gold chain so I could wear it around my neck. It was my prized possession. The one thing I had left of my mom. I only took it off when I was sleeping.

"Is she . . ."

"Yes. She passed away. So did my father. Car accident."

"I'm sorry."

"It's okay. It was a long time ago. Do you want to watch some TV?" I didn't want to talk about my dead parents. And I definitely didn't want *her* to feel sorry for *me*.

"Sure, that sounds good."

For the next hour, we sat side by side on our old beige sofa, snacking on popcorn and drinking Sprite from the can while we watched sitcoms. Until eventually my eyes became heavy and I was fighting to stay alert.

"You look tired," she said.

"I'm okay." I didn't want the night to end. I wanted more time with her. She seemed like the big sister I'd always wanted.

"I'm kind of exhausted myself."

"Oh, sure. Do you want to go to bed?"

"I think so. I want to get an early start in the morning."

"Okay. Follow me." I walked her into

Nana's bedroom. "I can try to find fresh sheets."

"Don't worry about it. I can lie on top of the covers. It's probably better that way."

"You can borrow a pair of her pajamas if you want." I knew she was way too tall to wear mine. "They're in there. Help yourself." I motioned to my nana's dresser.

"Thank you." She nodded. "You saved my life. I hope I can return the favor one day."

"It was nothing." I didn't need anything in return from her. "Can I get you some water? Or an extra blanket?"

"Don't suppose you have a lighter?" Jordan asked.

"I don't think so."

"Matches?"

"Maybe somewhere." I thought about where Nana might keep them.

"I guess you don't smoke, then?"

"I'm twelve," I replied, as if twelve-year-olds couldn't smoke.

"Don't start. It's a shitty habit."

"I can look in the kitchen drawers."

"No big deal." She pulled a pack of cigarettes from the back pocket of her blue jeans and stuck one in her mouth. "I can use the stove." She held the cigarette between her lips as she spoke. It looked so effortless.

"Okay, well then . . ."

"Good night."

"Wake me up before you go. I'll make breakfast."

"That sounds great." She smiled at me one last time. "And again, I really can't thank you enough."

"You're welcome." I smiled back.

I never did see Jordan the next morning. She never even slept over that night. It wasn't until 7:00 a.m. that I awoke to a cloud of smoke filling my bedroom and spilling through the crack beneath my door. I jolted upright, as mind-bending fright permeated every cell in my body. There was a fire somewhere in the house. My instinct was to scream for Nana, but Jordan and I were the only ones there. I couldn't open the door. And there was nowhere to stop, drop, and roll. That's the first thing they tell you to do in the safety drills at school.

I reached to grab my necklace off the nightstand, but it was gone. I didn't have time to look for it. I rushed toward the window, opened it, and climbed out, dropping the few feet to the ground, wearing only a knee-length T-shirt and no shoes. I thought about going back in. I'd saved Jordan once. She'd said it herself. How could I not try to save her again? But I knew better than to run into harm's way, so instead I raced around the exterior of the house frantically, shrieking and crying at the top of my lungs. My feet carried me this way and that, through the muddy grass, which was sodden with dew. Until I couldn't move any more. I just stopped in our front yard, fell to the ground, and hugged my knees to my chest, as I rocked back and forth, howling into the eerie silence. Why didn't anyone hear me?

I don't know how long I sat there alone, praying that she would appear. But eventually the blare of sirens sliced through the unnerving hush of my neighborhood as two fire trucks and a police car came pummeling to a stop outside. Before I knew what was going on, they'd invaded the house. I didn't tell them that Jordan was in there, even when the cops questioned me. I was too shocked, and also too afraid to betray her. It didn't matter anyway. She was already long gone. What I didn't know is that Nana had come home early from her shift. And by that time, there'd been no sign of Jordan. My nana lit two candles in the kitchen, as she so often did. Then she went directly to sleep, unaware that the dial had been left on low and the stovetop was emitting a steady stream of gas.

The fire never reached her room; they were able to put it out fast enough so that much of the house was still intact, including the dresser in her bedroom, *without* her hard-earned cash in it.

Still, my nana died that day. Of smoke inhalation.

And Jordan took everything from me. Nana's money. My mother's engagement ring. And the person I loved the most in the world.

I cannot let her get away with it.

The phone rang, jolting me from the past. Speak of the devil.

"Hello? Jordana Pierson Wedding Concierge. This is Olivia. How can I help you?" I answered through gritted teeth.

"Hi, Olivia. It's me." I seethed at the sound of her voice. It was impatient. As if someone was listening in. Clearly, she hadn't gone to Boston. I knew that was a lie the moment it escaped her lips. "I'm just checking in. How's it going?"

"All good here. Staying on top of everything."

"Wonderful, thank you." I heard her exhale.

"How are you doing?" I feigned concern.

"I'm okay. I guess."

"I'm here if you need to vent."

"Thank you. I really appreciate that." She spoke quickly. "I need you to do me a favor."

"Sure, anything."

"It turns out that I'm going to stay the night. I have an old friend in Connecticut and I'm planning to stop there on the way home. So I need a little bit of clothing and my toiletries."

"Absolutely." *An old friend?*

"Great. So can you please take a cab over to my apartment right now? I'll need my black silk pajamas. They're in the top drawer of the dresser in my bedroom. The one closest to the bathroom. My undergarments are also there. Then I need the darkest blue jeans you can find — in the third drawer down. And a white cream L'Agence blouse, which should be hanging in the closet near the bed. And my toiletries . . . You know what? I'll just text you a list. Okay?"

"Got it."

"I'll let the doorman know you're coming and to allow you upstairs. He'll have a spare key, too. Then if you could messenger everything to me, that would be amazing. I'll text you the address. Tell them I need it immediately. My friend's clothing is too big to borrow."

"No problem." I already knew the address.

"You're a lifesaver, Olivia."
Now, where had I heard that before?

27
KERRIE

When I arrived at Jordana's building, the doorman rushed to help me out of my taxi and then escorted me inside. So *that's* what doormen are for.

"Hi, I'm Olivia Lewis. Here for Jordana Pierson. She said you'd have a key for me." I smiled politely.

"Sure thing. Got it right here!" Joseph — his name was monogrammed on the breast of his starched gray uniform — smiled back. "Just return it to Bill on the way out. I'm off in" — he consulted his watch — "five minutes. Goin' home to the family. Six kids. Would you believe it?"

"Wow, that's a lot of kids," I acknowledged, and then headed straight for the elevator.

Upon reaching the eleventh floor, I found that Jordana's apartment was the only one there, unlike in my building where there are ten apartments, five on each side of the hallway. I turned the key in the lock and let myself in.

When I tell you that I gasped, I swear it's not an exaggeration. It's one thing to peruse photos in a magazine, but to experience the real thing — in person — is another story altogether. In a word, it was majestic. The entryway alone felt like the size of a football field. And *everything* was white. The floors, the walls, the furniture. I remember the article calling the style "enriched minimalism." I had no idea what that meant until now. I also remember it saying that the space was over four thousand square feet. *Four thousand square feet!* I've never been in a house that large.

I found my way into the kitchen, just to check it out. White marble everywhere. Or was it granite? I have a hard time deciphering the two. There was also the most amazing refrigerator I've ever seen. It had a glass front so you could view all the neatly organized bottles of Pellegrino and Dom Pérignon. I wondered if they'd notice if I swiped one.

I wandered around some more and then made my way up to the bedroom to pack Jordana's things. Her list and corresponding directions were so thorough it only took a few minutes, so — once I'd finished — I sat

279

down on her four-poster bed. I needed a moment to let everything sink in.

I felt more resentful than ever. And the need to leave before I did something I regretted to this apartment.

When I got downstairs, I left the bag I'd packed with Bill and let him know that a messenger would be by to retrieve it within the hour.

It had been my intention to head home so I could order in dinner and catch up on *Game of Thrones* before Sara came over. But instead, I had a better idea.

I walked a couple of blocks, hailed a cab, and took it straight down to Wall Street and Water. Straight to the Andaz hotel, where I planned to sit on a park bench outside and eat the roast beef sandwich I'd purchased at a nearby bodega. I thought maybe I could catch John in the actual act of cheating. Well, not so much *in the act,* but perhaps I could bear witness to a hasty departure — a march of dishonor, if you like.

Just because we're supposed to be targeting Arthur doesn't mean I can't go after Jordana in other ways.

Unfortunately, just as I was about to unwrap my sandwich, my phone rang.

"Hello," I answered, smiling once I realized it was William.

"Hey, friend. What are you up to?" I felt a little flutter in my chest.

"Not much." *You know, the usual, just stalking my boss's husband.*

"Can you meet me for a quick bite? I need to talk to you again."

"Um, sure, yeah. That's fine. Where?" I tried to sound casual, but I was more nervous than usual about seeing him. What if I unintentionally revealed something about our plan to ruin his future father-in-law?

"How about the Silver Star Restaurant on Sixty-Fifth and Second. Does that work?"

"Yup." No point in raising questions about why I was so far downtown.

"Great, I'll see you soon."

Twenty minutes later, I was back uptown, seated across from William in a torn, faux-leather booth.

"This doesn't strike me as your scene." I lifted a spoonful of onion soup to my lips and tried not to slurp. I may not be truly sophisticated, but I try.

"I wanted someplace where I wouldn't bump into a million people I know. And anyway, aren't diners everyone's scene?" William took a generous bite of his turkey club. A dollop of mayonnaise oozed out the

281

back and dropped onto his french fries. The rest was smeared across his cheek. I defied the impulse to reach out and brush it away with my thumb.

"You're asking the wrong person. I don't eat out much. And when I do, this is about as upscale as it gets." I glanced at the revolving display cases full of fluorescent-lit cake slices and tapioca pudding.

"Trust me, most of the fancy restaurants aren't worth their eighty-dollar steaks and fifty-dollar hamburgers."

"Fifty dollars for a hamburger?" I almost choked on a glob of cheese. "That's insane. What the hell is in it?"

"A little foie gras. Some truffles."

"They put chocolate in the burger?" Gross.

"Truffles, as in mushrooms." He laughed, bringing out his dimple. Again, I resisted the urge to reach out and touch his face. "You crack me up."

"So what's going on? You sounded upset on the phone."

He sighed and slumped his shoulders. "I'm struggling."

"With what?" I had an idea, but I wanted to hear him say it.

"With this wedding. With Tatiana. Things have been really weird lately."

"Weird like how?" I probed, but didn't push. William has enough pressure on him.

"Like, I tried what you suggested. I sat Tatiana down the other night and I said, 'Let's elope. Let's just forget the whole wedding, leave town, and get married on a beach somewhere. Just the two of us.' " Suddenly I was queasy. That wasn't what I'd hoped he was going to say.

"And?"

"And she wasn't into it."

"Were you surprised by that?" I caught my reflection in the mirror next to me. I looked tired, maybe even older.

"A little."

"I'm really sorry."

"She said it was out of the question. That her parents would be furious. That they've already spent far too much money. Not to mention the social humiliation they'd endure if The Wedding of the Century didn't go off without a hitch."

"We're still calling it that?" I wrinkled my nose, then took a sip of my Diet Coke.

"I know, right?"

"Okay, so I get what Tatiana is saying about the wedding. Because I agree that Caroline would freak out. But what does that have to do with your feelings? I mean, you did agree to the wedding in the first place." I wanted to get to the heart of it. I wanted him to tell me he didn't love Tatiana anymore. And not just so I wouldn't feel so damn guilty about possibly ruining his fiancé's father's life.

"It doesn't. Or maybe it does. It's all tied together. Money makes people act in ways they shouldn't. I promise you, Tatiana did not used to be this way."

"I know, you've told me that. But she's always been rich, hasn't she?"

"Yes. It just takes on more meaning as you get older. When you feel the pressure to define yourself in other people's eyes. I told you, when we were in college, she was pretty normal. She never said who her parents were or what she came from. It was almost like she was embarrassed by it. The complete opposite of how it is now." I watched as he tried to conjure other examples of her purported normality. "She used to go to the movies without having to wipe the seats down with sanitizer and bring her own sugar-free snacks. She used to shave her own legs. She once backpacked through Europe and stayed in . . . hostels."

"Come on."

"It's true. And despite what you may think, Tatiana is smart. She was an economics major and she got into Yale Law School."

"What?"

"Okay, so Arthur did go there. For under-grad, too. But even without his influence, she would have gotten in somewhere decent."

"I take it she didn't go? To Yale."

"Clearly not." Go ahead, twist the sword. "Can I tell you a secret?" His eyes locked with mine and a smile crept up behind them. I knew he was going to divulge something juicy. Something he knew I'd want to hear.

"You mean another secret?" I teased.

"Okay, ready." He paused for effect. "Tatiana used to be chubby."

"Shut up!" I looked over both shoulders. "Don't let the word get out," I whispered.

He grinned.

"I don't believe you anyway."

"I'm not lying. Cross my heart and hope to die!" He drew an imaginary *X* on his chest.

"Okay, so how chubby are we talking?"

"Don't get me wrong — she wasn't fat, by any means, just *solid*. A good ten to fifteen pounds above average." I tried to imagine Tatiana as anything but skin and bones. I couldn't. Her gauntness defines her. "And you know, the thing is, I liked her that way. She was natural. She was happy. Now she's

285

just distant. And cranky all the time. I'm not even sure she's in love with me anymore."

Oh wow. My heart ached for him. Who in their right mind wouldn't love William? He's perfect in every way.

"Maybe you need some time to think about things?" I nudged gently. I can't be the one to tell him to call things off with Tatiana. Even though I want to.

"I don't have time to think. The wedding will be here before we know it." We sat in silence for a minute. "Let's get out of here." He motioned to the waiter for a check.

"Sure."

"You live near here, right?"

"Not far."

"Great, I'll walk you home."

"You don't have to do that."

"I may not have to, but I want to. As long as you don't have a hot date waiting for you."

"Nope, no hot dates to speak of." *Just you.*

"Great, then we'll take the long route so we can grab some ice cream."

"Perfect." I smiled, as we exited the diner and stepped outside onto the sidewalk. It was a gorgeous night. The kind filled with promise. Still, I couldn't stop thinking about Arthur. And how the fallout — if there is one — will affect William. If he gets hurt in all of this, I'll never forgive myself.

"I wonder if all in-law relationships are a little awkward," I mentioned as we strolled up Second Avenue. If William thought the comment was out of left field, he didn't say so.

"It's not that I don't like them." He didn't sound convinced. "As you know, Caroline is a handful. But her bite isn't as bad as her bark."

"Really?"

"No, not really." He laughed. "Let's just say she's very different from how my own mother was."

"In what way?"

"My mother had a heart."

"Nice."

"Yeah. Don't get me wrong, she's as sweet as she can be to me. But that's because I serve a purpose for her."

"By marrying her daughter."

"Bingo." He smiled, but it was weighted with uncertainty.

"And Arthur?"

"Like I told you, he's not the greatest guy, to say the least. But he treats me reasonably well. We play golf together sometimes. He calls me 'son' when he's had a few drinks and there are other people around. That's

287

not the real Arthur, though."

"I've heard."

"Oh yeah?" He turned toward me.

"Just a little. Some stuff I've read online,"
I lied.

"I'm sure that barely scratches the surface.
He's *very* private. The one thing he hates
most is when people try to get into his business." *Great.* "He won't even stay at a resort
with other people. Doesn't like to be observed in a relaxed atmosphere. He thinks
it's a sign of weakness."

"So they don't go on vacations?"

"They have a number of homes, but
mainly they go to Camp David."

"Like, the *president's* Camp David?"

"No. Their Camp David. Ridiculous,
right?"

"Just a little."

"Anyway, that's where they escape to.
Even I've only been there once and that
wasn't until after I'd proposed. *And* it was
at Tatiana's insistence. I don't think Arthur
was too thrilled about it."

"Where is it?"

"If I told you I'd have to kill you." He
nudged me with his arm.

"Really?"

"Not really. But you get the idea." William
pointed to a small ice cream shop on the

corner, which brought an abrupt end to our conversation about Arthur. "This is the spot. It's a hole in the wall, but they have the best mint chip."

"Mint chip is my favorite."

"Mine too." He placed his hand on the small of my back to lead me inside. "We're a match made in ice cream heaven." Then he smiled at the man behind the counter and said, "The lady and I will each have a double cone of mint chip."

"Double?"

"Why not? Live a little." He passed me a stack of napkins.

"Double it is."

"So what's been going on with you?" he asked, as we left the ice cream shop and cut across to Third. "I feel like we always talk about me."

"I've been good. Things have been going really well with work. I can't believe I'm saying this, but I actually love the wedding industry. I've made some strong contacts, and I finally feel like I'm coming into my own. There's something so satisfying about orchestrating the most important day of people's lives." It's such a relief when I can discuss things that are actually true with William. It makes the friendship feel more real.

"I can imagine." He nodded. "What's your favorite thing about it?"

"Good question." I thought about it. "So, the other day when I was with one of the caterers, I sampled this unbelievable lobster dish, and I knew immediately that the groom was going to love it. And then last week, I saw one of our brides in her dress and I just knew it was perfect. I could tell from the expression on her face how happy she was. I guess it's those moments when things work out as they're supposed to or as we planned they would." We turned onto Eighty-Fifth Street and fell silent when I stopped in front of my building. "This is me."

"Thanks again for listening, Olivia. You're the best." We stood facing each other, close enough to allow the other pedestrians to pass around us.

"That's me. The best." I rolled my eyes and William leaned down to kiss me on the cheek. "Have a good night." I waved at him before entering my building.

That's when it hit me like a sucker punch. I'm *falling for* William. I'm doing exactly what Jordana warned me not to do. But I can't stop myself.

At the same time, I can't deny that my plan for revenge is going to injure him. All the lies I've already told. The depth of deception that's still brewing. I can't breathe.

But I also can't turn back.

Maybe I am just a horrible person after all.

28
KERRIE

Once I'd closed the door to my apartment, I erased the thought of William from my mind and shucked off my work clothes. There's nothing more gratifying than that moment when you unfasten your bra. I flung it onto the bed, then slipped into sweatpants and a hoodie while I waited for Sara to arrive, which didn't take long.

"You look comfortable." She shuffled in, wearing fluffy gray slippers and a pair of men's style pajamas.

"You do too." I poured two glasses of wine and handed one to her.

"How was your day? Did you find out anything?" We collapsed onto my couch and she got right to the point.

"I did. But I'm not sure it's worth much."

"What is it?" She sat up straight.

"Apparently, the Doonans have a vacation home called Camp David."

"You're kidding me."

"I wish I was."

"Where is it?" She leaned in closer.

"I don't know. William couldn't tell me."

"Couldn't or *wouldn't?"*

"What's the difference?"

"*Couldn't* means he'll never tell you. *Wouldn't* means there's a possibility."

"Somewhere in between, maybe." It's hard to judge how loyal William is to his future in-laws, despite his personal feelings. And I hate putting him in the middle.

"It could be a dead end, but it's worth looking into. I'll investigate."

"Okay. What about you? Anything?"

"I spoke to an old source from the newspaper. She said she can give me some access without raising a red flag, so I can start looking into Arthur's company. This way I can get myself up to speed on what's been going on during my hiatus. It's a first step, if nothing else. And who knows? Maybe I'll find some kind of clue or at least a lead. Sometimes even the craftiest criminals make mistakes."

"How long do you think that'll take?"

"Not too long, I'm sure, why?"

"Well, it's just that Tatiana and William's wedding is just a couple weeks away."

"That's *right*." Her eyes twinkled.

"And I was thinking maybe we could wait

until after that." I know William is having some second thoughts, but if he does decide to go through with marrying Tatiana, I can't, in good conscience, ruin the most important day of his life.

"You're fucking brilliant." Sara slapped one of my throw pillows.

"Why is that?"

"If we can implicate Arthur within the next couple of weeks and get an article published on the morning of the wedding, that will take this to a whole new level. It will be explosive! There will be Doonan shrapnel all over Wall Street and beyond."

"Wait, no, that's not what I said."

"It's still genius, my friend."

"I don't think so." I shook my head. "Why do we have to drag Tatiana and William into this?"

"Tatiana and William are going to be dragged into this no matter what."

"Yeah, but we don't have to intentionally screw them. That's just adding insult to injury. They didn't do anything wrong."

"Olivia." She held my gaze. "Stop worrying about everyone else. When we pull this off, it'll be *our* moment. *Your* moment. Finally getting what you deserve. I can't believe I'm the one saying this to you, but are you in or are you out? There's no room for wishy-washy."

"Of course I'm in. But my focus is on Jordana and Arthur. Not William."

"Oh my God."

"What?"

"You have a crush on him." She pointed at me. "I can see it in your face."

"I do not!" I objected. Even though I'd give my left arm to marry someone like William (or William himself), I'm also not naive enough to think he would ever consider being with someone like me.

"I think you do."

"Well, you're wrong." I looked away. I knew I sounded unconvincing. "We never become invested in the relationships of our brides and grooms. We're not marriage counselors. Our job is to execute the wedding itself." I repeated Jordana's cardinal rule verbatim, which sounded idiotic.

"Honey, that may be a nice motto, but it's not real life."

"This is silly. Just because I don't want to ruin William's wedding doesn't mean I'm interested in him romantically."

"Whatever you say." She held her hands up. "All I care about is whether you're in or you're out. And *in* means doing whatever we have to do, even if it fucks with William."

I waited a beat before saying anything. I

thought about my nana. I thought about Jordana's lavish apartment. And I thought about the woman I want to be. "I'm in."

29
JORDANA

"Jordana." My mother came knocking at nine o'clock this morning. I haven't slept that late since I was a teenager. "Are you up?" I heard the knob turn and the door open just a crack. It was refreshing to be awakened by a soothing voice in my old home — not my father's ominous roar. *You lazy little bitch. Get the hell out of bed and make yourself useful around here. You think this a free ride?* he'd shout, and then rip the covers off me. Fond memories.

"Yup," I croaked, sitting up and stretching my arms overhead as she lifted the blinds on what appeared to be a beautiful sunny day in Connecticut.

"I made you French toast for breakfast." She was already showered and dressed in pleated beige slacks and a red sweater. Her auburn hair was pulled into a ponytail, highlighting her cheekbones and radiant complexion.

"I'm not hungry."

"But it's your favorite," she pressed.

"Mom, please. I said I'm not hungry." Despite ten hours of sound sleep — more than I've had since I married John — I was still tired. Thankfully, she noticed that I was somewhat irritable so didn't push the issue any further.

It's pretty amazing that my mother can still measure my moods. That eighteen years later, she still knows me that well. Honestly, I'm flattered.

There's no more accurate description for yesterday than to say it was surreal. Kind of like when you're roused from a dream and can't escape the notion that it wasn't just a delusion. You can smell the dream. You can taste it. That's what it's like to come back home after nearly two decades. To walk through the front door. To sit at the kitchen table. To sleep in my own old room, which is the only space that my parents left un-touched.

My creaky wooden bed is still intact and uncomfortably restrained by my old blue flannel sheets and red-and-gray striped comforter. My white wicker glass-top bu-reau is also in one piece, which is pretty remarkable given that it continues to lean to the left.

And then there's the life-size stuffed tiger slumped in the corner of the room. I won him at the state fair for tossing a baseball into a jug in one try. I witnessed my father glow with pride that night. He'd never done that before, at least not about me. "That's my girl," he'd crowed. Of course, he later chalked it up to beginner's luck and told me not to be a braggart.

It's strange without him here. The house is more relaxed. So are we.

I told my mother that I needed the remainder of the morning to catch up on work. She said she understood, but I could sense her disappointment. However, when it came to lunch, she wouldn't take no for an answer, which is what landed us at Frankie's Diner. It's been open twenty-four hours a day, seven days a week since the 1930s. But that's not why my mother picked it. I'm wise to her plan. You see, Frankie's Diner is less than half a mile from Bridgeport Hospital, where my dad is dying. How's that for convenient?

Despite this knowledge, now — sitting across from my mother — I'm still less anxious than I was earlier, because I had the chance to speak to Olivia, who continues to be the best decision I ever made. She has the uncanny ability to anticipate what needs to be done, without being a know-it-all. Thank God. I don't work well with know-it-alls.

With Olivia by my side, I'm going to be able to grow the company by leaps and bounds. Maybe even take on twice as many weddings. I'm seeing green. And you know what green means? Freedom. Whoever said independence was red, white, and blue had it all wrong. Believe me. This lady of liberty likes cold hard cash.

My mom has been quiet since we sat down. She's thinking about something. Hiding something, if my instincts are correct.

"How's the coleslaw?" She motioned to the small bowl next to my plate, a heap of carrots and cabbage drowning in mayonnaise and vinegar.

"I'm not eating it. Would you like some?" I edged it toward her. She knows I hate coleslaw. Or doesn't she remember?

"No thank you. Though if you're not going to eat your pickle . . ." I handed it to her even though I wanted it, because *I know* that she loves anything briny. When I was a child she used to dip pretzel rods in sea salt.

"Are you sure?" She took it before I could answer.

"Yes, I'm sure." I offered a charitable smile. One minute I want to tell her that I

300

forgive her. That everything is going to be okay. Better even, once my father is officially ridden from this universe. Unfortunately, the next minute I want to berate her for never being the mother she should have been.

"I can't believe you're really here." It's the umpteenth time she's said it.

"Me neither." I dunked the corner of my tuna melt in ketchup and took a bite. The grilled bread, the cheese, the savory fishiness, and the tang of the ketchup melted in my mouth. "So do you want to tell me what's going on?"

"What do you mean?" She concentrated on her Greek salad. Even the grape leaves couldn't save her from my interrogation.

"Mom. You know exactly what I mean."

"Okay, okay. It's just that . . ."

"What?"

"It's a lot." She set her fork down and strummed her fingertips agitatedly on the table. "And I'm not sure how you're going to react."

"Well we won't find out until you tell me, will we?"

"I don't know." She fretted some more, as she twisted her napkin into a baton. I looked to my right at the lady in the booth next to us. She was rocking back and forth and chanting something under her breath. "Don't mind her. That's Cindy. She sits there all day."

"That's weird." I watched her some more. How do people get to the point that they're alone in a diner for twelve-plus hours just swaying and muttering? No one to talk to, even though all of the regulars know who they are. That could have been me if I'd stayed. If I'd let my father drive me crazy.

"There's something a little off with her." My mother snapped the slice of pickle with her front teeth. "She never bothers anyone, though, and —"

"Okay, Mom," I interrupted. "Let's not get off topic here. Just come out and say whatever it is you've been holding in. On the count of three. Are you ready? One, two . . ."

"Your father can't walk," she blurted, and then looked up at me to appraise my reaction.

"That's it?" I shrugged. "What's the big deal? The man is dying. I'd hardly expect him to be dancing on the ceiling."

"No, you don't understand. He's . . ." She inhaled a long deep breath, as if air was a precious commodity. "He's a paraplegic. He has been since . . ."

"Since what?" My stomach stirred in

warning.

"Since you left. Well, actually, we didn't have his diagnosis until the next day."

"What are you saying?" I lowered my voice like it was some sort of secret. Like Cindy might overhear us. "I'm sorry. I'm going to need a little more of a clarification."

"When you came at him with the chair . . ." She treaded carefully. "He fell pretty hard. He was unconscious." She paused.

"Okay. And?"

"And I called an ambulance, but it was taking so long. It felt like at least an hour had passed."

"An hour?"

"I don't know how long it actually was. But anyway, I was afraid to wait. So I dragged him to the car and lay him across the back seat."

"You dragged Dad that far? He weighs twice as much as you do!" Not to mention that you're supposed to keep people as stable as possible after a blow like that. Although the image of my mother towing my six-foot-three, two-hundred-and-sixty-pound father from the kitchen to the drive-way and then hauling him into the car is sickly amusing.

"You'd be amazed at the strength you can

303

summon in an emergency."

"Apparently." I nodded, as the thought of me tugging John's limp body anywhere flashed through my mind. "Then what happened?"

"Then I drove him to the hospital, and the next thing I knew, the paramedics were lifting him onto a gurney and whisking him away. A day later the doctor told me that he was paralyzed from the waist down due to a spinal injury. Something about the roots of his nerves." My mother tipped her head downward again.

"So it was my fault."

"*No.* It was an accident." She didn't sound so sure.

"It wasn't an accident. I meant to push him. You know that."

"You didn't mean to paralyze him, honey. You were just defending yourself. I called the police. I tried to get them to find you, but they said it was too soon to consider a seventeen-year-old a runaway. I wasn't sure I could do it on my own. I thought you were already gone." Only I wasn't. Not yet. I was with Kerrie right down the street. And while she doesn't know specifically where I was, she does know that I came back to our house and left a diamond ring and some cash in our mailbox.

"I'm so sorry, Mom. I shouldn't have left so abruptly. I should have helped you more." I wasn't sure I believed that, but it seemed like the right thing to say in the moment.

"Jordana. You did what you had to do. I know that now."

"It must have been a huge burden for you. Everything with Dad."

"A burden?" She sniffed. I thought she was about to cry again. But when her face rose back up to greet mine, all I saw was a sly smile. "Are you kidding?" She laughed giddily. "It was the best thing anyone ever did for me."

"What?"

"For one, it afforded us more money in disability payments than he'd ever have made on his own." That explained the home renovations. "But more important, it gave me the upper hand. After all those years of . . ."

"Abuse?" I supplied, and she nodded almost imperceptibly. Clearly, she can't bring herself to say the word.

"He couldn't touch me anymore. Not in the same way."

"That must have made him even angrier, though. And resentful."

"At first, yes. The initial days, weeks, and

months were a challenging adjustment, to say the least. But then something must have clicked inside him. It was like he all of a sudden accepted his handicap. He needed me more than I needed him. And he recognized that. He was still mean at times, don't get me wrong. Although he never laid a hand on me again. He couldn't. He knew I'd leave."

"You should have left."

"I couldn't."

"Why not?"

"Because I loved him, Jordana." She refused to look me in the eyes. "I still love him."

"Why?" I wanted to shake her. "I don't get it."

"I have my reasons."

"Which are?" I needed to know how someone like my mother could possibly love someone like my father. "Forgive me, but it's hard to see why anyone would even like a man so vile."

"I was young when I fell in love with him. He didn't start out mean." She sighed. "I didn't realize how bad things had gotten until I was suddenly in charge. I knew I had a choice to make, but I decided it was too late to leave. I picked your father. And he picked me. We committed to each other.

For better or for worse. That vow was important to me. More important than the allure of freedom. I didn't want to have to start over. I was scared. That may not make sense to you, but it's how I felt."

"You're right. It doesn't make sense to me." It never will.

"Please just come with me to see him."

"I can't."

"But you're here. And this is the end."

"You do understand that he abused me. That I loathe him, right?"

"Yes." Did she really, though?

"Then why?"

"Why what?"

"Why is it so important to you that I see him?"

"Because it's important to him. And because I honestly think you'll regret it if you don't. He's the only father you'll ever have, Jordana." The waiter appeared at our side with a check, and my mother tried to hand him her credit card.

"I've got it." I gave him mine instead. "Mom, I said good-bye to him nearly two decades ago when, apparently, I paralyzed him. I don't regret that, and I won't regret not visiting him today."

"How do you know?" She wasn't going to let it go. "If there's one thing I've learned, it's that sometimes, once you realize you've made a mistake, it's too late." She was talking about both of us. "I think he wants to apologize to you."

"I just . . . I don't know." Could I go see him? Let him grovel and then give him a piece of my mind? Slap him around a little, so he can see how it feels.

"If not for him or for yourself, then do it for me. I know I already asked you to stay the night when you didn't want to. And I know you don't owe me a single thing, much less two things. But I'm asking for this, too. Please."

"I don't know." She was right that I didn't owe her a thing, but — still — how could I deny her?

"*Please,* Jordana."

"Fine, let's go." I stood up abruptly. "Before I change my mind." I slapped a ten-dollar bill on the table. "I want this over with."

30
JORDANA

As soon as we arrived at the hospital, I regretted my decision. The corridors smacked of urine and beef stew, and I had to divert my eyes at every turn for fear of exposing myself to something unsettling.

When we got to his room, I didn't walk right in. I wasn't sure I could. *I don't want to be here. I don't want to say good-bye.*

"Go ahead," my mother urged, standing behind me.

"You're not coming with me?" I should have known she'd expect me to do it alone.

"Not right now. You should see him privately first."

"Great." My teeth were chattering, even though my palms were lubricated with sweat.

"You can do this," she encouraged.

"I don't want to."

"I know." She nodded.

"I don't have to."

"I know." She sat down on an errant plastic chair that someone had left in the hallway. Probably for situations just like this.

"Fine." I pushed the door in, unprepared for what confronted me. A man who I didn't recognize at all. So small. So insignificant. So fragile.

"Well, look what the cat dragged in." He whistled through the oxygen tube.

"Hello." I refused to call him Dad. I didn't want to provide him the satisfaction of hearing me say it. "How are you?" A silly question, I knew, but what else to say?

"How the fuck do you think I am?" he barked. His skin was pallid beneath patches of white hair covering his chin and cheeks. His arms and legs were limp, very nearly comatose beneath the thin white sheet. I felt nothing. No sympathy. No empathy. No remorse. Certainly no love or even affection. He looked like a dead man already.

"Fair enough." I stood over him, but not within reach. I didn't want him to touch me.

"You look well."

"Thank you."

"Your mother said you're doing real nicely for yourself down there in New York City."

"Yes."

"That's good." He tried to sit up, but he

310

couldn't. I didn't offer to help. "Can't say the same for myself."

"I can see that."

"So, uh, tell me how you've been." I assumed he was kidding. We're about eighteen years past idle chitchat. *Well, let's see. I got my hair styled last Monday. And on Tuesday, I had swordfish for dinner. Two great cuts in one week!*

"I've been fine."

"That's all? Just fine." I could see by his expression that he didn't like that answer, but he was trying his best not to be a complete asshole. Valiant.

"That's it."

"You've got nothing else to say?" he grumbled.

"You look like hell." How about that?

"Is that any way for you to talk to your old man?" It took all of my willpower not to suffocate him with his pillow. To watch him wriggle and writhe until his body went flaccid.

"Is that what you call yourself?"

"I'm your father, whether you like it or not." He started coughing and couldn't stop. He motioned to the water on his nightstand, but I remained still.

"As far as I'm concerned, you were a sperm donor."

"You were always so moody. I see nothing has changed."

I reached for the water. "Is this what you want?"

"Just give me the fucking water," he rasped. I did. He didn't say thank you. "I thought you were coming here to apologize."

"You thought *I* was coming here to apologize?" I took a step closer to him. "I'm not sure where you got that impression. But I sure as hell have no intention of saying I'm sorry for a damn thing. *You* are the one who should be sorry. I thought I was coming here for an apology from you. Not the other way around." My mother had set us up. She'd duped each of us into believing the other one felt remorseful, perhaps in an attempt to assuage her own guilt.

"Well, I guess it's your unlucky day, then."

"Any day that you're a part of is unlucky."

"You're the one who left. *You* ran out on your family."

"You gave me no choice. You ruined my childhood, and I wasn't going to let you ruin my entire life."

"You were an ingrate," he barked.

"You were an animal. An abusive husband. An abusive father. And a sorry excuse for a man."

"You think you're better than me?"

"Oh, I know I'm better than you are." I smiled. "Do you know where I live now? In a ten-million-dollar apartment on Park Avenue." I puffed my chest, because money signifies independence. He knows that and I know that. "I own a company, did you know that? I'm a success. I'm living the fucking dream. Unlike you ever did."

"Snooty bitch." He tried to raise his voice but he couldn't. That incensed him even more.

"I've waited two decades to say these things to you. To tell you that you repulse me. And that you treated me and Mom like the piece of shit you were." I took a breath. I didn't want to let him rile me any further. He didn't deserve that. But I couldn't help myself. "How did it feel to be in a wheelchair all these years? To not be able to walk or run or loom over Mom before you punched her in the face? To have to look up at everyone you spoke to? How did that feel? Huh? Tell me. I want to hear you say 'I'm a sorry excuse for a man.' Once and for all. So I can stroll — yes, *stroll* — out of here and never look back. Say it. Say 'I'm a sorry fucking excuse for a man.' *Now!*"

His eyes widened with rage just as one of the machines he was hooked up to began beeping. Faster and louder until it was pulsing inside my head. Within seconds a nurse was at his side frantically jabbing at buttons and adjusting dials.

She turned to me, her face alarmed and apologetic at the same time. She was under the mistaken impression that I cared about him. "I'm sorry, sweetie, but you need to leave."

"What's happening?" I moved a little closer to get a better look.

"You need to leave *right now.*" Somehow he managed to grab my arm with what little strength he had left in him, but I squirmed free, and then I did exactly what I said I was going to.

I strolled right out of the room and never looked back.

An hour later, he suffered a massive heart attack. There were multiple attempts to resuscitate him, but they were in vain. My father died that day. No, my mistake. A stranger died that day. He died angry. And sour. He died knowing that I'd held him accountable for his sins. That I hadn't apologized or forgiven him, and I certainly hadn't forgotten.

That is what I call closure.

31
KERRIE

"Yes, that's correct. Size ten, black leather wing tips. The bow tie with the pinstripe. No cummerbund. No vest. Plain white shirt. Thank you, Daphne. Grey will be in next Monday to try everything on. Five o'clock. Excellent." I hung up and took a bottomless breath as I shuffled through a stack of papers Jordana had left on my desk with a sticky note that read: TOP PRIOR-ITY in all caps. Despite our hyper focus on the Doonan-Blunt wedding, our other weddings still need some attention. And with Jordana out of town, it's my job to concierge the shit out of them.

She called this afternoon to say that she'd be on her way home in a few hours and that she'll be in first thing tomorrow morning. She also said that we're going to be taking on two more major weddings (two more than the three she already told me about) and that she'll be giving me much more responsibility due to the fact that I've proven myself over the last couple of months. She even promised me a promotion, which I couldn't believe would happen so soon, despite the fact that I think I've earned it.

In the meantime, I've been keeping tabs on everything, fielding maniacal calls from Caroline, and I have an appointment at Harry Winston with William in forty-five minutes to *finally* select a wedding band.

I'm also supposed to meet Sara for dinner tonight.

And on top of all that, I'm making regular trips to the bathroom with an upset stomach. Fine, it's diarrhea. Is this what they call stress?

Just as I was about to grab my purse and head out to meet William, my cell phone blared Sara's number on the screen.

"Hey, what's up?"

"You ready for some sushi and sake?"

"Not yet."

"I'm starving already. This kid sucks the life out of me and all I want to do is shove some rice in my face." I heard Dante wailing in the background, which would typically make me feel grateful for my single, childless existence. But lately I've been thinking about what it would be like to have a real family of my own. I've never had that. Not in the traditional sense.

Once my nana was gone, I figured I'd be shipped off to Florida to live with my father's sister Ronna. She was my only living relative, and it never occurred to me that there would be another option. Ronna lived in Palm Beach with the "fancy folks," as my nana called them. We visited her every now and then, marinating in the luxury of her waterfront condominium with its hand-painted pink Pelicans on the kitchen wall and its white and black lacquer furniture positioned around her sweeping, sunlit living room.

Ronna let me soak in her whirlpool tub for hours and scoop peanut butter out of the jar with my fingers. She called herself a tough cookie, which I admired. Her teeth were tarnished beyond bleaching, thanks to twenty-five years of smoking a pack or two a day, and she wore frosted peach lip gloss that coagulated at the corners of her mouth, but I didn't care. Ronna had no husband or children of her own, though she was a natural at the art of nurturing. I wondered why Ronna didn't take me in when my parents died, since she was much younger, but never asked.

While the time in my life surrounding

Nana's death is foggy, due to the trauma and the overwhelming guilt that I was to blame, I do recall feeling relieved to leave everything behind and start fresh. I remember thinking *Florida is sunny,* which was a metaphor for what I believed my future would hold. Brightness.

Only that's not what happened. Instead, it was decided by someone — I'm not sure whom — that I would be taken in by the assistant principal and his wife, who were already certified foster parents. I was told it would be better for me not to have my life upended again. I needed continuity. I needed to stay where all of my friends were. Except, what they didn't understand was that I didn't have any friends. In fact, there wasn't one person who'd miss me if I never came back.

But I kept my mouth shut, even though I was raging inside, and I spent the next four years with my head down.

There was nothing *wrong* with Martin and Jean Splain. They were kind to me. They provided for me as best they could. They wanted so badly to be the parents I never had, which — to their disappointment — pushed me further and further away. Jean bought me pretty pink dresses. She'd leave them on my bed and ask me why I never

318

wore them. She tried to re-create my nana's chicken pot pie.

Some might say they were saints; they just weren't my saints. And they certainly weren't real family.

"We're still on though, right?" Sara asked, drawing me back to our conversation.

"The thing is, I'm really swamped. Jordana is out of town, so everything is falling on me. And I still have to meet a client. I'm not sure I'm going to be the life of the party after that."

"I don't need you to be the life of the party. We need to strategize. The clock is ticking."

"I hear you. It's just —"

"It's just *what*? This comes ahead of everything else, right?"

"Yes, yes, but —" I thought about William.

"But *nothing*," Sara cut me off. "I already have a babysitter lined up, so you have no choice."

"Okay, okay."

"I'm not hanging up until you say yes."

"Fine, yes."

"Great. See you at seven o'clock. With any luck, I'll have some news on Arthur by then."

32
KERRIE

By the time I'd made my way across Central Park, William was already waiting for me outside Harry Winston. He rushed to open the door of my cab and offered me his hand as I stepped onto the street. What a gentleman.

"Hey there." He smiled, as a construction worker whistled at me. Not only have I gotten used to this sort of reaction from strange men, I've come to expect it. Believe me, I never thought I'd see the day. "Ignore him." He positioned a protective palm on my back.

"So, are you ready?" I smiled at him too.

"Actually, no. I'm not." He scratched his head as we stood facing each other on the sidewalk, with pedestrians zipping past us.

"What do you mean?" Jordana made me swear not to leave the store without a wedding band.

"We're not shopping today." His eyes met

mine. And for the first time I noticed an aching that I'd never seen before. An almost imperceptible splinter of pain. "I need to talk again."

"Okay, but what about our appointment?" He'd made it himself, which I found strange. We never let our brides and grooms do that sort of menial work.

"There's no appointment."

"I'm not sure I'm following."

"Come with me. There's a little bar about seven blocks away. Nothing fancy, but we definitely won't run into anyone we know." Clearly, that was not a risk for me. "You okay to walk?" He looked down at my four-inch heels.

"Oh yeah, I'll be fine."

Ten minutes later, William and I were seated across from each other, beers in hand, in an establishment that can best be described as a dive, which is what I love about Manhattan. Gazillions of dollars of jewels within a hop, skip, and a jump from a bar that reminds me of home — where your feet stick to the floor and white wine spritzers are not on the menu. Jordana would sooner be caught buying flatware at Target than spotted here.

"So what's going on?" The music was a

little too loud for a heart to heart — and it was country, which was pretty unforgiveable in and of itself — but I certainly wasn't going to complain. "You don't seem like your usual happy self."

"Am I making a mistake?"

Yes. "You know I can't answer that."

"We're friends, right?" He finished his beer in three swigs and motioned to the waiter for a shot of tequila. "You want one?"

"Oh, no thank you." If I started downing shots, I'd never make it to dinner with Sara. Also, I still have to maintain a degree of professionalism with William if I want to keep my job. Which I do. Until all of this is over, and I've ruined his life. Or saved his life. It's amazing how fine the line might be between those two.

"So, as I was saying, we're friends, right?"

"Yes, we are friends." I savored that thought, even though, in my heart, I wished we were so much more.

"Then tell me. Should I marry Tatiana? I just need someone — *anyone* — to tell me honestly." He kicked back the tequila and politely requested another.

"Do you want to maybe slow down on those?"

"No." Got it.

"Why don't you give me a sense of why

you're asking this? What exactly is on your mind?"

"It's all just too much." He shook his head.

"Okay, so I remember you saying that Tatiana is different than she used to be and that she's been extra irritable lately." I started to walk him through it. "And I know you've had some doubt, but — again — I want to assure you that it's completely natural to have jitters this close to your wedding day. I know Jordana's seen it with plenty of our brides and grooms. It's nothing to be ashamed of." I hated myself for sounding like a PSA. *This is your brain. This is your brain on marital bliss.*

"It's more than that." Another shot down the hatchet. "It's become very clear to me that we're not headed in the same direction. We want different things in life."

"Are you sure?" I asked. "You both enjoy spending time at the country club." It was the only thing I could come up with.

"I hate it there."

"Come on, that's not true."

"No, it is. I hate the country club. And everyone who belongs there." He was slurring now, as the waiter brought another shot. "What am I doing, Olivia? How did I get to this place?" I've wondered the same thing about myself.

"You got here because you love Tatiana. You said you did."

"It feels like another lifetime."

"But you didn't propose in another lifetime. That was only a few months ago."

"That's not exactly what happened."

"I don't understand."

"The proposal wasn't really my choice."

"Don't tell me *she* asked *you* to marry *her*? No way."

"No. But she did ask me to ask her to marry me. She said all of her friends were getting engaged and that it would be humiliating for her to be the last one married. Caroline was really pushing for it too. We'd been together for so long. It was almost like if I didn't do it, I'd embarrass myself and everyone else." He shrugged, defeated. "It just seemed like what was supposed to happen. Like it was the next natural step and there was no sense in delaying it. Isn't that a great reason to commit your life to someone?"

"And, again, I'm just playing devil's advocate here. You've had months to change your mind. You could have backed out at any point."

"Ha!" He laughed cynically. "Once Tatiana and her mother started planning the

324

wedding, it was all over. I was either on the train going full speed or I was stranded at the station." Another shot.

"Okay, you really need to stop drinking. For one, you can't think lucidly. And beyond that, I'm not strong enough to throw you over my shoulder." I smiled and placed my hand on top of his.

"Tatiana doesn't want children," he blurted, and then looked at me with sad eyes.

"What?" I was stung on his behalf. On my own behalf. "How do you know?"

"She said it last night. She'd spent the day with her brother's kid. Nico. He's two. She said it was a *total fucking nightmare* — those were her exact words — like she'd had a bad bout of food poisoning." I thought about Dante and how difficult he can be. Still, even on his worst day, Sara adores him within an inch of her life.

"Ouch."

"Yup. So there's that."

"And you definitely do want kids?" I imagined William cradling a baby in his arms. I envisioned him encouraging his son to take his first steps. Or watching his little girl twirl around in a pink tutu. There's no doubt in my mind that he'll make an amazing father.

"Of course I want kids. And she knows that."

"I'm sure she'll come around."

"Are you? What if she doesn't? And what other bombs is she going to drop *after* we get married?"

"I don't know."

"Well, neither do I. And I'm afraid to find out. What am I doing?"

"Okay, listen. Calm down. This is all going to be fine. You need to go home and tell Tatiana how you feel. You need to explain to her how important it is for you to be a father and that one tough day with a child doesn't mean anything. She'll hear you. I'm sure of it." I wasn't sure of it. And there was a part of me that didn't want him to say any of it. Tatiana doesn't deserve him.

"You really are amazing, Olivia," he said, but I knew it was the booze talking. "Maybe you're right."

"Okay, let me ask you this. Are you *in love* with Tatiana?" *Please say no.*

"I don't know."

"You don't know?"

"I'm so confused." He folded his arms on the table and slumped his head on top.

"Oh, William." I wasn't sure what else to say. "Let's get you home so you can sleep it off. I bet things will look clearer in the morning."

"I don't think so." He shook his head as I helped him to his feet. And then he held on to my hand as we made our way out of the bar and into the light of day. I checked my watch. There was no way I was going to make it in time to meet Sara for dinner. With any luck, she'll cut me some slack.

"Let's get you a cab." He followed me onto the street, as I held my arm up and a taxi pulled right in front of us.

"Thank you." He stumbled.

"I'm coming with you."

"You don't have to do that."

"Yeah, I do."

"I don't know what I'd do without you, Olivia."

"You'd be just fine." We both got in, and I gave the driver William's address.

Once we'd rolled to a stop outside of William's apartment building, I watched him fumble to find his wallet in his jacket pocket, to no avail.

"I've got it, don't worry." He didn't put up a fight this time. He didn't have it in him.

"You're such a good person." He leaned toward me until I could feel his breath on my skin. I should have backed away. But I didn't. I couldn't.

Instead, I did something icky. Only because I knew he wouldn't remember it the next day.

I said, "Hey, you never did tell me where Camp David is."

His expression was bewildered, eyes half-closed, but he didn't hesitate. "Private island, not far off Grand Cayman."

"Are you going to be okay?" I whispered, as the moonlight streamed through the window, casting its sultry glow on us.

"I hope so," he whispered, and cupped my face in his hands. My heart was trembling with anticipation.

"Come here." Without warning, he pulled me closer and touched his lips to mine. Quickly. Gently. Almost as if it had never happened. Then he got out of the taxi and walked into his building alone.

And I sat there. Overcome by the compulsion to tell him how I felt about him. To tell him to choose me. To forget Tatiana. To confess everything and beg for his forgiveness.

But I didn't. Not yet.

33
JORDANA

"What am I going to do with him?" my mother asked.

I was surprised to learn that my father wanted to be cremated. I figured a man like him would want to remain in one solid piece so he could terrorize people in the afterlife.

"Flush him down the toilet?" I suggested, thankful that I'd be long gone by the time she received his ashes.

"That's not funny," she scolded. I knew there had to be a part of her that was relieved he was gone, even though she'd never admit it.

"Well, I don't think I'm the right person to ask, then." We were walking side by side along Compo Beach in Westport — an affluent coastal town in Fairfield County where Manhattan transplants flock to greener grass, cleaner air, and sand between their toes. Where kids can ride bikes around their neighborhood, swim in the ocean on a weekday afternoon, and walk to their friends' houses without looking over their shoulders. John thinks I grew up here.

"I wish you wouldn't go yet." She'd asked for one more hour with me. I couldn't say no — the woman had just lost her husband.

"I know. But this is my busiest time at work." I paused for a moment to watch a young girl, no older than three, lapping a leaky ice cream cone until her chin was gooey and her shirt was stained with chocolate.

"You'll come back soon?"

"I don't think so." We continued on.

"But . . ."

"Don't worry, Mom. We'll find a way." I picked up a shell but it was cracked, so I let it drop. The truth is, I don't know if we'll find a way. One thing I do know is that I can't hold on to the anger I felt toward my mother any longer. Maybe she did do the best she could. It's just too complicated to think about now.

"Just stay for a few more minutes." She gazed out over the water.

"You'll be fine without him," I encouraged, as two women dressed in yoga gear sped past us, pumping their arms as they chatted easily. Not a care in the world. Or maybe it just seemed that way. Maybe they have secrets too. "You'll be better off."

"I'm not strong like you, Jordana." She shook her head.

"Yes, you are." She had to be to have survived him.

She faced me then. "I'm sorry. For everything."

"It's okay, Mom." And if it wasn't, it would be.

"No, it's not. I should have stopped him. I should have done something. Anything. I was hardly innocent." We came to a shack named Joey's that touted the best lobster roll in Connecticut and stood there for a few minutes, as a gaggle of shirtless boys in damp board shorts staggered themselves around a picnic table and shoved fried clams and potato chips into their mouths. Then we turned around and walked back in the same direction we'd come from.

"You couldn't have stopped him. Neither of us could." I draped my arm across her back. "He was sick."

"I know." She bit her lip to stop it from quivering. "But as you said, you were the child. I was the adult. It was my responsibility. Not yours."

"It's in the past. Let's leave it there, all right?" She didn't answer.

A minute passed as we carried on in

silence. A hush of sadness.

"Are you happy, Jordana?"

"What do you mean?" It was an unexpected question from someone who knows so much about who I was, yet so little about the person I am today.

"I mean, in life. Are you happy? I know you have a career. I know you have a lot of money, and a fancy car. But that can't be enough. I also know you're married, but I haven't seen you talk to your husband once. And he's certainly not here to support you. I also know you have no children. So I want to know if you're really happy with all of that."

"I'm not sure, Mom." It was the truth. Plain and simple. I've known it all along. It just never mattered before. Or I never let it matter. I was so focused on proving my worth. On achieving financial sanctuary. On being someone who people didn't pity. Maybe I forgot what it means to be happy. If ever I knew what it meant in the first place.

"Then do something about it."

"It's not that simple. I can't just snap my fingers."

"Don't make the same mistakes I did. Don't let anyone else ruin you. And don't ruin yourself. You're better than that."

"I tried to help you. I left you the ring and some money. Why didn't you run too?"

"Where would I have gone? What would I have done to survive? I didn't know anything other than what I had. And I couldn't just abandon your father when he got hurt." She reached into her purse and handed me a small velvet pouch. "This is yours."

I released the drawstrings and pulled out the ring. Kerrie's mother's ring, still strung on the gold chain she wore around her neck. "I can't believe you kept it all this time." It was just as I recalled: a simple round stone with two smaller diamonds on either side. Nothing like the rings my brides wear or my own six-carat cushion cut. But still perfect. I turned toward the ocean and held it in my open palm.

My mother stood next to me and said, "He loved you, Jordana. In his own way. And I love you too."

With that, she moved gradually toward the shoreline, her shoulders heaving. I listened to her quiet tears, but I didn't follow her. Then I closed my eyes and whispered, "Good-bye, old man."

34

JORDANA

By the next morning, I was back at work with my past safely in the rearview mirror.

My focus is fiery and fierce again. And all of it is on Tatiana and William's wedding, which is approaching *fast*. God bless Olivia for keeping everything in order while I was gone.

I still can't shake the feeling that there's something so familiar about her. Every now and then I'll spot a mannerism I'm faintly acquainted with, or she'll say something that almost harkens a memory. Almost. And then it's gone. Maybe I knew her in another life. Either way, I'm sure I can trust her, which is more than I can say for most people.

"Okay, so let's go over a few things." I sat down at my desk and gestured for her to sit across from me. "First, I want to say thank you so much for taking care of everything while I was gone. I truly appreciate it. You'll definitely be receiving the promotion I promised you, and a bonus. Second, I've noticed how devoted you've been to bettering yourself, not only on the job. And your confidence is on point. I know these things may seem superficial, but in this line of work, they can be everything. Really impressive, Olivia."

"Thank you." She smiled and rolled her shoulders back to illustrate my point.

"Getting down to business. What are the outstanding details for the Doonan-Blunt wedding?"

"For one, William still doesn't have a ring."

"You're kidding me. I thought you went with him yesterday."

"I did meet William, but it wasn't a successful trip."

"I don't understand. Doesn't he know he's getting married *imminently*?" Something isn't right about this. Usually the groom's band is the easiest thing to cross off the list. "What's he going to do when she has to place the ring on his finger? Use one from a vending machine?"

"I'll call him today and light a fire," she assured.

"Perfect. Moving on. Where are we with Caroline and Tatiana's dresses?"

"Tatiana's second and third dresses are

done. And her first dress should be done ASAP. Same with Caroline's. Her shrug did arrive, but she hasn't tried it on yet. She said she'll come in with Tatiana for her final fitting to firm everything up. And not to touch it. So I just left it in the garment bag the way it was delivered."

"Smart," I praised. "Caviar bar?"

"All good."

"Whiskey tasting for the rehearsal dinner?" I continued.

"Done," she acknowledged.

"Dominique Ansel is confirmed for desserts?"

"Yup."

"In person?"

"Absolutely."

"And every couple is taking home a miniature version of the wedding cake as a favor, right?"

"One hundred percent," she reassured.

"Fireworks at the after party?"

"Check."

"Excellent. Still, we'll need to follow up with all of these people again the week of. There is *never* too much follow-up. Dot every *i,* cross every *t.* And, always remember, mistakes will be made because vendors are not as invested in the success of the wedding as we are. No one else is. Except maybe Caroline."

"Got it."

"I think we've covered enough for now. I'll need a few updates on the other weddings once I've caught up on some paperwork." I exhaled for what felt like the first time since my return. It's amazing how being gone for two days can feel like a lifetime. "It's good to be back in the swing of things."

"Did you have a nice time with your friend?"

"Well, I wasn't actually with a friend." If not for the call from my mother, I may have gotten away with lying to Olivia too, although a part of me wants to confide in her. "I didn't have time to explain everything while I was gone."

"I kind of figured." But she didn't say anything. One of the many things I admire about her.

"It's okay. It's always better to err on the side of discretion," I confirmed. "I was actually home. I grew up in Connecticut. At the address you sent the clothing to."

"I see."

"My father passed away while I was there."

"Oh my God." Her eyes widened. "I'm so sorry to hear that. I had no idea."

"No one did. No one does. And it's fine. We weren't close at all."

337

"Still . . ."

"He wasn't a good person. To say the least."

"I understand." She didn't. She couldn't, even though it is nice to have another person in my new life, aside from Cathy and Stan, who knows what happened.

"He was abusive," I revealed. Maybe I just wanted to say it out loud. Or maybe I want Olivia to know more about me.

"That's so awful. I can't even imagine."

"Well, you should be thankful for that. It wasn't easy." My eyes stung. "I know it may seem like I live in this perfect world, but it hasn't always been that way. Appearances can be deceiving."

"I really am sorry." She reached out and touched my arm, as a few tears escaped down my cheeks.

"Anyway," I sniffed and wiped the tears away quickly, "I left eighteen years ago and I finally have the closure I need. I hope."

"I hope so too." She hesitated. "You can talk to me any time, you know."

"I do. At least now I do." I nodded faintly. "Thank you again, for being a friend."

"Of course. I just feel terrible for you, for everything you've been through. No one should have to endure that."

"Isn't that the truth." I took a long, deep

breath. "Please keep this between us. Not a word to anyone."

"I will. If there's anything I can do . . ."

"There's nothing to do at this point."

"How's your mother doing? If you don't mind my asking."

"She's heartbroken. She loved him, despite everything."

"I see."

"She'll be happier without him though." I smiled at Olivia.

"That's good." She smiled back.

"We both will be. Soon enough."

35

JORDANA

"You're going to have to meet me at the Doonan wedding." I sat up in bed, next to John, watching him scan through emails on his iPhone and occasionally murmur something tetchy under his breath.

"I'm not doing that," he answered moments later, as if he'd only just heard me.

"What do you mean?" It was midnight already, and I'd worked long hours to catch up on everything since my return from Connecticut. The first thing I wanted was a decent night's sleep before waking up early to get back at it. The last thing I wanted to do was argue with my husband.

"Jordana" — he turned to me then — "we're invited as a couple, and that's how we'll go. Anything else would be tacky."

"I have to get there first thing that morning so I can make sure everything is in place. And I'll be there all day. I'm just not sure I'll have time to come home in between."

"I'm sure you'll find a way." He picked up his reading glasses and set them on the bridge of his nose.

"Well, I'm not. And you know this has to go seamlessly. You do want that, right?"

"Of course I do," he grumbled. "I just don't see why *I* need to keep sacrificing for this silly hobby of yours."

"It's not a hobby." I pinched the underside of my thigh beneath the sheets.

"Oh really?" He placed his phone on the nightstand in a show of exasperation. "If it doesn't make money, it's not a job."

"Well, I'm hoping to turn a profit this year." *As I have every other year.*

"How much?" he challenged.

"I don't know." I wasn't prepared for such a direct question.

"You don't know?"

"Not exactly."

"Let me put it this way. Will it make a difference in our lifestyle?" He swept his hand across the room as if to say, *Look at all that I provide for us.*

"That's not a fair question, and you know that."

"Sure it is," he sighed. "Jordana, I'm sick of this. I don't want a wife who works late.

Or who goes out of town for business. I want a wife who accompanies me to my boss's daughter's wedding. I expect you to be by my side, literally and figuratively. This isn't what I signed up for."

"It's not forever." I tried to placate him. I'm not ready to leave just yet.

"No, it's not. This has to be it. You've been more invested in Tatiana and William's happiness than in mine, and I don't like it." He looked me directly in the eyes, a rare occurrence. "If the company doesn't make a significant amount of money by year's end, you're shutting it down. Understood?"

"John," I objected.

He shook his head to silence my protest.

"I'll meet you at the wedding. This once." He held up his index finger. "As long as we're in agreement."

"Okay," I relented, as resentment and fear rose in my chest. I refuse to be "the wife of." I won't.

"That's my girl." He smiled contentedly. "Now, come over here." He pulled me close to him and then climbed on top of me. John likes to be the one to look down.

One day, I thought, *one day soon. This will all be over.*

36
KERRIE

I was roused at seven this morning, first by the trill of my cell phone, and then to instant vigilance by the crash of Sara's deafening voice through the receiver. She explained swiftly and at the top of her vocal register that a contact at one of the biggest banks in Grand Cayman — someone with whom she'd worked closely throughout her years at *The Wall Street Journal,* someone who owed her a big favor — had given her a list of all the shell corporations that held accounts at the bank. And that after sifting through pages and pages of names, she eventually came upon one that stood out. *Camp David.*

"This could be it!" she shouted. "This is no coincidence. I'll let you know what else I find."

"Great," I said, as enthusiastically as I could. I wasn't sure how I felt about her revelation, but I didn't tell her that.

343

Tatiana's final fitting is this afternoon — precisely seventy-two hours before The Wedding of the Century. Since Jordana returned from Connecticut, we've been dousing fires left and right, some that I kindled myself, and others that ignited from the sheer volatility of Caroline's fluctuating whims. Miraculously, I haven't been held accountable for one misstep.

The phone rang for what felt like the hundredth time this morning.

"Jordana Pierson Wedding Concierge," I answered as naturally as I breathe. "I'm sorry, but the bride and groom have elected not to be interviewed by the media," I told the woman calling from News 12. It's our blanket statement to every writer, reporter, producer, blogger, and journalist of any kind. Tatiana and William are not talking.

Trust me when I say that the lead-up to a wedding of this magnitude is a healthy dose of adrenaline you can't spoil. Beyond the details inherent in such an elaborate affair, when the Doonans and Blunts are the key players, there are also issues of press and privacy to consider. Every outlet from *Vanity Fair* to the *New York Post* is vying for a slice of socialite pie.

"What is this about, then?" Jordana looked up from her computer with a questioning expression. "I see. I'll have to see if she's available. Give me a minute." I put the woman on hold and covered the receiver with my hand, just in case. "It's Jan Marshall from News 12. She said that our building manager contacted them to say that we're not paying rent and now they want to speak to you about a story they're doing about rich people who think they're invulnerable."

"You've got to be kidding me."

"Sorry, I'm not." I shook my head. "What do you want me to do?"

"Didn't he come by to get the check?"

"Yes, and I gave it to him. I put the check right into his hand," I lied, as the adrenaline pulsed through my veins. I did give him the envelope, but it was empty.

"Of course you did. How ridiculous. He's just trying to screw us for five minutes of fame." Since I've managed to convince Jordana that I can do no wrong, she didn't even think to blame me.

She stood up and walked over to my desk. "Give me the phone."

"Jan? This is Jordana Pierson. It seems you have some misinformation. We pay all of our bills on time." She paused. Presumably Jan had something to say about that. "No, I have no comment and I never will. Please do your homework before you decide to badger us with baseless accusations. We have real work to get done. Have a lovely day." Jordana hung up and stalked back to her desk. "I don't have time for this crap. If she calls back, don't answer."

"Okay." I nodded obediently, just as the phone rang yet again.

"Is that her?" Jordana was ready and eager to decapitate Jan.

"No, it's Caroline. I've got it." I picked up and in my sweetest voice said, "Hello, Caroline. It's Olivia. How can I —" Before I could finish, she'd taken off on a tirade about how fabricated sketches of Tatiana's gowns had been released, and that the rumor was she'd be wearing eight different styles between the rehearsal dinner, the ceremony, the reception, and the after party, when the reality is that there are only five. She said that TMZ had also reported (accurately) that there will be four-hundred-and-twenty-five family and friends in attendance, half of whom the bride and groom can't identify in a police lineup. "I understand that this is upsetting. Of course we're sensitive to your desire for privacy." Jordana rolled her eyes at me. "I believe Jordana is on the phone with TMZ right now." I took a chance, and Jordana smiled. "I assure you, this wedding is our sole focus . . . we're doing the best we can to keep things as discreet as possible . . . you're on your way here? Okay then, we'll see you —" The line went dead abruptly.

"That woman is batshit crazy," Jordana said as soon as I'd hung up. "I'm not kidding. She may need to be institutionalized."

"I hear you."

"I mean, how insane is it that she's trying to pretend she doesn't want everyone in the Western world to know about this wedding? She's thrilled that TMZ and all the others are broadcasting every last detail. I just wish she didn't have to go through the motions of pretending that she's up in arms. It's a waste of everyone's time, including hers."

"She probably doesn't have anything better to do."

"You're exactly right." She nodded. "Anything else of major concern that I should know about?"

"Still no wedding band for William."

"Is this some kind of sick joke? I don't understand why he can't just pick a platinum or gold band — he can choose sterling silver, for all I care — like every other groom on the face of the Earth. What's his problem?"

"I'm not sure." I was sure. But there was *no way in hell* I could tell Jordana that he was having second thoughts about marrying Tatiana. "I'm on it, though. You do not need to worry about it."

"Thank you. Because if one more thing goes wrong I might hang myself from our chandelier."

"Nothing else will go wrong," I said, even though I was thinking the exact opposite. With less than three days to go, there is a very real possibility that the proverbial shit is about to hit the proverbial fan. Fortunately, Jordana is the one whose reputation will be tarnished, and I'll remain completely spotless.

The thing is, while I still believe that Jordana deserves to pay for her mistakes, I do have the smallest amount of sympathy for her. Losing a parent is never easy. And I'm touched that she confided in me about it. I'm just trying not to let it set me off course, even though yesterday I thought, *What if I don't expose her at all?* I've finally reached an abundant place in my life and my career, if you ignore my dwindling funds. I could just go on this way. Take my raise. Take my promotion. I'd have to manage my money better, but so what? I like Olivia a lot more than I liked Kerrie, anyway. Maybe that's enough of a payback.

In other news, I haven't spoken to William

since he kissed me in the taxicab. He's called and texted — it hasn't been easy to avoid him — but I've had no choice. For one, I'm sure that it was just a drunken mistake, an intoxicated peck on the lips. How humiliating is that? Jordana *cannot* find out.

Don't get me wrong, there have been many moments when I've wanted to run to William and divulge everything. But I haven't. In part so I can see my plan through. And also because I *really* don't want to hurt him. Plus, I know he doesn't see me that way. He'd chalk it up to a silly crush, and I'm not sure my ego would survive that kind of rejection. Even though he's out of my league, a girl can still dream. The dream is always better than the reality.

"They're here!" Jordana called out suddenly, averting me from distraction. Then she got up, readjusted the two white leather coach chairs surrounding our long, rectangular glass coffee table, and waited for Caroline to burst through the door.

"I don't think it's the Doonans. They're not due for another ten minutes." Caroline is never late. But she's rarely early, either. I walked toward the door and spotted a young woman I didn't recognize, carrying two bulky garment bags, standing outside. "I'll get it." I let her in and relieved her of one of the bags.

"Thank you." She smiled gratefully. "These are heavy." I showed her where to hang them. "There's one more. I'll be right back." She left and reappeared again. "So now you have the two bride's dresses and the mother-of-the bride's dress. Can you please sign here?"

"What do you mean the *two* bride's dresses?" I pretended to be shocked, even though I wasn't.

"Is that not right?" She stared at me blankly. She was probably an intern or a low-level gofer. Bright eyed. Bushy tailed. And dressed head to toe in "designer" clothing she'd bought off the sales rack at someplace like Marshall's or T.J. Maxx. She'd touched up the scuff marks on her black leather pumps with a Sharpie.

"Not unless you're hiding one of the gowns somewhere. The bride is supposed to have three. I confirmed with Ilana." *You tell one lie, it leads to another . . .*

"Oh yeah, Ilana is no longer with the company."

"I see." *Duh.*

"What's going on here?" Jordana rushed over and unzipped the garment bags to reveal dress number two and dress number three. "Where is the main gown?" Her tone was arctic. My hands were on my hips in a show of solidarity.

"I . . . I don't know. I'm new. I . . . I just started yesterday," she stammered. Poor little lamb.

"Well, you better get your boss on the phone." The girl didn't move. "Now!" Jordana barked.

"Yes, yes, of course . . . I'll just be a minute." She stepped outside again. For fear we might eat her alive, one scrawny limb at a time. It didn't take long for her to return. "I'm so sorry, my boss said that there's been a little mix-up, but that she'll get to the bottom of it immediately."

"Listen to me." Jordana's eyes were ferocious. "I need you to go back to that store and find the dress *immediately*. Got it?"

"I'll try." She took a step backward. I thought Jordana might lunge at her.

"You'll *try*?" If it's possible to actually see steam coming out of someone's ears, I believe I did. Because that was when Tatiana and Caroline made their grand entrance and little lamb was hastily dimissed. All in the bat of an eyelash extension. I couldn't wait to see how Jordana was going to scrape her way out of this hole.

Needless to say, neither Tatiana nor Caroline received the information well. But Caroline was the one who launched a full-scale tantrum, especially once she realized there was a second mistake. That her shrug was made of velvet, not duchess satin. *Oops.*

"Let's speak privately," Jordana suggested to Caroline, before physically guiding her into the back room, leaving Tatiana and me, somewhat awkwardly, alone.

"What?" She caught me staring at her. It's so hard to envision her as William's wife. Sure, they look the part. But to know William is to understand that they don't make sense beyond aesthetics. It's not that Tatiana is a bad person — remarkable given her genetics — it's just that I don't think she's William's person. And the fact that she wouldn't want to have kids with him is unthinkable.

"Nothing." I shook my head.

"This must all seem outrageous to you."

"In what way?"

"I don't know — this larger-than-life wedding and everything that comes with it. I'm sure you deal with it all the time, but it's still over-the-top, don't you think?"

"I think if it's what you want, then it's as it should be." I hesitated. "Is it? What you want?" I asked brazenly. Strangely, she didn't appear at all surprised by my question. She even waited a few seconds before answering.

"I guess so." She shrugged. "Either way, it's happening. My mother's been planning it in her head since we started dating."

"I believe that!" I smiled.

"I know it may not seem like it, but she means well. She just wants me to be happy. And she does love to throw a killer party."

"I believe that too!" I laughed lightly. "Anyway, all that really matters is that you and William are madly in love."

"Right." She looked down at her feet.

"You are in love with William, right?" I couldn't help myself.

"Of course I love William," she answered, too quickly.

"But are you *in love* with him?" I nudged. "As in, are you prepared to spend the rest of your life with him?"

"Does anyone really know that?"

"I expect that they think they do."

"Maybe," she whispered. I'd struck a chord. "Or maybe not. Do you really believe every person who gets married is a hundred-percent sure?" In a way I felt sorry for her. In another way, I didn't. She still has time to make things right. To tell William how she's feeling, before it's too late. Although, it doesn't seem like she's going to.

"I'd hope so."

"Well, that's not real life," she stated plainly.

"You can still change your mind." I kept my voice low. The last thing I need is for Jordana to overhear me trying to convince Tatiana not to marry William. "You don't have to do anything you're not ready for." I saw what I hoped was a transient flicker of understanding in her expression. But then it disappeared.

"Are you kidding?" She turned away from me. "There's no way I could call off the wedding at this point. This wedding has to go on. Because if it doesn't, then everything will fall apart. It's not just William's and my relationship that's at stake here." Our eyes met in the mirror.

I held my tongue. Fine, so Caroline and Arthur would lose a few hefty deposits, but money isn't an issue for them. And perhaps they'd be embarrassed at having to explain the sudden split to their friends, even though their friends would probably delight in their misfortune. Does any of that really matter, though, if Tatiana and William aren't happy together?

"This isn't some run-of-the-mill social event. We're in the spotlight. There are expectations. A lot of them." I wondered what that must feel like. To have every move you make analyzed through a microscope lens. So much so that you'd go through with a marriage even if it didn't feel right. "Unfortunately, it doesn't matter if my feet are a little cold. Anyway, I'm sure it's natural."

Before I could respond, Jordana and Caroline reappeared.

"The misunderstanding has been resolved," Jordana announced. "They've found the dress. It will be here in twenty minutes. And the shrug will be remade today, with another fitting tomorrow."

"Perfect." Tatiana managed a faint smile.

"Let's try on the other gowns while we wait." Jordana turned to me. "Olivia, can you please grab them?"

"Sure."

Tatiana's indifference had instilled me with the courage to do what I should have done weeks ago. Suddenly, I felt as ready as I'd ever be. To tell William who I really am. And how I really feel about him.

37
KERRIE

By the time I left the office, I had three missed calls from Sara and one message saying she'd come up empty-handed. The Camp David account in the Caymans was legitimate. And she'd hit a dead end. She sounded agitated and impatient. We planned to meet at my apartment in two hours to brainstorm, because — ahead of that — I had something important to take care of.

I texted William to meet me in front of the Guggenheim as soon as possible. I figured I could walk there faster than he could take a cab, which would give me a few minutes to gather my thoughts and find an empty bench across the street, on the perimeter of Central Park.

I needed to get this over with quickly or it wasn't going to happen at all.

As I waited for William to arrive, I thought some more about how drastically things have changed in the last two months. I uprooted my life by moving from a small town in Connecticut to the second largest city in the world — in case you're wondering, the first largest is Tokyo. I left the guy I was with for three years. I found a new job. I partnered with Sara to execute a plan for revenge that would honor my nana. And I physically transformed myself into someone I like seeing in the mirror. It's been exhausting and humbling at times, but it'll all be worth it.

I tilted my face toward the sun as a flock of pigeons descended from their perch in the window of a Fifth Avenue building. New York City pigeons do not nest in trees. I watched them swoop onto the sidewalk and gather around a large chunk of blueberry muffin someone had dropped on the street. Only one smaller bird couldn't break through the huddle. *That used to be me,* I thought. *Always attempting to get what I deserved, but never succeeding. Those days will soon be over. I hope. There's not much time left.*

A few seconds later William appeared and sat down beside me. His shoulders were hunched. His skin was sallow. He was not the picture of a happy groom. In that moment, I knew I was doing the right thing.

"Hey." I turned toward him. "How are you?"

He exhaled. "I've been better. How are you?"

"I'm not great either." I cleared my throat. "I need to talk to you about something serious."

"Sure, of course." This got his attention, since it's usually the other way around.

"There's really no way to say this without just coming out with it."

"You can tell me anything." His expression was so earnest, I almost got up and left. "Go ahead."

"I'm not exactly who you think I am."

"What are you talking about?" His forehead wrinkled with concern.

"My name isn't really Olivia Lewis." I paused while he digested that first crumb of information. "Well, it is. I mean, it's on my birth certificate that way. But that's not the point."

"You're losing me here."

"My whole life, since I was two, I've always gone by Kerrie O'Malley. Kerrie is my middle name, and O'Malley was my nana's last name. She's the one who raised me."

"Right. In Palm Beach."

"William, I've never even been to Palm

Beach. I grew up in Bridgeport, Connecticut. Like I said, I'm not exactly who you think I am."

"Wait, you're confusing me." He shook his head. "So, did your parents really die?"

"Yes, that's the truth. As is everything else I've told you about myself." Thank God for that.

"Are you running from the law or something? If so, I can help you."

Of course he'd offer to help. "Thank you, but no, I'm not running from the law. I'm not running *from* anything. I moved here to seek revenge on someone who wronged me. And my family."

"Who? Who would wrong you?"

"It's not important."

"So why are you telling me this now?" He pressed two fingers into his temples.

"Because you should know that part of my plan to seek revenge indirectly involved sabotaging your wedding." Suddenly it sounded so much worse than the plan I'd justified in my head.

"I don't understand. What does my wedding have to do with your revenge?"

"I can't explain it to you. Not yet."

"So, what? I'm just supposed to say, 'Fine, no big deal?' "

"I don't know."

"Olivia, I'm going to need a little more information here. You're freaking me out." He placed his hand on my leg. "You can confide in me."

"I'm sorry."

"Sorry for what?"

"I can't tell you anything else."

"This is insane." He pulled his hand away. "I thought we were *friends.*"

"We are."

"It doesn't feel like it," he snapped. "I thought I could trust you."

"You can."

"Olivia. You just told me that you've been lying to me about your name. Where you're from. And that you've been trying to ruin my wedding in the name of seeking revenge on some mystery person. You sound a little crazy."

"I can see that, but I promise you it's not the case." Though honestly, I'm not sure if that's true anymore. What if he's right? What if I am crazy?

"Can you at least give me more of an explanation? Like, why are you doing this? How did this person wrong you? I want to be here for you, but you're not making it easy."

"I know that. And I swear I never wanted to hurt you."

"But you did anyway? I revealed things to you, Olivia. *Private* things. I told you stuff about my relationship with Tatiana that no one else knows. And obviously you took advantage of that. You used it for your own agenda."

"I never used those things against you. It wasn't like I knew you personally when this all started. I was only trying to get what I deserved."

"Oh, that makes it so much better." His tone was suddenly acerbic. He's never spoken to me that way before. "You say you were only trying to get what you deserved, but it's clear that you didn't care if you screwed with a bunch of other people's lives in the process. Maybe you should look into sainthood."

"I'm so sorry."

"You already said that. But a simple sorry doesn't cut it if you can't even give me the slightest bit of clarification." William looked at me through bloodshot eyes. "I thought you were different. But you're just out for yourself like everyone else." He stood up abruptly.

"Wait, there's more."

"I've heard enough."

"It's about Tatiana." *And us.*

"Save it. Why would I believe you anyway?"

"Please listen, William. You can't marry her. You can't go through with this wedding."

"I'm done here. You're not the person I thought you were." His phone buzzed then. "It's Tatiana; I have to go."

"Wait."

"I can't."

"Please, William."

"Good-bye, Kerrie." He hurried into the street and hailed a cab before I could say any more. I wanted to call to him, but the words didn't come fast enough. Sure, I could have gone after him, but I didn't.

Honestly, I'm not completely sure what I'm running toward anymore.

38

KERRIE

"Thank God you're here," Sara said when I finally arrived at my apartment.

The truth is, after my conversation with William, I wasn't in the mood for company. I'd taken the long way home, lurching through the streets of my extended neighborhood, intentionally avoiding speaking to anyone. You'd think anonymity would be easy to achieve in New York City, but it always seems that the very moment you want to go unnoticed is the very moment everyone wants to notice you.

"Come on in." I unlocked the door and reluctantly let her inside. My feet were swollen from pounding the cement sidewalks and my back was aching from a string of restless nights. Giving up had never seemed as seductive a prospect. But by the determined look on Sara's face, I knew she wasn't about to let that happen. "Let's sit at the kitchen table," I suggested, hearing the strain in my own voice.

"We have a huge fucking problem," Sara announced, as soon as I'd draped my cardigan over the back of my chair and slumped into it. She spread her arms to wings' length to indicate just how huge it was.

"What's the problem?" I asked, when what I really wanted to do was pour us each a glass of wine and confide in her what had happened with William.

"I'm at a standstill." Her fists were balled. "This asshole is clean as a whistle."

"You're absolutely sure?"

"Yes," she snapped. "Sorry. It's just that I've gone over everything I could find on Arthur. I've burned through all my contacts and pursued every single lead. And nothing." She leaned forward, ensnaring her fingers in a twitchy cluster.

"So then that's it?" I felt strangely relieved. I could still reveal Jordana's demons without taking down Arthur. And it wouldn't have to ruin William and Tatiana's wedding.

"No." Sara shook her head vehemently. "There has to be something else. *Anything.*"

"Maybe there's not. We knew this could happen."

"I refuse to believe that."

"I know you don't want to admit it, but isn't it possible that Arthur isn't a criminal after all?" I find it pretty ironic that, while I originally came up with the idea, Sara is now the rabid one.

She looked at me accusingly. "No. And you better not be throwing in the towel."

"I'm not." I could be.

"Then *think*," Sara pled. "Think of anything. Any little morsel of information that could mean something."

We sat quietly for a few minutes. Suddenly our plan felt so disconnected from my own motives toward Jordana, even though I know the consequences will achieve the same end.

"I've got nothing."

"Jesus, Olivia." She folded her arms across her chest. "The least you could do is try to participate. This was your mission to begin with."

"You're right. I'm sorry. I wish I could think of something. I need more time."

"We don't have time. We've come this far. Do not give up now."

"I already said I'm not."

"Good." She nodded briskly. "Because nobody respects a quitter."

39
KERRIE

By nine o'clock the following morning, with just over forty-eight hours left until Tatiana and William say their 'I Do's,' I found myself standing in front of the Stephen A. Schwarzman Building of the New York Public Library, commonly known as the Main Branch, waiting for Jordana to meet me.

The best and only way to describe the entrance to the library is *regal*, with its three-feet-thick marble, twenty thousand blocks of stone, and two arresting lion sculptures — which the website tells me are named Patience and Fortitude — trapping either side of the stairway.

"Sorry, I'm running behind." Jordana appeared minutes later, looking polished as ever in a royal-blue shift dress and nude, patent leather heels with red bottoms, which even I can now identify as Christian Louboutins.

"No worries." I saw her recoil a little. She hates that expression.

"Let's go." She walked ahead of me and I followed her inside. "It's imperative to see the rooms a couple of days before any event, even though they won't be entirely set up. It allows for last-minute alterations should any be necessary, which I hope they're not." She spoke quietly.

"That makes sense." I lowered my voice too, as a security guard approached.

"Hello." Jordana smiled politely. "We have an appointment to see the Doonan-Blunt wedding spaces." Clearly, anyone who worked at the library would be well apprised of the grand affair.

"And you are?"

"Jordana Pierson." Every time she says her name, I note the elegant cadence. It sounds so much better than Jordan Butler. In the same way Olivia Lewis turns her nose up at Kerrie O'Malley.

"Just a second." He held up his index finger before engaging in a swift and garbled dialogue on his walkie-talkie. "You're all set. You know the way?"

"Yes, thank you." Jordana lead me to the Celeste Bartos Forum, where the reception would take place. A seated dinner for four-hundred-and-twenty-five guests. I'll never forget that number, not just because it's astronomical, but because Caroline has continually lamented the fact that she had to offend at least a hundred others who didn't make the cut.

"Wow, this is spectacular." As we entered the cavernous space with its thirty-foot-high glass saucer dome ceiling and sixty-four-hundred-square-feet of real estate, it suddenly occurred to me that William is going to marry Tatiana. And that once they've been pronounced husband and wife, this is where they're going to celebrate their lifelong commitment to each other. With four-hundred-and-twenty-three of their family members and friends. I felt sick.

"Wait until you see it all dressed up. The vendors will be arriving this afternoon and working straight through the next two days. I'll be spending a lot of time here overseeing." Jordana wandered around, swabbing surfaces with her fingertip and scrutinizing *everything* within reach.

"Where did you and John get married?"

"The Metropolitan Club on Sixtieth and Fifth," she answered instantly and without emotion. "Let's move on to where the ceremony will take place."

"Right behind you." I trailed after her as she took off down the hallway to continue

368

her white-glove inspection.

An hour later — after she'd made note of two light bulbs that needed replacing — Jordana was finally ready to leave. She had a meeting with our bride, Lucy Noble, and since there was still plenty of follow-up to be done for The Wedding of the Century, I was anxious to get back to work.

"I'll be at the office in a couple of hours," she said, raising her arm to hail a taxi. "Would you please email me the file called NobleCooper3 when you get in? It's on my computer. This way I'll have everything in front of me for Lucy. Whenever I'm with her, I feel like I'm being cross-examined. Typical lawyer."

"Sure, no problem. But it should be in our shared files. I can send it right now from my phone."

"Yeah, I don't think so. There was a copy on my desktop so I just worked off that one."

"That probably wasn't the most updated version. But don't worry, I'll figure it out."

"Perfect." She smiled gratefully. "I'll see you soon."

Once Jordana was gone, I walked to the subway station at Forty-Second and Lex and took the train uptown. I was at my desk within fifteen minutes and ready to conquer the long list of tasks at hand, when I remembered the file for Jordana. I opened her laptop and waited for the screen to spring to life. Discouragingly, her desktop was still as big of a disaster as it was when I first met her. Random files and folders everywhere. Remarkable, since she's so particular about everything else.

I found the file she was referring to, but as expected, it was an old draft and needed to be revised, which would take time, assuming I could find where she'd saved everything else.

That was when it caught my eye. The folder titled CD. The one Jordana had told me contained some documents of John's. I opened it up and searched through a few of them. Just a lot of numbers, as she'd said. Numbers that made no sense to her or to me. But a nagging feeling had me on edge, so I emailed everything to Sara. Just in case.

Then I turned my attention to the chores that confronted me. And forgot all about it.

Four hours later, Jordana called to say that she wouldn't be returning to the office, that she had too many things to deal with. So once I'd tied up every loose end, I shut down my computer, turned off the lights, and locked the door behind me. There was one more thing I had to do before heading home. One last favor for William.

40
KERRIE

I didn't sleep last night. Not a wink. I
couldn't. Once Sara told me what she'd
unearthed in John's files, I knew that today
would be the day.

A day Jordana will never forget, because
the world as she knows it will be demol-
ished, the same way mine was eighteen years
ago.

It's a lot to digest, especially when I look
back on everything that's transpired over
the last few months. I'm exhausted, physically and emotionally. And I miss William. I
was an idiot to think there could ever be
something real between us, romantically
speaking, but that doesn't alleviate the pain.
If this is what heartbreak feels like, then
maybe love isn't worth it.

Still, despite my anguish, this morning a
lengthy piece will run on the front page of
The Wall Street Journal, outlining just what
Arthur Doonan is capable of, especially with

the assistance of his cohort John Pierson (the best surprise of all!). It turns out that CD, the name of John's elusive folder, stood for Camp David, where he and Arthur have been holing up most weekends for the last six months, pulling off the money-making scheme they've been cooking up for quite some time.

It's pretty amazing that a financial giant like Arthur, who's managed to skirt any sort of censure for his entire career, will be taken down over John Pierson's sophomoric mistake. It's even more amazing that the proof was right there in front of me all along. Regardless, it feels like a hollow victory.

I'm not going to lie, there were moments, as I tossed and turned in bed, when I doubted myself. When I thought about Jordana's pitiful marriage. The loss of her father. The fact that she doesn't know what it feels like to love or be loved. But as soon as I let myself feel a modicum of sympathy or compassion, I took out an old photo album of Nana's and reminded myself that Jordana was the reason her life was cut short.

Once the sun had risen, I dressed myself in a slim black pencil skirt and the same red blouse I wore to my interview with

Jordana. The one she didn't approve of. The one I haven't worn since. It turns out she was wrong, and Sara was right. Red is my color. It's the color of power, which is what I hold. Jordana will never see me coming.

Sara did ask if I wanted her to join me. I'm not sure whether it was a show of solidarity or because she was worried I wouldn't be able to hold my own against Jordana. Either way, I knew I didn't need her there. If there's one thing I'm ready for, it's this.

I arrived at the library by 7:00 a.m. — I wanted to be there before she was. I once read that the element of surprise is the most challenging art of war. I look forward to witnessing that firsthand.

I sat on the steps waiting for her with a copy of the newspaper in hand, counting on the fact that she hadn't seen it yet. She arrived minutes later wearing a tailored white pantsuit, with her hair pulled back into a tight chignon. Her expression was concentrated, not concerned. I took a long, deep breath. I didn't exhale until she approached.

"You're here early." She clearly wasn't expecting me.

"Early bird gets the worm." Jordana doesn't know she's the worm. Not yet.

"Excellent." She smiled proudly. I savored

her praise one last time. "Let's get inside." I followed her toward the entrance, where there was a guard waiting for us.

"Jordana Pierson, here for the Doonan-Blunt wedding."

"I'm sorry, Mrs. Pierson. We can't let you in."

"Oh, no, we're not here as guests right now." She laughed nonchalantly. "I'm the wedding planner." I've never heard her use the word *planner* before.

"I know who you are." His face remained stern. "I've been given express orders not to allow you in."

"What are you talking about?" I looked down at my feet and took another deep breath. It was go time. The moment I've been waiting on for months. Maybe even for the last eighteen years.

"Ma'am, I'm going to have to ask you to leave." His tone was unyielding.

"To leave? This is preposterous." She looked past him for someone else to appeal to. There was no one.

"I don't want to have to do it by force. And I'm sure you don't want that either."

"No, of course not." She shook her head in disbelief as we retreated down the steps onto the sidewalk, which was vacant, save for a few passing joggers. "I have no idea

375

what's going on here," she said to herself more than me. "What the fuck am I supposed to do now? I can't call anyone at this hour on a Saturday."

"I don't think you'll need to bother," I said, as my heartbeat trotted to a sprint and my armpits flooded with perspiration.

"What do you mean? We have to get in there. There's still a lot to be done." Her eyes darted around in search of anyone who could help her.

"It's over, Jordana."

"What's over? What are you talking about?" I handed her the newspaper with the headline A DARK DAY ON WALL STREET, with photos of Arthur and John beneath it, and watched as the realization seized her. Her mouth dropped open, but no words came out.

"I'd say I'm sorry, but —"

"But what?" She looked at me with a ferocity in her eyes.

"But I'm the one responsible for it. Although, come to think of it, I really have you to thank. All of the information I needed was right there on your desktop." I smiled smugly. "Oh, and I may have messengered a letter to Caroline Doonan last night saying that you were *The Wall Street Journal*'s source. I'm guessing that's why

376

they didn't let us in."

"Olivia. You better tell me exactly what's going on here."

"You should really be nicer to me. You once told me I saved your life. Don't you remember that?"

"This makes no sense." She shook her head. "I never said that to you."

"Sure you did. Eighteen years ago. When I invited you into my home, and you stole everything from me."

"Oh my God." She looked at me with widened eyes, as she studied my features one by one. "You're . . . ?"

"Kerrie. O'Malley. That's me."

"All this time . . ." She reached around for something to steady her, but there was nothing to hold on to.

"Yup. Surprise!"

"I've always thought there was something so familiar about you, but I could never put my finger on it." I watched her expression mutate from shock to fear, as everything began to fall into place. "You're a liar."

"You're catching on now."

"But, why? Why this?" She held up the newspaper. "It doesn't —"

"Add up?" I finished her sentence for her. "Sure it does. You ruined my life and now I'm going to ruin yours. Tit for tat."

"What the fuck?" I could see she was trying to calculate her next move. "What do you want from me?"

"I want you to pay for what you did to me. And for what you did to my nana."

"Which was what, exactly? What did I do to you that would warrant this?" I'd expected a bigger reaction. More drama.

"You stole from me!" I accused, hoping to rile her. I'd had enough of her demureness.

"I was *desperate.*" Her voice remained even, which provoked me even more.

"That's it?!" I cried, as a young mother pushing a double stroller crossed the street to avoid us. "*Desperate?* That's your excuse?"

"I took a piece of jewelry and some cash when I was a teenager, so you went and destroyed my husband's career and probably mine, too? What the hell, Olivia? Or Kerrie. Whatever your name is."

"Are you fucking kidding me? You stole my life! You completely screwed my whole fucking existence!" I gasped for air and kept going. "Oh, and that *piece of jewelry* you're referring to? That was the only thing I had left of my dead mother. Do you have any idea what that means to a twelve-year-old girl? You may have been desperate, but you were also a selfish bitch. You didn't give a shit about anyone but yourself!"

"You think I *wanted* to take your mother's ring and your nana's money?" Her lips were quivering as she spoke. She tried to still them. Because weakness is an admission of guilt.

"Yes! I do! Why else would you have done it?"

"Well, let's see, maybe because I had a father who abused the crap out of *my mother.* And I knew when I left it would only get worse for her. *I knew that if she stayed,* there would be times when there wouldn't be enough food to eat because he'd spent his paycheck on booze and bullets. *I knew that if she stayed,* she'd keep crying herself to sleep at night, because she was that lonely. Or battered. Or sick. *I knew that if she stayed,* one day he might beat her so hard that she wouldn't recover. That's the way it was for us. I wanted to give her an insurance plan. I had to. What's so wrong with that?"

"Everything!" I had to stop myself from lunging at her. *"Everything* is wrong with that."

"That's easy for you to say."

"Excuse me?"

"You had security."

"Plenty of people grow up in horrible

379

circumstances, Jordana. You're not the only one. But not everyone does what you did. At least you had parents. I never even knew mine."

"You were lucky."

"What?" My head jerked back.

"I said, you were *fucking lucky!* Okay? Is that what you want to hear?" Her voice was suddenly loud and urgent. And then she whispered, "I was jealous."

"Jealous of me?" I almost laughed at the absurdity.

"Yes."

"That's ludicrous."

"Is it? You had a grandmother who loved you. A nicer house than mine to live in. You never had to worry that if you said one false word, your father might give you a black eye."

"That doesn't mean it's okay to *rob* someone. I helped you that night. I saved your ass. You don't remember that?"

"I do."

"And here you were living this big fancy life in New York City."

"Kerrie —"

"No, shut up," I interrupted. "Believe me, I know it was tough, because I saw some of what went on in your house. And I still wanted to be just like you. I *idolized* you."

"I still don't understand why you came here and made up a new name. You could have just asked me for the money and the ring back and been done with it."

"Done with it?" I balked. "You killed my nana!"

"Killed your nana?" She took two steps backward. "What are you talking about? Are you out of your mind?"

"You left the gas on."

"What?"

"When you lit your cigarette. You didn't turn the gas all the way off. There was a fire. My nana died from smoke inhalation." I held her gaze, challenging her to deny it. "You did that to her. *You* are responsible."

She didn't say anything.

"And now you're going to suffer the way I did. I applied for this job so I could sabotage your life, the way you did mine. When I saw you on *Access New York,* it sparked something inside me. I knew that if I wanted to set myself on a better path, that I had to get back at you before I could move forward. I also knew that I had to honor my nana and all that you took from her."

"I . . . I don't . . ." she stammered.

"Don't say anything."

"Kerrie . . ."

"No." I held up my hand. "I don't want

381

to hear another word out of your mouth." I thought I would. I thought I'd want her to grovel. But I didn't. I'd finally satisfied my objective and that was enough. Well, except for one more little thing. "I also had a letter messengered to your husband. It explains who you really are, where you really came from, and what you did to me that night. He should be receiving it" — I checked my watch — "right about now." I waited a beat as she processed this new information. "I wonder how long it will take for such *explosive* secrets to reach the rest of the Richie-Riches. What do you think? An hour, tops?"

"I . . ." She started to speak again, but I cut her off a second time.

"Good-bye, Jordana. I truly hope you get everything you deserve," I said.

And then I turned my back on her and walked away.

41
JORDANA

As I boarded the plane, I thought about what I'd done to Kerrie all those years ago. And what kind of person that makes me. I also thought about John, what he'd done, and the litany of lies that had been sustaining us for too long.

My husband isn't just a philanderer.

He's a thief.

And with that realization, the storm subsided and the future became cloudless.

John's files revealed dozens of spreadsheets exposing that he'd helped Arthur defraud customers on bond prices by altering electronic chats to make it appear he'd paid more for bonds than he actually did. It sounds complicated, which it is, but the bottom line is that he and Arthur generated fifteen million dollars in illegal profit for A. Doonan, LLC. *I guess he really was with Arthur all those work weekends.*

It's one thing to be blind to the faceless.

To deafen yourself to the voices you can't hear. His personal affairs were inconsequential. But this is different. My husband is a crook.

I knew immediately what I had to do.

It turned out that the things that seemed the most important were precisely the things that weren't important at all. And that the determination that once impelled me forward was actually hindering me from attaining true happiness.

I found my seat in first class, by the window, and relaxed into it.

"Can I offer you a glass of white wine?" the stewardess asked.

"That would be nice, thank you," I answered softly. "Do you want one too, Mom?"

She turned toward me. "Oh, I don't know."

"Live it up a little." I smiled at her. "And don't worry, it comes with the ticket."

"Okay, then." She smiled back.

"Two glasses of white wine coming up." The stewardess walked away. She didn't recognize me, thank God. She probably doesn't read *The Wall Street Journal.*

It may be hard to believe, but in a way, I have Kerrie to thank. Her revelation was the final push I needed, although I would have preferred it to be on my own terms. John doesn't love me. He doesn't know how to love. Neither do I.

John isn't a cruel man. Nor is he an exceptionally kind one. We served a purpose in each other's lives. He'll miss the me he thought I was. For a little while. Then he'll find a replacement. Someone younger and more submissive.

Being Jordana Pierson has wearied me. And now things must change. They *will* change. But only if I'm the one to make that change. There's no turning back and there's no standing still. I scrambled to get where I am. I convinced myself that it would be sunny at the top. Only it isn't. It's fucking freezing. And I'm alone.

Once upon a time I was the girl who ran. Of course, I thought I was chasing something bigger. Something better. And I thought that bigger, better life would finally make me happy. I was wrong.

I won't make the same mistakes again.

"Passengers, please turn off all electronic devices and fasten your seat belts," the pilot's voice said over the loudspeaker. "Flight attendants, prepare for departure."

I closed my eyes and took my mother's hand in mine. "This time we're running together," I said to her. "The next chapter in our lives begins now."

42
KERRIE

A few days after the wedding — yes, William did go through with marrying Tatiana — I sat on my couch, staring at the headline on the front page of the *New York Post,* which declared: DOONAN IS DOOMED. The photo below it was of Arthur being hauled off in handcuffs with Caroline, venomous as always, in tow.

Behind them was John Pierson. Shackled as well. And all alone.

The article explained that they'd been charged with ten counts of securities fraud and six counts of relaying untrue statements to multiple clients, including large institutional investors. It said that the case was precedential because they'd been prosecuted for falsifying their own prior purchase price. Very clever. Until it wasn't.

On the next page, there was another snapshot. It pictured Tatiana and William, beneath a banner that read: BLUNT BLUSH-

ING BRIDE ANNULLED.

I couldn't believe it. But before I had the chance to read the full story, my phone vibrated with a text message from Sara, who ended up receiving over a dozen lucrative job offers as soon as the news about Arthur and John broke. Unexpectedly, she's back on the fence about leaving Dante to work full-time.

Meet me downstairs in five. Joel is home early. Let's grab a drink.

Just as I was about to write back, my buzzer rang. I walked over to the intercom and pressed the button. "Hello?"

"Is this Kerrie O'Malley?"

"Who's this?"

"My name is Cathy Paulson. I'm an old friend of Jordana's. I have some things she left for you."

"Sorry, but I don't need anything from her."

"It'll only take a minute. I come in peace. I really think you'll want this stuff."

"I highly doubt it."

"Please. Nothing fishy, I swear."

"Okay. I guess," I relented, and reluctantly let her in. A minute later she was at my door.

"Can I come inside? I promise I won't be long."

"Sure." She looked harmless enough, like

an old hippie, so I took a few steps back. I didn't offer her a seat.

"This belongs to you." She placed a small velvet pouch in my palm. I knew immediately what it was.

"I can't believe she kept it all these years." I shook my head as I examined my mother's ring and tears flooded my eyes.

"Apparently her mom did."

"Wow."

"There's this, too." She handed me a check. "Jordana said the amount will cover the money she took from you, with interest."

"Thank you." I nodded.

"One more thing." She gave me a thick manila envelope.

"What's this?"

"You'll see." She stood there for a moment and then said, "She's not a bad person."

"I think that depends on your definition of bad," I replied. "Either way, she seems to live a pretty charmed life, so it's hard to feel too sorry for her."

"Looks can be deceiving."

"Can they?"

"I've known Jordana since she moved here when she was a terrified seventeen-year-old girl. I've watched her transform herself into a completely different person over the last two decades. She's had some high highs and some very low lows. I've had to peel her off the floor more times than I care to recall. I bet you didn't know that."

"No."

"I'm not expecting you to pity her. I know what she did to you. I'm only telling you that she's troubled. She always has been and she probably always will be. I'm just glad she finally left."

"Left what?"

"That disgusting husband of hers. That ridiculous facade of a life."

"She's gone?"

"Oh yeah. After your confrontation, she came straight to me and then went directly to the airport."

"Where did she go?" I hadn't expected that. I don't know why. I suppose once a runner, always a runner.

"I don't know."

"I doubt that."

"Does it matter?"

"Not really."

"What about the company?"

"It's all in the folder. You'll see. I'm not sure she appreciated your approach, but she obviously had great faith in you, even after everything." She smiled faintly. "If you ask me, you did her a favor."

"How so?"

"She wouldn't have survived in that world for much longer. It was eating her alive. She was ready to go. Just scared. Deep down, she knew it. I'm glad you did too." Cathy turned toward the door, which was still open. "I'll be going now."

"Thank you for all of this."

"You're welcome." She paused for a second and then looked back at me. "For what it's worth, Jordana really liked you."

EPILOGUE

Three months later, I sat at my desk half expecting Jordana to storm into the office and declare that it was all a mistake. That I'm the one who has to leave. But that never happened. Though the business is thriving, she has yet to return, and I doubt she ever will.

While there is a part of me that misses working with her, my sense of satisfaction at running the show buoys me even more. I finally found the purpose I've been seeking for so long.

If there's one thing I've learned from this journey, it's that life doesn't follow a pre-meditated pattern. You can't control your destiny.

Do I forgive Jordana? I don't know. I do feel sorry for her, though, and I hope she finds what she's looking for.

Inside the envelope Cathy gave me, there was paperwork from Jordana indicating that her payback to me — in addition to the money and the ring — was the company she grew from the bottom up. It's now called Olivia Lewis Wedding Concierge. I think it has a nice ring to it. So did Lucy Noble and Donald Cooper and Alexa Griffin and Grey Wilder. They stuck with me, despite Jordana's absence, because I'm good at what I do. And because they trust me. Thankfully, their loyalty was the catalyst for the company's growth.

I suppose my gift to Jordana is guiltless, unencumbered freedom. I'm not looking to go after her for anything, not anymore. I've learned my lesson. Quit while you're ahead.

Anyway, like my nana said: "Senseless revenge will whip its neck and snap you on the bottom."

As I finished tying up some loose ends before closing up for the evening, my cell phone rang. The number was international, probably a misdial, but I answered anyway.

"Hello?"

"Olivia?" The connection was fuzzy, but the voice familiar. "It's William. Can you hear me?"

"Barely." I smiled.

"I'm calling to say thank you."

"For what?"

"The ring. *Everything.*" Despite the fact

that I didn't approve of William marrying Tatiana, I did go to Harry Winston to pick out a wedding band that I knew he would love, and then I left it with his doorman. No matter what he thought of me, I had to do that for him. Not because I felt I owed him, but because I wanted to.

"You're welcome. Although it looks like you won't be needing it."

"You tried to tell me."

"I did."

"Listen, Olivia. I'm not sure whether the reception will hold up. I'm traveling in Africa with my father for another few weeks. I needed a break. Some time to think. And you've been on my mind."

"Really?" I shut my eyes to drown out my surroundings. I needed to hear everything he said as clearly as I could.

"Can I see you when I get back?"

"I don't know." I wanted to say yes. I wanted to jump up and down and scream it. But, what if revisiting the messiness of the past prevents me from moving forward? I made that mistake once already.

"Come on, I thought you were my faithful servant." He laughed.

"Well, when you put it that way."

"I'll be in touch."

"Okay." The line went dead then. And all

that was left was silence. Along with the delicious realization that William will come back to me.

As it turns out, happiness *is* a choice. It's just not for sale.

ACKNOWLEDGMENTS

People often assume that writing a book is a solitary effort. But the truth is, by the time my novels reach the world, they've been touched by so many talented individuals in a variety of different ways.

Thank you first and foremost to my brilliant agent and cherished friend, Alyssa Reuben. I can say with absolute certainty that *Pretty Revenge* would not be what it is or where it is without your tireless efforts, not to mention your unyielding support.

My deepest gratitude also extends to my rock-star editor, Kate Dresser. You took what was a *very rough* first draft, saw exactly what needed to be done, and then guided me every step of the way, until the book was where we both wanted it to be. I'm so thrilled to be working with you and I look forward to shaping many more books together. As you say, Huzzah!

Many thanks to the team at Gallery and

Simon & Schuster for welcoming me with open arms — Jen Bergstrom, Aimée Bell, Jennifer Long, Molly Gregory, and Michelle Podberezniak. Stacey Sakal, you are an eagle-eyed copy editor; I'm so grateful for that!

Kathleen Carter, my publicist and friend for many years, you are a gift to authors. No one works harder than you do, and I appreciate your efforts more than you know.

Katelyn Dougherty, you are a gem! Without your sage advice and phone-call therapy sessions, I would not have survived this process.

To the many authors who support and inspire me: Jane Green, Elin Hilderbrand, Lauren Weisberger, Alisyn Camerota, Emily Giffin, Sarah Pekkanen, Sarah McCoy, Lynne Constantine, Brenda Janowitz, Liz Fenton, Lisa Steinke, Jamie Brenner, Abby Fabiaschi, and Susie Orman Schnall.

Thank you, also, to the readers' groups, devoted book bloggers, and event hosts: Robin Kall, Vilma Gonzalez, Melissa Amster, Jenny O'Regan, Courtney Marzilli, and many more. Andrea Katz — you are a dream. Wise, kind, thoughtful, and beyond knowledgeable. Thank you for being you.

My readers are everything to me! Please keep reading and I'll keep writing. Deal?

To my friends, who always lift me up: Melody Drake, Sara Haines, Kerry Kennedy, Jordana Gringer, Emily Rosnick, Allison Walmark, Anya Pechko, Stephanie Szostak, Heather Cody, Simona Levin, Andi Sklar, Kristina Grish, Anne Epstein, Jen Goldberg, Jenn Falik, Heather Bauer, Anne Greenberg, Teresa Giudice, Margaret Josephs, David Goffin, Susie Landau, Michele Weisler, Andrea Buchanan, Karen Sutton, Devin Alexander, Marni Lane, Jamie Camche, Amy Falkenstein, Rachel Golan, Andrew Kindt, and Laura Laboissonniere, and special thanks to my first reader, Shari Arnold.

Maria Manzi, you keep everything running smoothly in our home and beyond. We could not love you more.

To my family, whom I'd be lost without — my parents, Tom and Kyle Einhorn; my grandmother, Ailene Rickel; my brother, Zack Einhorn; my soon-to-be sister-in-law (yay!), Nayani Vivekaandamorthy; and all of the Lieberts.

Finally, to my boys — my husband, Lewis, and our sons, Jaxsyn and Hugo. I love you all to the moon and back.

ABOUT THE AUTHOR

Emily Liebert is the author of four novels and has been featured in publications such as *The Wall Street Journal, Ladies' Home Journal, People, HuffPost,* and many more. Emily lives with her husband and sons in Connecticut.

The employees of Thorndike Press hope you have enjoyed this Large Print book. All our Thorndike, Wheeler, and Kennebec Large Print titles are designed for easy reading, and all our books are made to last. Other Thorndike Press Large Print books are available at your library, through selected bookstores, or directly from us.

For information about titles, please call:
  (800) 223-1244

or visit our website at:
  gale.com/thorndike

To share your comments, please write:
  Publisher
  Thorndike Press
  10 Water St., Suite 310
  Waterville, ME 04901